TRUST HIM

BOYS, DADDIES, SNUGGLES AND MORE 2

ELOUISE EAST

CONTENTS

AUTHOR NOTE

If you would like to see any potential triggers for this book and any other books I've written, please go to this link on my website: https://elouiseeast.com/triggers

LIST OF CHARACTERS

Beatrice, Ollie's mother
Ben, Gareth's boyfriend, BBoy22
Bernie, Ollie's deceased father
Denny, Ollie's best friend
Don, Toby's father
Enno, Ollie's best friend
Fletcher, Toby's brother
Gareth, Ben's boyfriend, DaddyG, Owner of Boys, Daddies, Snuggles & More
Imogen, Ollie's sister
Nigel, Toby's brother
Ollie, mechanic, D-Mad79
Preston, Gareth and Ben's friend
Rio, mechanic
Sally, Toby's mother
Sarah, Toby's best friend
Toby, dog walker, Oh2Bs3xy
Vince, Gareth and Ben's friend

1

TOBY

Hi, Oh2Bs3xy! This is DaddyG's boy. I saw your comment on the blog. I'd love to help you if you want me to. Message me back, okay? Ben.

Toby Neesham stared at the message, his heart in his throat. Could he do it? Could he reply and get some help in finding the elusive Daddy he belonged with? Could he trust Ben? He didn't know him from the next person who messaged, but the reply had come through the blog under DaddyG's username. People can hack into things like that, but would they do it with something as benign as dating?

He groaned and dropped his head into his hands. He needed to stop second-guessing everything he read, saw and did. There had to be a happy medium somewhere. He clicked reply and typed as quickly as he could before he changed his mind.

Hi, Ben. Thank you. I would love some help.

He didn't put his real name, not wanting that to get out yet. It wasn't that he was ashamed of who he was—he wasn't—but until he knew he could trust the person on the other side of the screen, he would hold back a little.

Clicking out of the message board so he wouldn't keep checking for a reply, he finished getting ready for work. Not that it took much. Navy khakis and a tan-coloured polo shirt were his uniform. He grabbed the lunch he'd packed and headed to his car. On nice summer days, he walked to work, but on chilly, blusterous days, he caved and took the car instead. Within fifteen minutes, he walked into the building to the resounding chorus of barking and grinned. Dogs could make anyone smile; he was sure of it.

Once he'd put his things in his locker, he headed for the kennels, checking who he was looking after that day.

"Ooh, Luna, Goldie and Bella. You're mine today, sweethearts," he called as he entered. He received several barks in response, though which dog they were from was a mystery. "Hey, Jem. How're things?"

"All good, Toby, my lad. All good."

"Glad to hear it. Any issues over the weekend that we know about?"

Jem shook her head, her greying curls bouncing. "All quiet on the canine front. Peppa's owners left her here for another week." She rolled her eyes. "They extended their holiday. Again."

Toby sighed, peering into the kennel the gorgeous poodle stayed in. "Poor girl. Good job she has us to love her. How long has she been here now?"

"If you don't include this week, it's five weeks."

"Toby! I need a word."

He sighed, and Jem stared at him. "Hold your ground, my boy. You do enough around here without doing more."

Toby sent her a small smile and headed for the manager's office. "Yes, Clara?"

"I need you to work an extra shift this week. Sarah has asked for Friday off, so I need you to cover."

No please or thank you. "Sure."

"Good. There's a list of things that needs doing today."

That was a dismissal if ever he heard one. He stalked back to the kennels and rolled his eyes at Jem.

"You said yes, didn't you?"

"Of course I did. I love these dogs, and anything that keeps me here is wonderful because then I'm not wallowing at home." He grabbed the leads for Luna, Goldie and Bella and headed for their kennels. "Who's a good girl, Bella?"

He let himself into the kennel, allowing the West Highland Terrier to greet him, then clipped on the lead and let him out. Following the same routine for Goldie, a mischievous Dachshund, and Luna, the show-ready Labradoodle, he waved at Jem before heading out of the gates on their usual walking route. He was glad for his coat because it was an awful day, but the dogs didn't seem to care.

How was he ever going to find someone who would take him as he was and not try to use him or change him into something he wasn't? He didn't want to be at someone's beck and call. He wanted someone to care for him, to know what he needed even when he didn't know himself, and to love him. It was probably too much to ask, but it didn't stop him from wanting it. Decent Daddies were too hard to find, but at least he had DaddyG's blog to help him, and if Ben was being truthful, him as well. Maybe they would have the magic touch.

When he got back to the boarding kennels, Sarah was there.

"What's this I hear about someone wanting the afternoon off on Friday?" He put his hands on his cocked hips. "Where do you think you're going without me?" he asked his best friend.

Sarah chuckled. "Mum set up a spa day without telling me and, being typical, booked it for a day I was working. Let me guess. You've taken the shift."

Toby snorted. "Of course."

"You need to stop!" Sarah huffed. "She's working you to the bone."

"At least I'm getting paid for it."

He led the three dogs to the respective kennels, leaving them with fresh water and a treat for being good, then headed back to her.

"I'm taking you out for dinner on Saturday," Sarah said. "It's the least I can do. Unless you want to try a club."

Dread curdled in his stomach. "No, thanks. Dinner is more than enough."

"He might not even be there." Sarah slid her arm around his shoulders.

"And if I don't go, I won't know. Win, win." He diverted to wash his hands.

Unfortunately, his best friend was tenacious. "I hate that he's making you miss out on something you need. He's such a jackass."

"Truer words have never been spoken, but it doesn't change my answer." He debated whether to tell her about Ben, then shrugged. She knew everything about him. "You know that blog I read? DaddyG?" She nodded. "I received a message from DaddyG's boy. He's offered to help me find a Daddy."

Sarah frowned. "How does he plan to do that?"

"I've no idea yet. I got the message this morning."

"What are you going to say?"

Toby licked his lips. "I've already said yes." He sighed. "I'm not doing well enough on my own, so I need help. Even if he can't do anything, at least he's tried."

Sarah crossed her arms and bit her lip—her thinking pose, as he called it. "It won't hurt to get help, especially when I can't do anything. I know nothing, even with research and your explanation. I'm useless in this respect."

Toby hugged her. "But you're my best friend, and you're there whenever I need you to be. Listening to my crappy woe-is-me tales. That's priceless in my book."

"What are you buttering me up for?" she joked.

"Well, you're already paying for dinner. I'm wondering if I can persuade you to stretch to dessert." He laughed when she threw something at him as he walked away.

He loved Sarah, but she was truthful with her words. As much as he explained being a boy and needing a Daddy, she just couldn't understand his draw to it, and that was fine, but it didn't help him. She was a fantastic cheerleader, though.

His shift ended quickly, and without Clara calling to ask him to work later, which was a miracle in and of itself, he headed home. He could've checked his emails at work, but he didn't want anyone else to see them, so he waited until he was at his computer. Once he logged on, he found another message from Ben.

Hey! I'm glad to hear from you. I thought I might scare you away by being so upfront about it. To help me get started, I need to know something about you. What you need from a Daddy and what you enjoy doing. If you're happy to send me that information, I will see who I can find for you. It might be trial and error to begin with, but I will try my hardest. Ben.

Trial and error were what they all had in their lifestyle. No one ever knew exactly how well they would mesh with someone until they tried it, and it either failed or succeeded. He would see what Ben could come up with. No harm, no foul. He sent a message back, giving as much information as he was comfortable giving to a stranger, then closed it down.

Now, he could spend the rest of the day playing his game and getting lost in the animated world with his friends. He climbed the stairs and headed to his bedroom, which held not only a double bed but a desk, a gaming chair, a game console and two monitors. As he settled into the comfortable chair, he relaxed more than he had anywhere else, except when he walked the dogs alone. Those two places were his peace, his haven. Though he would be the first to agree that once he got lost in the game, time had no meaning. Hours passed without care, mealtimes came and went, toilet breaks were a thing of the past, and he ignored the needs of his body. It wasn't the best, but it helped keep the loneliness at bay.

When he finally came up for air, unable to ignore his bladder, it was dark outside, and his eyes were sore from staring at the screen. He yawned and said goodbye to his friends before logging off and running to the bathroom. Once that need was satisfied, he raided the kitchen cupboards for something quick and easy he could eat before he crashed into bed. A pain au chocolat, some dried apricots and an apple wasn't the best meal, but it also wasn't the worst he'd come up with before. He added in a biscuit, then carried it back upstairs to bed.

He ate while he changed into his pyjamas, then brushed his teeth straight after. Once he finished, he climbed into bed and was asleep before his head hit the pillow.

It hadn't seemed like five minutes before his alarm blared through the silence. He slammed his hand down on the bedside table, trying to find his phone to turn off the horrible noise, but when he couldn't locate it, he had to sit up. The noise wasn't coming from his bedside table like it should've been. It was coming from his desk, so he scrambled across the distance and snoozed it. If he turned it off, there was a chance he'd fall back to sleep, and then he'd be in trouble.

Mornings were the worst. Why couldn't mornings start at midday?

When he was ready, he gulped down some apple juice while he checked his emails. His heart raced at Ben's reply.

Hey. Thank you for that. I'll get on it. I have high hopes, but bear with me, okay? While we're waiting, I wanted to let you know a bit about me...

Ben continued, and Toby found it easier to believe him when he was so easygoing. At the end of the message was Ben's phone number. Toby didn't think he was ready for that yet, but he'd keep it in case he ever was.

As the week continued, he looked forward to Ben's emails each day. It was only one email a day, but it seemed to set his day on the right path, keeping him upbeat about the future, and he held on to that thought. And when he met Sarah for dinner on Saturday, he had so much to tell her. After he finished spewing all the details he could, she smiled at him.

"It sounds like you've found another friend. I'm glad."

Toby hadn't thought of Ben as his friend until that moment, but Sarah was right. He talked with Ben about the same things he talked to Sarah about. Was he ready for an actual voice conversation with him? It was almost as nerve-wracking as meeting someone face-to-face. But as the dinner continued, he knew he had to do it.

The following day, he sat with his phone in his hand and stared at it as if it was a snake waiting to bite him. He took a deep breath and dialled, putting it on speaker so he didn't have to hold it in his clammy hands.

"Hello?"

"Uh, hi. Uh, is this Ben?"

"It is," the hesitant voice answered.

"It's Toby. We've been emailing. You gave me your number. Is it okay that I called? You're probably busy, aren't you? I can call back another day." He inhaled.

"Toby! Hi! I wasn't expecting to hear from you, but I'm so glad you called. I'm not busy at all. Daddy is out at the minute, so I'm on my own." Toby didn't know what to say. "Are you okay, Toby?

I know it's a lot talking to someone new."

Those words did more than anything else could've, and he relaxed. "Yeah, it really is. I'm okay. Just nervous."

"You have nothing to be nervous about. You mentioned you liked video games. Do you do streaming or anything like that, or is it just playing with your friends?"

Toby settled onto the sofa. "I occasionally stream, but not very often. I find it too stressful because there's so much to think about. I much prefer being able to play and forget about everything else."

Ben hummed. "I agree. Letting your mind roam free is nice, isn't it?"

"Nothing can reach you when you're there," he murmured.

"We'll find someone for you, Toby. I promise we will. We have things in the works that I can't talk about at the moment, but it will make life easier for us all." Ben sighed. "Would you like to meet up at some point?"

Toby choked on his spit, and he coughed. "Uh, maybe. One day."

"One day soon, I hope."

They spent the next twenty minutes talking about Toby's job and what he loved about looking after dogs, but that he didn't have one of his own because he worked too much. Maybe one day.

When they finally ended the call, Toby felt lighter than he had for a long time. He had another ally in his fight against loneliness, and he couldn't wait to get started on a life that was closer to what he wanted his future to look like. Now, he just needed to find the Daddy to complement that image.

2

OLLIE

Ollie Young wiped his oily hands on a rag and studied the engine before him. He'd fixed a couple of small issues, but as the customer hadn't been willing to explain what the noise problem was, only that it was coming from somewhere at the front of the car, there wasn't much more he could do without hearing it himself, and when he'd driven the car for a test run, he hadn't heard anything.

A long, loud trilling noise rang through the garage, and he winced. His dad had been hard of hearing and needed the extra volume to ensure he heard the phone, but Ollie could turn it down now that his father was no longer with them. The familiar ache pressed against his chest, and he breathed through it, knowing it would ease with time but also hoping it never would. It had only been four months since Bernie had died of a heart attack—quick and painless, he'd been told—but there was an enormous gaping hole in his life, and he wasn't sure he *wanted* to fill it.

"Ollie! Phone call!"

Ollie threw the rag on top of the tools he'd been using and jogged over to the office.

"Hello?"

"Mr Young?" the nasal voice said.

"Yes."

"I'm calling from Smithson and Ryatt. We need to arrange an appointment to continue going through the probate information for Mr Young, Senior. Are you available on Friday at eleven o'clock?"

Ollie bit back a sigh, knowing it was necessary but wishing they could get it done already. "Yes, that's fine by me. I'll check with my mother, but we should be okay with that."

"Wonderful. I'll put you in the diary, but please let us know if you need to change the appointment."

"Will do."

"Thank you, Mr Young. Bye."

He replaced the receiver and sank into the chair, rubbing his forehead. Most of the details of his father's belongings were easy to sort because they went straight to his wife—Ollie's mum—but the garage was a different matter. Bernie had put it in his will that he wanted to transfer the garage to Ollie, which was a whole other ballgame than giving it to his wife. Hopefully, it wouldn't take much longer to get it completed because it was a ballache of how many phone calls, letters, emails and in-person meetings they had to have to get it sorted.

Checking the clock, he sighed at the impending end of the day. There was no way he'd stop when everyone else did. Instead, he'd do what he usually did and close the main doors and keep working on his current project. He might as well use the hours he had nothing else to do by making extra money. And if he managed to get the bike finished ahead of schedule, it could only do him favours.

He headed back to the main floor and checked in with each of his mechanics on where they were with the car they worked on. He was glad to hear three out of the five would be ready for collection at the close of the day, and he went back to contact the owners to let them know to pick the car up before the garage closed.

After the three finished cars and four mechanics left, Ollie stared at Enno, one of his best friends. "No."

Enno smirked. "Yes. Get your ass cleaned up. We're going for a drink."

Ollie sighed. "Have you told Denny? You know how he gets when he misses out." He stomped down the steps and headed for the second set of stairs at the back of the building.

"Yes! He's meeting us there!" Enno called.

Ollie shook his head and climbed the stairs to his home. He'd been living above the garage since he'd moved out from his parents' house at twenty years old. He'd wanted independence, and although it was still close, he'd found his feet there. Now, he was reluctant to find anywhere else.

He showered, scrubbing at his skin as best he could to remove the oil and grease from his hands. It was a hazard of the job, and his hands never looked perfectly clean, but he knew they were. There were soaps and cleaners out there that could get rid of it all, but he'd found he was allergic to a lot of them and had stopped using them. People could take him as they saw him or not at all, as far as he was concerned.

He dressed in black jeans and a brown T-shirt with a hoodie over the top. He clicked his watch into place and ran his hands through his dishevelled hair and over his goatee. It was the best he could do. No, that wasn't true. It was all he could be bothered to do. He was sick of trying to find the right boy for him, and he'd given up after several relationships had fizzled after weeks or months.

It was one reason he didn't want to go out with Enno. He loved the guy, but he'd found his forever boy, and they were perfect for each other. But every time he saw them together, Ollie was envious. He didn't want Enno's boy, Rick, but he wanted what they had together. And fuck, did it hurt some days.

"Stop being a grumpy asshole and smile, for fuck's sake. No wonder no one wants to be with you with a face like that."

The pep-talk didn't help, so he shoved his wallet and phone in his pocket and locked up before heading to the car park where Enno waited.

"About bloody time. I was seriously wondering if you were getting in touch with your feminine side with how long you took."

"Fuck off."

They climbed into Enno's car and headed to Enno's place to pick up Rick before continuing to their usual haunt, The Dog and Duck. It wasn't busy, but it would be before the night was through. They had a darts competition, quiz night and all manner of different events scheduled throughout the week, making it the place to be for all ages. The owners had done a brilliant job of creating a cross-ages business.

"Two Fosters and a vodka and orange, please, Gail," Enno requested of the bartender.

"Make it three," Ollie said, spying Denny working his way towards them, stopping every two seconds to greet someone.

"Hey, man. How's it going?" Denny asked, not expecting an answer from him. His best friend hooked his arm around Ollie's neck and brought him in for a brief hug, and Ollie slapped his back.

They grabbed their drinks and found their usual seats—although they weren't always available.

"So, what's new?" Denny asked.

Ollie shook his head. "I saw you yesterday. Same old."

Denny raised his eyebrows, and Ollie's shoulders dropped. He was being an asshole. More so than usual.

"Sorry. The lawyer called for another meeting. It's dragging out, and I'm fed up with it."

Denny squeezed his shoulder. "I know. Not much longer."

Ollie took a mouthful of his beer and wiped his mouth while he studied the customers. He didn't expect to see anyone who screamed boy, but it didn't hurt to look. Even though it crushed him every time he went home alone.

His friends left him alone for the most part, and he added his comments to the conversation when he could be bothered. He hated feeling that way. Like he didn't have enough energy to even converse with someone because it didn't feel like there was any point to it. He knew he was still grieving, but everything felt like so much work. He'd be happier staying at home with his bikes and cars and hiding away from the world. Maybe then it would be easier to cope.

He gave up after a couple of hours and left Enno, Rick and Denny to their evening, opting to walk home rather than getting a taxi. He pulled his hood up to ward off the chill and set a fast pace. What usually would take about forty-five minutes took around half an hour, and Ollie dripped with sweat when he arrived. Instead of going to his apartment, he slipped into the back of the garage, where he kept his custom bikes. It was a side job he'd been doing for around five years, and he had plenty of work to keep him busy. His calendar was full for the next year, if not longer.

Settling in front of his current project, he set to work, not even putting music on. Just the clank and click of what he was doing. Almost therapeutic. When his hands cramped, he stopped and sighed. It was eleven o'clock, and he needed more food before he crashed and repeated the same day over again.

He showered again, scrubbing clean, then made a sandwich and headed for his laptop. He checked his emails while he ate before reading the latest blog post from DaddyG. Ollie's heart fought between hope and envy as he read that DaddyG had found his boy. He'd been struggling as Ollie had been, but now he'd found someone. He hoped they worked out. Ollie posted a comment on the blog post.

"I'm so pleased you've met your boy. You deserve it after all this time. I wish I could find my boy. Everyone around me seems to be able to find their forever except for me. Keep your fingers crossed, eh?"

He didn't want to bring people down or make them pity him, but he couldn't help the tone or the pleading need for his boy to arrive. He was forty-three years old. How much longer could he wait before he gave up all hope?

The following days were more of the same thing, but he was in his element at the garage. It was all he'd known, and he loved it to the depths of his soul. He would love to have someone to leave it to, but that wasn't looking likely.

He finished the custom bike he'd been working on, and when the guy arrived to pick it up, he was overcome. The bike had been his brother's, and it had needed some work to get it up to rideable condition, but the owner had wanted something else added. A memorial paint job to remember who it had belonged to. Now, the sleek black bike had a phoenix flying almost the entire length of the bike.

"I can't even explain how much this means to me. It's absolutely perfect. Phoenixes were his favourite, and this means it'll always be his, regardless of his current owner. Thanks, Ollie."

The man, Gray, held out his hand, and they shook. Gray paid for the job and added a bonus for it being completed early, despite Ollie's protestations.

"You deserve it, Ollie. And I'll make sure to recommend you everywhere."

"Thanks, Gray. I enjoyed doing it."

Instead of relaxing when Gray disappeared with the bike secured on the back of the truck, Ollie pulled the next bike into place. He always kept one bike he was working on and the next bike waiting in the corner, then he could get started as soon as the previous one was done. He also called the owner to say he was starting work on the bike and asked if there were any changes he wanted to make to the original order. Luckily, it was fairly straightforward, and he only needed to restore it to its former glory.

"Bloody hell, Ollie. Enough already. Let's go to the club," Denny said several nights later. "You can have a boy for a night if nothing else."

Ollie rubbed a hand over his face. "I don't want one for a night, Denny. I want forever."

"Well, you'll have to deal with one night for now. You can't keep suppressing your Daddy needs. You need to let them out, and why not do that on someone who doesn't have a Daddy? It's fair play. You help them, they help you."

He made sense, though Ollie was reluctant to admit it. "Fine."

He wasn't a hardcore BDSM Daddy where he dressed in leather, so he wore his usual uniform of jeans and a shirt. There was no denying the frisson of "what if" that fluttered in his stomach as he entered the club with Denny at his side.

It was the same style club someone could find in any town or city, with dark furniture and decorations and low music, but with the added extra of slapping skin and moans. They continued through the club to the back, where they had a separate area for those interested in Daddy scenes. Some scenes included sex in the mix, and some didn't. Everyone was different, after all.

There were several boys without Daddies and several Daddies without boys, but the longer Ollie sat there holding his drink, the more uneasy he felt. He couldn't find the inclination to play with any of the boys, and when he finally pushed to his feet, he apologised to Denny and left.

At home, he sat in front of the TV, mindlessly staring at the pictures but not taking anything in. His brain was tuned to what he wanted from a boy. Someone he could give rules to and know the boy would be safe whenever Ollie wasn't there. Someone he could hold and look after and feed. Someone he could cherish and love. He needed to open his horizons if he was going to find that special someone. But how? And where? And when?

His mind went to DaddyG's blog. Could he help him find someone? It wouldn't hurt to ask.

He logged onto his laptop and brought up the blog, following it down to where it said "Contact Me" and clicking. It opened a blank email, and he started typing.

Dear DaddyG,

Thank you for the blog. It's been so helpful to me.

You probably receive a lot of emails asking for help, and I suppose I'm no different. I've tried everything I can think of to find my boy, but other than several failed relationships, I have nothing to show and so much to give. Do you know anyone who's looking for a Daddy? I know it's a huge generalisation, but I'm desperate. I feel like I'm missing a limb, and I'm not sure how much more my heart can take before it shuts down completely.

Thank you, even if you can't help.

D-Mad79

He clicked send before he could change his mind and stared at the screen. What more could he do except maybe move? He didn't want to do that. He didn't mind travelling, but at that moment in his life, he couldn't see himself giving up the garage and his family to move somewhere else. Maybe that was his problem.

Either way, something had to give. He could stay alone for the rest of his life, or he could move and potentially find a new life. Each had pros and cons to them, but how could he weigh them when they just about balanced each other? He rubbed his hands over his face, then switched off the laptop. His mind in turmoil, he did what he always did and headed down to the garage, his heart as heavy as his steps.

3

TOBY

“I can't believe I'm doing this. I must be mad.”

Two weeks later, after being talked into it on call after call with Ben, Toby clenched his fingers around the steering wheel and negotiated the roads his phone told him to until he pulled up outside the house Ben told him was his Daddy's. He didn't know DaddyG's real name, but he was sure he'd find out. He stared at the house for far longer than he should have, trying to find the courage to climb out and knock on the door, but the decision was taken from his hands when a guy with black hair and glasses came running out of the house. The guy opened the passenger door and settled into the seat.

“I'm hoping you're Toby, and I haven't just climbed into a stranger's car. I'm Ben.”

Toby chuckled. “I'm Toby.”

“Oh, thank god.” Ben grinned. “Come on. Daddy's making us spaghetti bolognese for lunch. He has to work tonight.” He climbed out of the car again and waited for Toby.

Toby couldn't leave the man standing on the path, so he got out and locked his car, fiddling with the keys as he joined Ben.

“I know it's scary, but we're all friends here. Daddy knows you're coming, and he's not an ogre." He leaned forward and lowered his voice. "Unless I misbehave. Then all bets are off. But I will be on my best behaviour, I promise. Scout's honour."

"You weren't a Scout," a man said from the doorway, and Toby jumped.

"You scared him!" Ben slid his arm around Toby's shoulders, which settled his nerves a little. They entered the house, and Ben said, "This is Daddy. Daddy, this is Toby."

Ben's Daddy was a little scruffy looking, but he had lots of laughter lines around his eyes, making him seem nice, and Toby relaxed.

"You might need to give him my other name, sweetheart. I don't think he'll want to call me Daddy all day."

Ben laughed. "Oops. This is Gareth."

Toby held out his shaking hand. "Nice to meet you, Gareth."

"You, too. Lunch will be about twenty minutes, so have fun, but remember the rules." He waved his hand and disappeared into what Toby assumed was the kitchen.

"We don't have a games console, but would you like to play a board game or watch TV or something?" Ben led the way into the living room and sat on the sofa.

Toby joined him. "I don't mind."

"I want to get to know you, but I know you have questions, too. Would it be easier to talk if you're doing something else at the same time? I know I get stuck in my head sometimes, and I need something to distract me before I can start figuring it all out."

Toby nodded. "I get like that, but mainly I *avoid* talking or thinking about it."

Ben chuckled. "Well, if you want help to find a Daddy, we can't ignore it."

"A film, maybe."

Ben grabbed the remote and brought up the film choices. "We won't get to see all of it before lunch, but maybe Daddy will let us watch it after."

Toby settled back on the sofa and tried to relax. Ben wasn't pushing him to talk, which was nice, but he found he wanted to. "How did you meet your Daddy? He didn't mention it on the blog."

A mischievous smile crossed Ben's face. "I'm his boss."

Toby gaped. "What?"

Ben giggled. "Yes. He started working for the supermarket I'm the manager of. And things went from there. It was a unique meeting. I didn't think I liked him to begin with, but then he grew on me."

"That's great." Toby sighed. "I struggle to trust people, Ben. It's why it's taken so long before I arrived at this point with you. The only Daddy I ever had was...unkind. Well, I suppose unkind might be the wrong word. He wanted sex and a slave, and he thought having a boy would give him one. It took me far too long to realise he didn't want me, only what I represented to him."

"Idiot. He didn't know what he had and lost." Ben squeezed his hand. "I can't promise there aren't more like him out there, but between us, we should be able to find a decent Daddy."

"How?"

Ben bit his lip and glanced towards the kitchen. "I have to ask Daddy before I can say anything."

Toby smiled. "It's okay."

"Food's ready!"

Ben paused the movie they hadn't been watching, and they entered the kitchen. The scent made Toby's stomach growl, and he covered it with his hands, wanting to cover his face instead. They settled at the dining table, and Gareth put a steaming plate of spaghetti bolognese in front of him. He closed his eyes and inhaled.

"It smells wonderful. Thank you. You didn't have to go to any trouble."

Gareth smiled. "It's no trouble. I always cook for Ben at

lunchtime when I'm working in the evening." He put a glass of milk next to each of their plates, but Toby ignored it.

The conversation was easy while they ate, getting-to-know-you questions Toby could answer with no stress. But when Gareth reminded him to drink as well as eat, Toby shuddered.

"I don't like milk. Sorry."

Gareth smiled. "It's fine. Do you like juice or water?" He stood.

"Juice would be good, thanks." He glanced at Ben. "I hate being a pain."

"You're not a pain, Toby. You have to admit to things when you don't like them; otherwise, how can people learn about you?"

He knew Ben was right, but it wasn't easy. He could stand up for himself when he needed to, but he preferred not to. It's something he hoped his eventual Daddy could help him with. Gareth returned with a glass of juice, and Toby thanked him and drank. After they finished eating, Ben helped Gareth with the plates, and they had a quiet conversation that Toby couldn't hear. But when Ben returned to the table, he was grinning.

"Daddy says I can tell you. Let's go back into the living room." Ben tugged on Toby's hand and dragged him towards the door.

"But what about tidying up?" Toby glanced at Gareth.

Gareth waved them away. "It's okay. Today, you get a pass." He winked.

Ben pulled him to the sofa, and once they settled, he clapped his hands. "So, we're creating a dating app for Daddies and boys."

Toby stared at him. "Seriously?" Ben nodded. "Is that how you're going to find me a Daddy?"

Ben nodded. "We're putting the app into beta mode tomorrow, and Daddy will post on the blog about it. We need to get a certain number of people to sign up to test the app works as it should and to find any bugs with it. Would you like to join?"

"Yes!" Hope flared inside him.

Ben smirked. "I already have someone in mind for you, but I'm going to leave it up to the app to see if it matches you before I say anymore."

"Oh, wow. This is so exciting. And not just for me. What made you decide this?"

Ben sighed. "The immense need for it. There are other similar apps out there, but we thought we could help fill a void. And here it is. Daddy's Boy."

Toby smiled. "Is that what you're calling it?"

"Yes. Shall we get you set up? You can be our first guinea pig." Ben chuckled.

"Why not? I've nothing to lose."

Gareth joined them, and they worked for the next hour on his profile. Toby downloaded the app to his phone.

"Now, bear in mind," Gareth said, "you're the first person on here. It won't have results for you for a few days at the earliest because we need to get other people signed up. But I'm sure Ben will keep you up to date."

Ben slung his arm around Toby. "Of course!"

✦

"Mum! I'm here!"

Toby entered the kitchen the next day, having followed the scent of a Sunday roast, which was why he was there. He loved his mother and his brothers, but no one would turn down his mum's roast dinner.

"Took you fucking long enough, Toto," Nigel said. His brother took after their mother, just like Toby did, and so did Nigel's twin, Fletcher. They weren't identical twins, but they were close enough there was no way they could disown each other.

"Lunch isn't ready, is it?" Toby raised his chin and his eyebrows.

"Well, no—"

"Then I'm not late, so shut it." If he didn't stand up for himself around his brothers, they'd never stop. They were younger than him by seven years, but their personalities were so big everyone else could easily disappear when they were around.

He kissed his mother on the cheek. "Looking good, Mum." He laughed when she hip-checked him while still stirring the gravy.

Sally had curly greying hair tucked into a ponytail as she always did, but she wore a dress he didn't recognise.

"Have you been on a shopping spree?"

"Don't be daft. This was a gift from your aunt. What better time to wear it than when my boys come home?"

Toby grinned at her and went to find his father. Don was usually in the garden, tending to the vegetables he grew all year round. Even when it was raining, he'd be out there in his waterproofs and wellies, making sure the plants were surviving. Luckily, today was a dry day.

"Hey, Dad. How are they coming along?"

"Good, good. No issues with them yet. We'll see how they fare during the winter."

Don had retired almost five years ago, and his mother had confided that she wasn't sure how well he'd take it, but by focusing on his plants, he was surviving—at least, that was what Toby thought.

He got shoved from behind and nearly ended up faceplanting in the soil. "Fletcher!" He raced after his brother, not too old to roughhouse when the idiot needed it. His brother was halfway up the stairs when he got to the bottom, and he gave up, determined to get him back later.

"Boys! Lunch is ready! Clean hands, clean minds and clean mouths at the table, please!"

Toby smiled at the words she said before each meal, knowing each of them needed the reminder to keep their swear words to a minimum—or even better, zilch. Sally hated swearing, so they all tried their hardest. Nigel and Fletcher had the worst time because they used them more often than anyone else Toby knew.

Once they sat together and started eating, Sally started in on the ritual inquisition.

"Any new relationship options?" she asked.

Fletcher and Nigel shoved food into their mouths, and Toby narrowed his eyes at their devious plan. Their mum wouldn't let them talk with a mouthful of food. Which left him. He sighed.

"Not really. I have signed up for a dating app, though. Just to try. I have a friend who created it, and he wanted me to be one of the people to test it. We're just waiting for more people to sign up before the first potential matches come up."

Sally frowned. "Are you sure that's a good idea? I hear so many things about meeting people from an app. It's how people kidnap others."

"It can be dangerous if you don't take precautions, but I know my friend. He won't let anyone on the app who hasn't been vetted."

The frown didn't leave her face, but she nodded. "Don't you dare, Nigel."

Nigel paused with his fork halfway to his mouth and groaned, putting it back on his plate. "I have a date with a girl next weekend."

That was probably worse than not having anything to say because his mum asked question after question, which Nigel couldn't answer because he barely knew the girl.

"How's work?" his father asked him while their mum hounded Nigel and Fletcher.

Toby smiled. "It's good. I love the dogs, and even cleaning up after them isn't so bad." He forked another bite into his mouth, trying to disguise the vegetables with potatoes and gravy. Despite him being an adult—and a grown-ass adult at that—his mother still gave him vegetables. And he ate them every bloody time. Evil woman. "How's retirement?"

Don hummed, and Toby assumed it was anything from "It's okay" to "Not bad" to "Hate it." Toby chuckled.

They all stayed for a movie afterwards, as usual. This time, it was *West Side Story*. His mum and dad loved musicals. Nigel and Fletcher? Not so much. Toby could take them or leave them, but seeing his brothers uncomfortable was worth it.

He kissed his mum goodbye, hugged his dad and headed for the door with his brothers on his tail.

"So, what's this app you were talking about?"

Toby knew what they were after, but they didn't know anything about his lifestyle. "Nothing you'd like. You'd bring the tone of the app down."

Fletcher gasped as if he was affronted, then laughed. "Probably. See you later, Toto."

Toby held up his finger, but he couldn't be mad at them when the nickname reminded him of when they couldn't say his name when they were little. It was cute. Even when they were dickheads.

His mind wandered to the app as he drove. Could it be his saving grace? He hoped so. He itched to open it and see what was happening with it, but Gareth only posted on the blog about it that morning, and he knew it wouldn't have had enough time to vet the applicants before sending them through, so although he wanted to see who was on it, he waited. Ben had said he would call him when there were enough people on it.

How amazing would it be if there was someone close who matched with him? He didn't mind travelling, but it would be easier for them if they were closer. Long-distance relationships were difficult to maintain, or so he'd been told. He didn't want to move away from his family, but maybe that would be something he'd need to consider. He couldn't expect the other person to move just because Toby didn't want to. Relationships were about compromise, after all. He'd have to cross that bridge if it came up.

When he got home, he showered, dressed in his pyjamas and settled in front of his screens, logging on and losing himself in the games until his alarm reminded him to sleep.

But for the first time in a long time, he couldn't.

After two hours of tossing and turning, he gave up and went back to his games, pulling an all-nighter, as he used to in college. There was one positive thing about it. He didn't get to experience the usual case of having to wake up in the morning because he was already awake.

4

OLLIE

Boys, Daddies, Snuggles and More

Who wants to be a guinea pig? By DaddyG.

Good news! The app will be entering its beta stage, and we need some volunteers. At the bottom of this post is a form you'll need to complete if you're interested, but there's no guarantee you'll be picked for the beta testing version. As soon as the beta stage is complete, we will set the app free into the world.

I just wanted to take a quick minute to say thank you to everyone. Your support, both the blog and the app, means a lot to BBOy22 and me. As something we wished for on a whim, it has blown our minds to think it's a wish coming true, and not just for us. I hope this app does what real life has not been able to so far—bring you closer to your HEA.

Ollie couldn't believe what he'd read. Had he made it up? He refreshed his screen to make sure he didn't imagine it. But no. There it was in black and white. An app that might just save his sanity. He clicked the link and filled out the form. When he hit send, a weight lifted from his shoulders. Maybe this was the way to find his boy—his HEA as DaddyG had said. Now, he just had to wait and see if he was chosen. He wouldn't hold out for a miracle, but even if he had to wait until the app was out of the beta stage, he would.

Working on the custom bike that day wasn't distracting him enough. His mind was still in his apartment, at the screen, waiting for his answer. Luckily, most of the work he did he knew like the back of his hand, so he could do it without needing to focus completely.

After stopping for a drink, he hesitated in the doorway. If he went left, he'd go to his custom bike. If he went right, he'd go to his apartment. Before he made his decision, he heard a couple of thumps and Denny shouting his name. He unlocked the door that he used for his apartment when he wasn't in the garage to see his friend holding a shit ton of beer.

Ollie took some of the load. "What's this for?"

"Thought we could lose ourselves in alcohol and come up with a plan for world domination."

Denny's deadpan delivery meant he could've been completely truthful about that, but thankfully, Ollie knew Denny well enough to understand he couldn't be arsed to conquer the world. He'd rather someone else do it, and he'd be their minion.

He carried the beer up the stairs and put it on the table. "Drink?" Denny raised his eyebrows and glanced at the beer. "I meant, other than beer. I'm starting with tea."

"Sure. I'm always up for trying new concoctions." He opened a beer and guzzled some.

Ollie shook his head and filled the kettle, the mindless tasks not distracting from the need to open his laptop and see if he'd received an answer from the app.

"Have you decided about the college reunion?"

Ollie groaned. "I'm not going, Denny. I don't care if it's been nearly twenty-five years since we left college. There's no one there I want to remember."

"Not even Frankie Roberts?" Denny snorted.

"Why would I want to remember his closeted ass? I spent far too much time on that asshole."

"In more ways than one." Denny waggled his eyebrows.

Ollie grunted. "That was more of a reminder than I wanted. Thanks for that."

"No problem." Denny disappeared, leaving Ollie with the chance to open his laptop. He logged on as quickly as it would allow, doctoring the drinks while he waited, then clicked on his emails. He purposefully hadn't installed emails on his phone because he hated seeing the bloody icons telling him how many he'd received, so he kept it to his laptop only, but at that moment, he wished he had. It would've been quicker.

Finally, it opened, and he scrolled down the unopened emails from that day. Nothing. He tried not to let it bother him because he knew there would probably be a huge influx of volunteers, and they probably needed to be checked out as well. It wasn't a quick job for them, but his nerves still vibrated with impatience.

He slammed the lid shut and grabbed the drinks, carrying them to the living room. Denny had made himself comfortable as always, feet resting on the coffee table, remote in hand.

"What're we watching?" Ollie asked though he wasn't bothered. He doubted he'd be able to concentrate on anything onscreen.

"Are you up for a *Marvel* or *Fast & Furious* marathon?"

"Vin Diesel."

"Technically," Denny said, "he's in both."

"Fuck off. You know what I mean. Hearing his voice is not as satisfying as watching him."

Denny held up his fist, and Ollie bumped it with the side of his own. It was something they could agree on.

They managed to get through half an hour of the first movie and two cans of beer before Denny set in about the reunion again.

"Why do you want to go to the reunion so badly? You didn't

enjoy college any more than I did," Ollie asked, staring at him.

"I'm curious what others have done with their lives."

Ollie snorted. "Can't you find that out on social media?"

"Probably, but it's not the same as seeing it in their faces when they try to make themselves look better than anyone else."

"So, you just want to see everyone squirm and make them uncomfortable."

Denny bellowed a laugh. "Pretty much."

"I'm not saying yes." He sighed. "But I'm not saying no."

Denny pumped his fist in the air. "Progress! Woohoo!"

"Just watch the damn film," Ollie grumbled, getting up. "Want food?"

"You cooking?"

Ollie glared at him. "When don't I?"

"When you're lost in your bikes?"

Ollie put his middle finger up as he walked away. "Cooking for one, then."

"You dare!" Denny shouted.

He couldn't help his smile at the response. He chose beef stir-fry and set about chopping vegetables. His gaze kept snagging on the laptop, but he refused to check it before he'd finished getting the ingredients ready. Once they were sizzling in the pan and the rice bubbling away, he opened the laptop again and logged in. He stirred the food while he waited for it to load, wishing he'd caved and bought a new one like he had planned to but never got around to. When the emails loaded, his heart raced, and he clicked on the one from Daddy's Boy.

Dear Mr Young,

Thank you for your interest in the app. We are pleased to offer you a position on the beta team. If you are still interested, please download the app and log in using the details below. As soon as you set up your profile, you'll be available for matches.

Please be patient with us. As the app is new, it may take a while before there are enough people signed up before matches are found. This will not stop you from being able to view who is on there, but the app will not match you with them unless it thinks you are suitable. You, obviously, have the chance to make your own decisions. Feel free to contact anyone you wish, but remember to be kind and courteous.

If you find any bugs with the app, please use the feedback option in the main menu or, alternatively, email us.

Finally, welcome to Daddy's Boy.

Sincerely,

Gareth and Ben

(DaddyG and BBoy22)

Ollie took his eyes from the screen and focused on the stir-fry so it didn't burn, but his heart pounded. Was this the miracle he'd been waiting for? He grabbed two plates and set them on the counter, dividing the rice and stir-fry between them both. He shoved a fork in each and carried them to the living room.

"Awesome, thanks." Denny dived into his straight away, but Ollie was slower, his mind still reeling. "What's wrong?"

"Nothing." Should he explain it to Denny or leave it for now? Ollie almost rolled his eyes at himself. He never kept anything from Denny or Enno—well, almost nothing. "I've been accepted into a beta group for a dating app."

Denny rested his plate on his lap and sipped his beer. "And?"

"What do you mean?"

"What are you worrying about?"

Ollie sighed. Trust Denny to pick up on that. "I'm scared to hope."

"What's the app?"

"Daddy's Boy. You know the Boys, Daddies, Snuggles & More blog?" Denny nodded. "The owner of the blog created it. He asked for volunteers, and I got accepted. What if there's no one on there for me?"

"Then you won't be any worse off than you are now."

He had a point, though Ollie didn't want to say it. "What if it's someone on the other side of the country?"

"Then you travel and do long-distance until you find out whether you're compatible. Then you figure out who wants to move."

"I don't want to move."

Denny sighed. "What do you want more, Ollie? Love or the garage?"

Ollie didn't reply because he didn't know the answer. He ate in silence, eyes on the screen, but his brain was on the app. When they'd finished, he took the plates back into the kitchen, filled the dishwasher, and then wrote down the login details for the app. He settled back on the sofa with his phone in his hand.

"Here goes nothing."

"Or here goes everything."

He downloaded the app and logged in successfully, which was a plus in the new apps pro column straightaway—no fumbling with the correct details. He didn't have any other option than to create a profile, which made sense if they didn't want random people looking at the other men on it before they could be identified themselves.

He chose a picture with Denny's help. It was one they'd managed to make him smile in, which wasn't a regular occurrence at the moment. He filled in his likes, dislikes, hard limits and several other questions he remembered from when he'd completed the application form for the club. When it was done, he clicked to save it, and it showed a big green tick before opening a menu page. He saw the feedback button the email mentioned, and there was a search button.

"Should I search now, or should I wait to be matched?"

Denny shrugged. "It wouldn't hurt to look."

He pressed to search and was given options to put the users in different orders, such as distance, alphabetical or based on certain criteria. Ollie clicked distance, and within seconds, eleven profiles were returned with the option to search further afield.

"Not bad, but that's within twenty miles," Denny said. "I suppose you could go further afield if none of these is what you're looking for."

Ollie hovered over the view button but closed down the app instead. "I'm going to wait."

"You've waited this long."

The phone burnt a hole in his pocket as he watched the films and drank. After finishing film three, Denny stood and yawned.

"I'm going. Don't stay up too late staring at your phone. A watched kettle never boils," Denny hollered as he disappeared.

"I've never understood that saying," Ollie murmured.

To distract himself from checking the app, he went through his emails. Then he went through them again and unsubscribed from far too many that he'd never managed to do before. He couldn't even remember signing up for most of them. Then when that wasn't enough of a distraction, he went through his spam folder and bin, clearing out everything he didn't need. After that, he switched off his laptop and went for a shower. His hands itched to open the app and see if any of those eleven men were compatible, but he didn't want to be disappointed. Waiting until he had a match would at least make things easier because they would be suitable according to a computer.

He barely slept that night, and the following day was more of the same—itching to open it. But he resisted. Denny must've opened his mouth, though, because Enno asked him about the app. Ollie explained about it, then hesitated.

"What's really got you worked up, Ollie?" Enno asked after

pulling him into the office.

"What if I'm not a good enough Daddy?"

Enno sighed. "You won't be good enough for some people, and you'll be too good for others. But there will be the ones who you're perfect for. You like spoiling your boys, and some boys need a stricter hand, like Rick. Those aren't for you."

"I feel like this is my last chance, Enno. I don't know why, but I do."

Enno opened his mouth to answer, but Ollie's phone chimed. Ollie frowned, not recognising the tone and pulled it from his pocket. He stared at Enno. "I have a match."

Enno grinned. "Look at it, then!"

Ollie blew out a breath, his heart missing several beats as he logged in with shaking hands.

Congratulations! You have a match!

He clicked to view the profile, and a man with short brown hair and a layer of scruff on his round face filled the screen. His nose was fairly prominent, but it was his eyes that held Ollie. He couldn't tell the colour, but they were dark. His lips were thin, but they were curved up at the corners in a shy smile that had an ache starting in Ollie's chest.

"He's nice," Enno said over Ollie's shoulder.

Ollie clicked on the profile.

Username: Oh2Bs3xy
Likes: Dogs, Biscuits, Tea, Video games
Dislikes: Vegetables, Milk, Jelly (just no!)
Hard limits: Anything harder than a spanking, bondage I can't get out of myself, exhibitionism.

Ollie licked his lips. He sounded perfect if he ignored the

vegetable thing. He checked where the guy was from.

"He's thirty miles away."

Enno squeezed his shoulder. "Not impossible. It'd take between half an hour and an hour, depending on where exactly he is. It's doable. What have you got to lose?"

For the first time in such a long time, Ollie allowed himself to hope. Could this be who he belonged with? Only time would tell, but at least he had a match.

"Send him a message. Start a conversation. See where it goes."

Ollie closed the app. "I will. But I need to let this settle first. I'll message him tonight."

"I'll ask you to prove it tomorrow." Enno stared at him, trying to look stern. It might work on his boy, but it didn't on a fellow Daddy.

Ollie chuckled, a sound he hadn't made for a while. "Deal."

The rest of the day was a whirlwind of emotions as he came to terms with what was potentially in his future. Now he had someone who might be interested in him, he hesitated, although he knew it was only temporary. When he settled that night, he would put it all on the line and hope he wasn't making a huge mistake.

5

TOBY

"Toby! It worked!" Ben's words gushed into Toby's ears, and he tried to unpack everything he'd said while juggling the leads and the phone.

"What?"

"The app! It matched you with the guy I told you about the other day! I knew you'd be perfect for each other!"

Toby filtered out anything else Ben said as his mind tried to acclimatise to the idea of someone being what he needed and wanted. Could it be that easy? If the app matched them, then they must have something in common. But where did they go from here? They'd have to meet at some point. The thought soured any joy he'd felt from the news. He hated meeting new people on the best of days. Would the Daddy be open to chatting online for a while before they met? Or would they expect a meeting straight away?

"Toby!" Ben shouted, garnering his attention.

He gripped the phone tighter and pressed it against his ear. "Yes?"

"Are you okay?"

"No. I'm having a freak-out."

Ben chuckled. "I thought you might be. What's worrying you?"

"Everything. Talking to him, meeting him, interacting with him on any level." He exhaled, feeling lightheaded.

"Breathe, Toby. Breathe. I don't need you collapsing somewhere, and I have no idea how to find you."

Toby concentrated on his steps, heading back to the kennels. "Okay. Who is he?"

"You can look for yourself. You'll get a notification from the app, and he'll be front and centre."

"Can't you just tell me about him?"

Ben sighed. "Fine." Toby heard clicking, and then Ben came back on. "He is forty-three, has black closely cropped hair with streaks of grey, I think, and has a goatee. Aww, he has crinkles around his eyes, just like Daddy does. That means he's happy a lot. That's good. He has a lovely thick bottom lip, too. Just big enough to bite down on."

Toby giggled. "You're crazy."

"Maybe so, but it got you to laugh. He likes tea, just like you, bikes and toffee popcorn—a man after my own heart. He doesn't like coffee, fizzy drinks or, uh oh, a mess. You might be in trouble with this one." Ben chuckled. "I think you'll like him, Toby."

He didn't want to get his hopes up when they hadn't even spoken yet, but everything so far sounded wonderful. "Where does he live?"

Ben hummed, clicking again, then said, "About thirty miles from you. So not far."

"So close? I was expecting someone from across the country. It would've been just my luck if they had been."

"You need to message him or wait until he messages you. But if he doesn't, you do it. He might be as nervous as you are."

Toby bit his lip as the kennels came into view. "It'll have to wait until later. I don't finish until five o'clock today."

"That's okay. He's not going anywhere. Just don't leave it too long because you'll chicken out. Call me if you want a push."

"I will. Thanks, Ben."

"You're very welcome, bestie!"

Toby chuckled and ended the call. They were far from best friends, but he could see them getting there at some point. He let the dogs back into their kennels and wrote on the paperwork that they'd been walked and the time. Then he set about cleaning the empty kennels ready for the new dogs arriving the following day.

His phone chimed at him on the way home, but he didn't look at it until he'd closed his front door behind him. The notification came from the Daddy's Boy app. His thumb froze over the logo, but then he took a breath and pressed it.

Congratulations! You have a match!

He clicked to view, and D-Man79's profile picture came up. Ben had been right. He was nice to look at, and that lip was ready for biting. But it was the kindness in his eyes that held Toby still. He couldn't see any of the anger or nastiness from his ex, and that, more than anything else, settled him. A message icon popped up, saying he had a message, and he stared at it as he clambered onto the sofa and curled up in the corner. He pressed it.

D-Mad79

Hi there. We've been matched on here, and I wanted to say hello. I hope we can chat and get to know each other, and maybe, if we find out we're compatible, we can meet soon. Ask any questions you want to ask. I'm a completely open book to you. No matter how silly you think your question is, I promise I will answer it. Hopefully, speak to you soon. Ollie. P.S. I'll start. What is your favourite colour?

Toby smiled at the reassuring tone, along with the random dating question. He bit his lip, trying to stop his smile, but he couldn't. He pressed reply.

Oh2Bs3xy

Hello, Ollie. I would love to chat. I will start by saying I'm a nervous nellie when it comes to meeting new people, and it takes me a while to pluck up the courage to meet someone. If you can be patient with me, I'll get there, but if you want to find someone who can meet you sooner, that's fine. No hard feelings. In case you're still interested, my favourite colour is teal. Some people say it's the same as turquoise, but I'll stand on that hill and argue all day long. Turquoise is lighter than teal. Question: What do you do? Toby.

He pressed send before he could read it over and clicked out of the app because he would've second-guessed his words for the next three hours if he'd stayed on it. He messaged Ben to say the Daddy had messaged, and he'd sent a reply. He put his phone down and closed his eyes. Exhaustion pulled at his body. He guessed it was from all the excitement of the day. It was wonderful to think this could be the start of something big.

He groaned and got up, heading for the kitchen to heat some soup. He didn't enjoy cooking and made his dinners as easy as possible, especially when he'd been working all day. Soup, toasties, tinned ravioli or beans on toast were about his limit when he had no energy. On other days, when he finished work earlier, he could usually manage something like spaghetti bolognese or throw something in the oven like a frozen pie and chips. It wasn't the healthiest, but he'd not died yet.

As he slurped his soup, his phone chimed again, and his stomach swooped when he saw it was from the app.

D-Mad79

Hey, Toby. Thanks for replying. I have no problems with chatting on here for a while. You don't need to be nervous. Although saying that, I am a little too. I want this to work so badly, but I don't want to put pressure on either of us. I probably have done that now I mentioned it. Sorry! I agree that turquoise and teal are different. Turquoise is more of a blue-green, whereas teal is more of a green-blue. To answer your question, I'm a mechanic. I have a garage where we work on several cars a day, but I also make custom designs for motorbikes. Your turn. What do you do?

Toby's cheeks were aching by the time he finished reading, and he rubbed them to ease the ache. Toby wasn't particularly interested in cars or bikes, but he could appreciate how pretty some of them were. They didn't have to have the same interests, though. He wasn't sure if to reply straight away or wait a while, so he finished his soup first, then got ready for bed before picking up his phone again as he waited for his game to load.

Oh2Bs3xy

Hi. Congratulations on passing the turquoise/teal quiz. I bet customising bikes is a tricky but rewarding job. I can't begin to understand where to start with that. I can barely change a tyre. I can do it. I just don't find it easy. As for me, I'm a glorified dog walker. Lol. I work at what the company calls "doggy daycare," although that makes me think of American kennels rather than British. In other words, I look after dogs while their owners are on holiday or away on business or something like that. They truly have personalities of their own. Question: Why do you dislike fizzy drinks?

Again, he didn't re-read his message. He was finding it easy to talk to Ollie, and he didn't want to jinx it by making himself nervous. He put his phone aside and joined his friends online. As was usual, he lost himself in the game, and everything else faded away. His phone alarm roused him at bedtime, and he rubbed at his eyes. He probably should've gone to bed instead of playing, but he didn't want to miss out on his time with his friends, even if he didn't speak to them much during the game.

He brushed his teeth and climbed into bed, remembering to put his phone to charge on the bedside table before snuggling down. He was dozing when he remembered about Ollie. Reaching blindly for his phone, he squinted at the bright screen. Turning down the brightness, he noticed the Daddy's Boy app icon and pressed it.

D–Mad79

Most of the custom jobs are changing the paint job. But I do get some who want all the bells and whistles. I'm always up for a challenge, though. It's not for everyone. There's a reason they say a dog is a man's best friend. You get to be best friends with them all. As long as you enjoy the work, it doesn't matter what job you have. As for fizzy drinks, I don't like the bubbles. Call me strange when I admit this though...I don't mind beer. I'll hold my hands up and say I have no idea how that works. Maybe it's not the bubbles at all. Maybe it's the additives or something. I don't know. I gave up trying to work it out myself years ago. What's your favourite dog breed?

Toby smiled and replied.

Oh2Bs3xy
Seeppy wwll msesssaege tmoorrwo.

He turned his phone off and gripped it, which made it even more difficult to find when his alarm woke him. He shoved at the pillows and covers until he found the wayward phone. Why was his phone in bed with him and not on the bedside table as it should be? He blinked at it, then unlocked it. Palming his forehead, he read the message from Ollie.

D-Mad79

Lol. That's so cute. I'll leave you to sleep. Sleep well, Toby.

Toby snorted. Cute. Not quite the impression he was going for, but he'd take anything other than what he'd experienced before. He checked the clock and scrambled to get showered and dressed. The day was warmer than it had been, so he grabbed a coat and walked to work, chomping on a banana and a croissant as he went. He wanted to reply to Ollie, but he also wanted to think through the interactions they'd had so far. It was so easy to talk to him, and Toby didn't trust it. Was he trying to find trouble where there was none? Or was there some little niggle telling him something wasn't right?

"Sarah!" he called a couple of hours later. "I need your help."

"Sure. What's wrong?"

Toby shook his head, having turned himself into a right mess with his thoughts. It was a never-ending circle, and he needed to talk it out. "Not here. My house after work."

"I have the late shift tonight, remember?"

"I'll be up. No way I can sleep yet." He twined his fingers together.

Sarah hugged him. "Are you sure I can't help you before? You're a mess, Toby."

"I just need to make sense of it all."

"Is there someone else you can talk to before I finish? Maybe someone who can help calm you down. I bet you haven't had anything to eat or drink today, have you?"

Toby shrugged. "Maybe Ben, but I don't know if he's at work."

"Try him, at least. I'll still come round after work, but he might be able to help in between."

She hugged him again, and he inhaled her scent, trying to calm himself. "I'm heading out. See you later."

He dragged his coat on and set a punishing pace home. Then he exhaled, slowed and pulled out his phone. Dialling Ben, he held his breath.

"Toby! I'm glad to hear from you. I wanted to find out what happened yesterday with D-Mad79 but didn't want to interrupt."

"Ben," he mumbled.

"Toby, what's wrong?" Toby swallowed but couldn't voice his fear. "Toby, you're worrying me now. Can you tell me what's wrong?"

"I don't know if I can do this."

"Do what, sweetheart?"

Toby pulled his coat tighter around him. "I don't know what to believe and what not to. It gets mixed up in my head when I think about it too much. It's like going round in circles and never coming to a conclusion, let alone a right one."

"Jeez, Toby. You scared several years off my life, I think." Ben blew out a breath. "Look, from my point of view, trust is a tricky subject. There are no hard or fast rules or a checklist you can use to figure out if someone is telling you the truth or not. But usually, if I look into someone's eyes, I can see their sincerity. Or not, as the case may be." He paused for a moment. "I think you need to just try. Don't worry about the little details. Get to know him using what he's giving you, then meet him and see if the visual he gave you matches with reality."

"I don't know if I can meet him."

"Would you like me to come with you?"

Toby's breath caught. "You'd do that?"

"Of course, I would. This app is not supposed to make your life more difficult. I'd do anything to help."

Toby chewed his lip, wishing he could curl up on the sofa to think about things, but Ben told him not to do that too much. "That would definitely make me feel better about it."

"Set it up then, Toby. Set up a meeting, and Gareth and I will be there with you. You won't have to worry about a thing."

"Thank you, Ben. I feel much better now."

"Good! I think I need a vodka after that scare!"

Toby chuckled, the first he'd managed that day. He could do this. He could. Maybe.

6

OLLIE

Oh2Bs3xy

Hi, Ollie. Sorry for not replying sooner. I had a bit of a wobble, but I'm fine again now. I'd like to meet you if you still want to?

If Ollie still wanted to? Of course, he did. He was enjoying their conversation, but he'd expected it to be a lot longer than a day before Toby said he was ready to meet. He'd mentioned having a wobble—did that mean he'd had second thoughts? Ollie wouldn't blame him. It was a trust-heavy situation they were in, and Toby needed to feel safe.

Maybe if Ollie offered to go to a cafe in Toby's town instead of them meeting in Ollie's. However much he wanted to show off his garage, it could wait for another time. Toby's nerves were the most important factor.

D-Mad79

Hey. I hope you're feeling better. If it was something I did, please let me know. I don't ever want to make you feel uncomfortable. I'd love to meet. Would you like me to come to a cafe close to you? We can meet in public where lots of people can see us and maybe have some lunch. How does that sound?

He sent the message and closed the app. He had nothing to do that night, but if he kept the app open, he'd be checking it every minute. Instead, he set it on the worktop and sat beside the bike he'd been working on. The paint job was coming along nicely, a rather unique skeleton, flowers and flames combination. It wasn't something he would have on his own, but it was nice all the same.

When his phone dinged, he shot up from the floor and checked it, unable to pretend he hadn't been waiting for it.

Oh2Bs3xy
That would be great. Thank you so much for understanding. What day is best for you? I know you have a business to run.

The boy was so thoughtful of others. Why hadn't he been snapped up already?

D–Mad79
Sunday is the best day for me as the garage is closed, but I can come any day that's good for you. I can make sure someone covers for me.

Enno was more than capable of looking after the place for a few hours or a day, even. He knew the ins and outs of the garage as well as Ollie did.

Oh2Bs3xy
Sunday is good. Let me know a date, and I'll give you directions to the cafe.
D–Mad79
Is this Sunday any good for you?

Oh2Bs3xy
Sure. How about eleven o'clock at the Waterside Cafe?
D-Mad79
I'll be there. Looking forward to it.

Ollie couldn't keep the grin from his face, and he forgot all about the bike and headed to his apartment instead. He had far too many days in between now and then, and he knew he'd sleep for shit. They didn't have to end their conversation. Ollie opened up the app again and clicked on Toby's icon.

D-Mad79
You never did tell me which breed of dog was your favourite.

He didn't wait for the answer, instead heading for a shower. There was a deep need inside of him that nothing but a release would help him with. He stripped down after starting the water, already imagining having a boy on his knees. Wrapping his hand around his cock, he gave a few leisurely strokes as he stepped into the spray. He closed his eyes and let the water flow over his head and neck, bracing one hand against the tiles.

The boy licked at his crown, gathering the precome already leaking, a hand encircling the base while he sucked the head into his mouth and used his tongue to massage the underside. The other hand fondled his balls, squeezing and tugging, sending spikes of fire up his spine. The boy slowly took him further into his mouth, inch by inch, until his nose nestled in his groin. Then he gazed up at him as if he had given him everything.

Ollie's release painted the tiles, his chest heaving. He wanted that. So much. He wanted a boy to give everything to. And he might just get his chance.

Sunday dawned bright but breezy. Ollie would know because he woke before the sun peeked over the horizon and couldn't get back to sleep again. Instead, he cleaned. The house wasn't dirty by any stretch, but he did jobs that he'd put off for weeks, like the inside of the kitchen cupboards. He'd had enough hours to do them all before he needed to leave.

By the time he climbed into his car, his body was thrumming with a low-level buzz. He wanted this to work. He wanted them to get on well in person. His phone told him it would take him about forty-five minutes to get there, traffic permitting, so unless he met Sunday drivers along the way, he should be early enough to park and get a table and a tea before Toby arrived. Enough time to settle his emotions.

He set the radio to play in the background as his mind whirled with thoughts of "what if" and "what could be." He hadn't wanted to get his hopes up, but he couldn't help it.

The world helped him out, and he made it on time, found a parking space close by and entered the Waterside Cafe—though why it was called that, he had no idea. There was no water to be seen except what people drank.

Ordering a small tea, he chose a table close to a window but not right next to it, not knowing if being right in front of one would make Toby's nerves worse. There was plenty of light and space and lots of wooden, well-cared-for furniture. On the other side of the room were several sofas with a small coffee table in between them. It was a quaint place, and Ollie liked it a lot.

He saw the moment Toby entered the cafe, hand gripping another man's arm, his head swivelling around. Ollie half-stood and waved, and Toby froze. The other man leaned close to his ear and said something, and Toby relaxed, though Ollie could see he was still tense. They wandered closer, another man following, and Ollie frowned. Why were there three of them? Was this some sort of scam? He tensed, ready to fight or leave—he wasn't sure which.

"Hi," Toby said, his voice small and quiet.

"Hey." Ollie glanced at the other two men.

The one behind Toby and the other man came to the side and held out his hand. "I'm sorry for the ambush. I'm Gareth or DaddyG." He smiled. "Toby was a little nervous about meeting you, so we offered to come with him to make things a little easier for the first few minutes."

Ollie shook his hand, his shoulders dropping. "Nice to meet you. I've read your blog since the beginning."

Gareth nodded. "I remember you messaging in."

Ollie's face heated, and he cleared his throat. "Seems like you answered with way more than I expected."

Gareth rested his hand on the other man's shoulder. "This is Ben, my boy. And you already know Toby."

"Nice to meet you, Ben."

Ollie scooted across to the other seat at the table, giving Gareth the seat next to him while Toby and Ben settled opposite. Toby's demeanour blared, "I want to hide," but he didn't leave. A server came and took their drink order.

"Hey, Toby," Ollie said, taking control of the conversation. "Thank you for inviting me here. I love this cafe. Do you know why it's called the Waterside Cafe? I didn't see any water near here." He thought talking about something benign might help to relax him.

Toby licked his lips, his face pale, but he glanced up. "The owners have a few other cafes in different towns. The first one they opened was beside a river, and they called it the Waterside Cafe. They kept the name for all the businesses to keep it on brand."

Ollie nodded. "That's a sound business decision. I bet trying to differentiate between them in the accounts is difficult." He chuckled and mimed typing, affecting a slightly different tone. "'Waterside Cafe, invoice six-five-two. Which blooming Waterside Cafe?'"

Toby cracked a smile, his teeth scraping his bottom lip, and Ollie's heart ratcheted up a notch. "They must have some sort of coding system or something. Or abbreviations, like WCMK for Milton Keynes."

Ollie shook a finger at him. "Good thinking." He wrapped his hands around his mug after the server brought their order. "You said your favourite dog is a Great Dane. Have you looked after any through your job?"

Toby nodded and smiled, and Ollie exhaled at the spark igniting in his eyes. "We've had several over the years, but the one I remember the most was called Boris. He was huge but had the softest personality. Whenever we walked past a child, he'd lie down to be stroked. As if he realised his large body made children wary. He was adorable."

"He sounds it. Clever, too."

Toby grinned. "He really was. We have this cute little poodle called Peppa with us at the moment. She's been with us for about two months now. Her owners are away on business, and they keep extending it. We don't have a problem looking after her, but I can tell she's missing them. Dogs love their owners, after all."

Ollie sipped his tea. "As much as the owners love their dogs."

"Some of them, anyway."

"True." He was aware of Gareth and Ben murmuring beside them, but he focused on Toby. He was who Ollie was here for. "How are your games going? Are you still beating your friend?"

Toby chuckled, and Ollie smiled in response to the carefree act. "Yes! He's not at all happy with me, but he needs to stop getting grumpy about it. I've been practising enough now."

The games were a huge part of Toby's life. How long did he play them? It wasn't his place to ask. Yet.

"Toby?" Ben murmured, and Toby glanced at him. "Are you okay if we head out now?" Ben glanced at Ollie, then back to Toby.

Toby curled his shoulders, his eyes darting to his hands, and they all let him have the time to think. Finally, he exhaled, straightened his back and smiled. "Yes. I'll be fine. Thank you so much for coming with me."

Ben tugged at him, and they embraced. "You're welcome. You know I'd do anything for you."

Gareth stood and held out his hand. "Nice to meet you, Ollie."

"You, too." He turned to Ben. "And you, too."

Ben smiled, slipping his arm through Gareth's and resting his head on his shoulder. "I look forward to seeing you in the future."

Ollie grinned at the implication of his words. They headed out, and Toby watched their progress, rolling his shoulders when they exited the cafe.

"You can call them back if you want to," Ollie murmured. "I don't mind. I want you to feel comfortable."

Toby sighed. "I do. That's why I let them go. I just struggle to know what to talk about." He threaded his fingers together, and Ollie took a chance. He surrounded Toby's hands with his own and stared into his eyes, noticing the small frown as Toby glanced at their hands.

"We talk about whatever you want to talk about. Dogs, games, Milton Keynes, Daddies and boys, TV. You name it, we can talk about it. Nothing's off limits. If you have questions, ask me. I'll answer anything." Toby smiled. "But first, would you like to get an early lunch?"

Toby nodded. "I'd love that."

Ollie let go, missing the warmth of his hands at once, and grabbed the menus, passing one to Toby. "Do you know what's good here?"

"Everything."

Ollie chuckled. "Noted."

They perused the menus and placed their order. Ollie chose the chicken tikka roll with salad, while Toby decided on the sausage sandwich, which he proceeded to drench in ketchup. Ollie grinned at the display.

"Do you like some sausages with your ketchup?"

Toby glanced at him and licked his lips. "A little."

Ollie was so proud of him for making a joke. "Glad to hear it. I know you are averse to vegetables. Any reason?" He took a bite of his roll.

"I've never found a way to make them taste nice, either raw or cooked. Life is too short to eat disgusting stuff."

Ollie tilted his head from side to side. "Yes, but you also need to be healthy." He held up his hand. "I'm not nagging. I'm just saying."

"I eat fruit, and I eat vegetables when I'm at Mum's house for dinner."

Ollie frowned. "Why do you eat them there and nowhere else?"

"Because she gives me them. I don't like leaving anything, so I disguise them with potatoes and gravy or some other combination, then I don't taste them as much."

"You could hide vegetables while you're cooking. Grating carrots into a bolognese sauce is one way."

Toby scrunched his nose. "I don't cook often. Well, I do, but not from scratch. I use a lot of tinned and jarred food."

Ollie nodded. "That's okay. Not everyone likes to cook. I love it, but I can understand how annoying it can be if it's not something you enjoy."

They ate in silence for a few minutes, and then Toby asked about his current project. "Have you finished the bike yet?"

Ollie shook his head. "I still have the paint job to finish, but I've done all the other modifications now." He pulled out his phone and swiped to a photo, turning it to show Toby. "It's a beautiful bike, even before the changes. It has a sidecar that attaches to it, too."

"I don't know much about bikes, as I mentioned, but it does look nice." Toby wrapped his hands around his glass of water and held it to his lips.

Ollie couldn't help watching him swallow. Toby wasn't feminine in any way, but there was an elegance to his movements. If Ollie was in a historical romance novel, he'd say Toby was part of the upper echelons of society.

They finished their lunch in comfortable conversation, and Ollie was glad that Toby seemed to relax completely. After the server had taken their empty plates, Ollie took another chance.

"Would you like to go for a walk and continue our conversation?"

Toby tilted his head as if checking in with his brain to see if he could do it. "Yes. I'd love to."

"You can show me what's around here."

They stood and pulled on their coats. Ollie insisted on paying for their food, and though Toby declined at first, he thanked him. He was glad they'd bundled up when the breeze hit them. Toby pulled a woolly hat from his pocket and tugged it on, and Ollie couldn't help but tweak his nose.

"That hat suits you."

Toby's face reddened, and he dropped his gaze, but not before Ollie saw his smile.

7

TOBY

Having Ben and Gareth with him when he met Ollie was the best idea Ben had ever had. It had made meeting Ollie so much easier. And as they walked side by side down the street, he was relaxed and content. He had no worries that Ollie wasn't what he said he was, but the lingering doubt that Ollie could change was still there. Toby wasn't sure if he would ever get rid of it completely. But for now, at least, he was enjoying Ollie's company.

"I'd like to talk about Daddies and boys now if you're okay with that?" Ollie said.

Toby had known it was coming, and he was ready for it. After all, it was the reason they were there. "Sure."

"Have you been in this kind of relationship before?"

Toby nodded slowly. This was the bit he didn't want to do, but he needed to explain. "My story's not great, but you need to know." He fell silent, trying to figure out where to start, and Ollie never once pushed him to talk. "I've been single for five years, but before that, I was with a 'Daddy.'" He held up his fingers to make air quotes, so Ollie could see his meaning. "I was with him for about two years, and when we first started, it was great. He took care of me, kept me on an even keel, and in return, when I moved in with him, I helped around the house. He worked twelve-hour

59

shifts over four days, then had four days off. It worked well. Until it didn't." Toby blew out a breath and stared into the distance.

"I can see you're struggling with this. Can I hold your hand?" Ollie asked.

Toby frowned. "Why?"

Ollie's eyes widened. "To offer comfort?"

Toby's heart raced. "Holding hands gives comfort?"

Ollie stopped walking and faced him, eyebrows drawn close over his eyes. "Usually, yes. A show of solidarity, of giving you a tether to keep you in the present while you have to relive the past. To know you're not alone." He blinked. "Have you never held hands with someone before?"

Toby tried to remember if he had. "Maybe when I was a teenager, but no, not really. I've seen people do it, but I never considered why."

Ollie's nostrils flared, and then he smiled. "Shall we try it? If you don't like it, you can pull away. I only want to help, not make things worse."

Toby held out his hand, and Ollie threaded the fingers together, holding them between them. Their fingers were cold, and it was a bit strange having his fingers spread to accommodate Ollie's, but as they warmed, it didn't feel so weird.

"Shall we keep walking?" Ollie asked, and Toby nodded.

It took a minute to get used to walking beside someone while holding their hand, but when he did, he found he enjoyed it. "He never held my hand. If he ever needed to keep hold of me, it was always my wrist. I just thought that was usual."

Ollie squeezed his hand, and Toby smiled as a hint of warmth flowed through his stomach.

He sighed and continued his story. "It took far too long for me to realise I wasn't an equal partner in the relationship. That he was using me like a slave. I was doing so much around the house. Cleaning, cooking, maintenance, that kind of thing. When he came home, he'd fuck me, then go to sleep. On his days off, I'd fetch and carry for him and let him fuck me whenever he felt like it. It was my best friend who made me see what was happening."

Needing a brief break, he tugged Ollie towards an art shop he loved looking in the window of.

"Do you want to go in?" Ollie asked.

Toby shook his head. "I just love looking at the displays. The colours are amazing."

"Are you interested in art?"

"Not to create myself, but to look at, yes. I just love how they use the colours of whatever painting they're displaying that week in the surrounding area." He pointed at the bottom. "See those ribbons? They're a deep red colour, and it matches with the splash of red in the sunset."

"I see that. It's beautiful."

"Every week, I make sure to check out what they've done. I love it." He sighed and turned to continue walking. "Sarah is my best friend. She questioned me when she saw how tired I was. I think it was because I was so tired that everything came tumbling out. She was horrified. When I think back on it now, I can see why, but at the time, I didn't think it was wrong. The first time I tried to leave, he stopped me. It was then I saw the change in his eyes. He was no longer the easygoing 'Daddy' I'd met. Instead, he was a..." He couldn't think of a word good enough to describe him.

"Asshole," Ollie spat.

Toby chuckled. "That'll do. After a failed second attempt, I began making plans. He went out with his friends one night and forgot to take the keys to my car. He usually took them so I couldn't leave. Where we lived at the time, I needed a car to get into town. The moment I saw them drive away, I didn't hesitate. I took whatever I could carry and shoved it in the car, not wanting to take too long, and then drove to my parents. I got a restraining order, and he's never tried to get to me. But I won't go to the clubs here just in case he's a member."

Ollie blew out a breath. "I'm so damn proud of you," he said. "So damn proud. You're amazing."

Toby licked his lips, his heart missing a beat. "Why?"

Ollie pulled them to a stop. "You're a fighter, Toby. Yes, you found yourself in a bad situation, but instead of putting up with it, you fought to get free."

"It took me long enough."

"It doesn't matter. You did it." Ollie brushed his thumb across his cheek, then continued walking. "I can understand why you struggle to meet new people. Trust is a big thing. To have someone's trust is amazing, but to give it means everything. I hope someday you can trust me."

Toby couldn't answer, and Ollie didn't seem to need one. "I can't remove this need to be a boy, though. So, I have to be able to trust at some point. I don't know how long that will take, but," he licked his lips, "if you're willing, I'd love us to get there."

Ollie smiled at him, the crinkles around his eyes deepening. "I'd love to." Toby's heart skipped a beat. "Can you tell me what you see as a good relationship to you? I mean, what you'd like to see as a boy."

"Making sure I don't work too much. I have a tendency to say yes to extra hours. When I'm playing my games..." He paused, not sure if he wanted to admit his bad behaviour.

"I won't tell you off. We're not there yet."

He took a breath. "I get lost in the games and forget everything."

"What do you mean by everything?"

Toby stared at him. "Everything. To eat, to drink, to go to the toilet, to move. Everything. I can spend hours there, and only my phone alarm blaring to me can interrupt the flow."

"How long do you play for?"

Toby winced. "Five or six hours, depending."

Ollie cleared his throat. Was he swallowing down his instinctive words? "Hmm. That's something we can work on."

Toby couldn't help the laugh that escaped. "That's not what you wanted to say."

"No, it wasn't." Ollie grinned. "Anything else?"

"I don't eat healthily, as you know. I get plenty of exercise and fresh air, though."

"You need someone to keep you on an even level. Making sure you get to do all the things you enjoy doing, but without hurting yourself in the process?" Ollie succinctly summed up Toby's needs.

"Yes. But I love the idea of comfort from a Daddy. Of him taking care of me...in all ways." Toby could barely get the words out.

Ollie squeezed his hand again. "Sounds good to me. What do you think about punishments? For example, if you spend too long on the game without stopping?"

"I don't mind being spanked, but I don't like anything harder. I don't like exhibitionism or humiliation. Other than that, I don't really know."

"Okay, I can work with that."

"What do you want from a relationship?" Toby asked.

Ollie smiled. "Someone to spoil. That's pretty much everything. I want to look after a boy, hold him, comfort him, help him, feed him, everything. I'm not one for having a bratty boy, but mischievous I can deal with."

Toby giggled, his hand covering his mouth. "I'm definitely not bratty, but I can't say for the second."

Ollie glanced at him. "I can tell you have a mischievous streak when you want to." He grinned, then sobered and pulled Toby to a stop. "I'll be honest with you. I want to try this. I think we could complement each other and work well together. What do you think?"

Toby searched Ollie's face and his own head. "I want to try." He frowned and shivered. "How would this work, though?"

"First, let's get back to the cafe or somewhere else if you want to. We need to get you warm."

"Yes, please." He laughed. "It's colder than it was this morning, I'm sure."

They walked fast back to their original meeting point, and they settled with tea on the sofa part of the cafe. Ollie had bought him a slice of chocolate flapjack, too. Toby broke a piece off and ate it.

"Thank you. It's delicious."

"You're welcome." Ollie sipped his drink. "The way I see us working at the moment is by doing what I call a 'weekend Daddy' trial. Either you come to me, or I come to you, and we spend the weekend being Daddy and boy. I don't have to stay the night with you if you'd prefer not. I can get you into bed, then leave. Whatever works best for you. But I think, because we live nearly an hour away from each other, this is our best option while we're still figuring things out."

"And after? If things go well?"

"Then we'll need to discuss our options. But don't worry about that yet."

Toby nodded, eating another piece of the flapjack while he considered what Ollie had said. He couldn't see any other option. They both had to work. His head snapped up. "You said the garage was open on a Saturday."

Ollie's mouth curved. "It is, but I know someone more than capable of looking after it for one day a week. It'll probably do me some good to give responsibility to someone else."

Toby tilted his head. "Why?"

Ollie huffed. "I work too much."

Toby narrowed his eyes. "How much is too much?"

"Fifteen hours a day sometimes."

Toby gasped, mouth gaping as he stared at him. How were they going to work when he worked that long?

Ollie rested a hand on his shoulder. "Don't worry, Toby. That wouldn't happen if we were together. The only reason I do that now is that I've been waiting for my boy. I needed something to distract me, and work was it."

Toby sighed. "Blimey. I thought I was bad. When did you open the garage, anyway?"

Ollie stared at his mug and worked his jaw. "It was my father's. He opened it over thirty years ago, and I grew up with it. I started working there straight after college and never looked back."

Toby scooted closer, wanting to comfort him but not sure how. Then he remembered Ollie holding his hand and reached for him, threading their fingers together.

"Is he gone?" he murmured.

Ollie nodded. "Five months ago."

"Oh, I'm sorry, Ollie."

"Thank you. He wouldn't want to see me working so many hours, either."

Toby smiled. "I think we've found the perfect way to help each other."

Ollie put his mug on the coffee table and reached forward to brush his thumb against Toby's cheek again. "I do, too."

Toby's stomach somersaulted, and he blurted out, "Will you kiss me?"

The tempting curve of Ollie's mouth drew closer, and Toby held his breath, wanting to remember everything about this kiss. Ollie's lips pressed against his, and Toby tilted his head so their noses didn't bump and opened to him. It was soft, but he felt every press of skin, every brush of air. His eyelids fell shut, and he concentrated on his Daddy. His Daddy. His *Daddy*.

Ollie pulled back, cradling Toby's jaw, eyes tracking over his face. "Okay?"

"Yes, Daddy," he breathed.

Ollie's smile lit up his eyes. "Yes, my boy."

He tugged at Toby and pulled him into his arms as he settled back against the sofa. Toby closed his eyes and rested his head against Ollie's shoulder. It had been a while since he'd been held like this by someone other than Sarah or his family. Or Ben. It was nice. Ollie's hand rubbed his arm.

"Would you like to come over next weekend?" Ollie asked.

"I would. Are you sure it's not a problem with the garage?"

"I'm sure. If Enno needs anything, he can call me."

Toby lifted his head. "Enno?"

Ollie smiled. "My best friend. He works at the garage with me. Has done for years. My other best friend is called Denny. He's a pain in the ass, but I put up with him because I've known him since pre-school."

Toby chuckled and sat upright, reaching for his forgotten flapjack. He picked up the plate and raised his knee onto the sofa so he could see Ollie easier. "I bet he would have stories to tell."

Ollie snorted. "He would. Enno, too, probably. Hopefully, you can meet Enno and Rick. They have a Daddy and boy relationship. Rick is a boy."

"I've never had any 'boy' friends when I was with him."

"We can see to that if it's something you want to look at changing."

"Maybe."

He ate the last piece of flapjack after offering it to Ollie, then settled back against his chest. He could get used to being this close to someone. The platonic cuddles and touches were as wonderful as his memories of sex. And holding hands... Well, that was something he intended to do a lot more of.

8

OLLIE

Ollie was on a high for the next couple of days. But the closer the weekend came, the more he worried he couldn't be what Toby needed. After all, several boys had left him before, so didn't that prove he wasn't enough of a Daddy for them? By Friday, he was back to being a grumpy asshole, and Enno finally pulled him into the office and slammed the door to separate them from the rest of the garage.

"What the fuck is wrong with you today?"

"Nothing," Ollie said, settling behind the desk. If he couldn't be in the garage, he'd work there instead.

"Bullshit! You've been like a bear with a thorn in its paw. I thought you were looking forward to Toby visiting tomorrow."

"I was." God, was he. He'd been so excited.

"What's changed?" Enno rested his ass on the corner of the desk.

Ollie wasn't sure he wanted to explain, but maybe it would be the only way to understand the mess that was his brain. "I'm no good as a Daddy, Enno. All those other boys proved it. Why am I doing this to Toby? He doesn't deserve to have a shit Daddy who can't look after him."

Enno chuckled. "Ah, it's nerves, eh? At least those I can work with." Ollie frowned, but Enno continued. "You are not a shit Daddy. Those boys were not the right ones for you. As you've told me several times, you don't want a boy who misbehaves and that you have to punish daily. You want someone to spoil, and from what you've told me of Toby, he's that boy. He needs someone to spoil him, to make sure he has everything he needs, everything that other guy didn't give him."

Enno had been as pissed off as Ollie was when he'd explained what Toby had been through. Ollie hadn't wanted to break Toby's confidence, but Ollie had needed to let off steam after the sheer anger at the ex had boiled inside him.

"But what if we don't work?"

Enno sighed. "Then you don't work. There're no guarantees in this life, Ollie. You know that. But don't borrow trouble. Enjoy learning about him, being with him. Stop having one foot out of the door."

That hit home harder than anything else he'd said. Ollie was always concerned about things not working, and he was always waiting for the car to drop on him. Was that why things hadn't worked out before? Was he not giving them his full attempt, always expecting them to leave? It sounded about right. Unfortunately, that niggle of doubt was always present. Could he push that aside and give things with Toby the best chances possible?

He shut his eyes and scrubbed hard at his face and head. "You're probably right."

"I'm always right." Enno stood. "Now, stay in here and get some paperwork done. No one wants you out there with the mood you're in."

"You're only the boss on a Saturday," Ollie complained.

"So you say." Enno laughed and left the office, closing the door and leaving Ollie to his thoughts.

Pushing the dominant worries aside was harder than it

should've been, but by the time Saturday morning arrived, he had some semblance of control. He needed it because he was supposed to be Toby's Daddy that day, and he couldn't let himself second-guess everything all the time. He wanted Toby to enjoy their time together without an underlying current of uncertainty.

He started pacing outside the garage ten minutes before Toby was due to arrive, trying to settle his nerves. When ten o'clock came and went, his heart pounded harder. He'd spoken to Toby the previous evening, and Toby had told him he was still visiting, but he could've changed his mind by that morning.

An engine interrupted his worries, and he glanced as Toby's car pulled into the car park. He didn't wait for Toby to get out, knowing how nervous he probably was. Ollie strode over to the car, locking gazes with Toby from several feet away. The poor boy looked terrified. Ollie opened the door and crouched beside him, taking his hand.

"Are you okay?"

Toby exhaled shakily and nodded. "I kept thinking I wouldn't get here or that you wouldn't be here."

Ollie smiled. "And I kept thinking you wouldn't come. We're both as bad as each other."

At that, Toby's shoulders lowered, and a small smile crept across his face. "We are."

"Would you like to see the bike I'm working on?"

Toby glanced over Ollie's shoulder to where the garage was. "There's a lot of people there."

"We can go around the back. You don't have to meet anyone if you don't want to. Though I can introduce you to Enno if you want."

Toby curled in on himself, something Ollie was beginning to understand meant he was uncertain. Almost as if he was trying to make himself smaller.

"Maybe later."

"Sure. Do you want to see the bike?"

Toby nodded, and Ollie tugged him from the car, pulling the keys from the ignition when Toby didn't. Ollie locked the car and slid his fingers through Toby's, leading him around the side of the garage to the back entrance and avoiding everyone. Toby gasped when they entered, staring at the Harley Davidson in the centre of the space.

"It's enormous!"

Ollie chuckled. "To you, maybe. Other people are a lot taller than we are. They need something bigger, and also, this is great for cross-country travelling. So I'm told, anyway."

"Have you never done that?"

Ollie shook his head. "I've not wanted to. I love my bike, don't get me wrong. But I love it here." He gestured around them. "Not just the garage, but the town. It's home."

Toby nodded. "It's similar to what I pictured."

"Is it?"

Toby's face flushed, and he pulled his hand free, rubbing at his cheek as he wandered to the bike. "I tried to imagine what you might look like when you're working on the bikes." He reached out a hand and paused several inches away from the bike, glancing back at Ollie.

"You can touch."

Ollie would be lying if he said he didn't have a response when Toby's fingers drifted along the shiny black metal. His pale skin contrasted with the dark colour and set Ollie's blood alight.

"Would you like to ride on one?"

Toby licked his lips, and he stared at the bike. "I don't know."

"We can visit the dog shelter here. Maybe take a couple on a walk?"

Toby glanced at him, a light in his eyes, and Ollie knew he'd won. "You'll have to go slow. I don't want to fall off the back."

Ollie grinned. "You can hold on to me really tight." He moved over to the cupboard, which held spare motorbike leathers. The smallest would still be too big for him, but he wasn't getting on the bike without them. He held them up and chuckled when Toby stood next to them.

"They're going to drown me."

"But you'll be grateful for them. You can take them off when we get there and put them on again for the ride back." Toby grabbed them, but Ollie held onto them and crouched. "Let me help. Use my shoulders for balance."

He removed one shoe and slid the leathers over Toby's jeans, then pulled the shoe back on before he put his foot down. Repeating the action on the other side, he then stood, pulling and tugging to get them over the denim fabric. Toby threaded his arms into the leather jacket, and Ollie settled it on his shoulders, tucking the jumper inside before zipping it up. He stared at Toby, the sight of him in leathers highly arousing.

"Crap." Ollie cleared his throat. "You look too good like that." He turned away and found a helmet that should fit, handing it to him. "Keep hold of that for a minute." Grabbing his own leathers, he stripped off his jeans and slid the leathers on, hiding his grin at Toby's gaping mouth. He slipped the jacket on over his T-shirt and then grabbed his helmet. "Are you ready to see *my* bike?"

Toby nodded and followed him through another door to a small room where Ollie kept his bike and car—the car he didn't use often. As for his bike, the gleaming dark blue machine was his pride and joy. He glanced at Toby to see his reaction. Toby smiled.

"It's gorgeous," he whispered.

"Thanks." Ollie's heart swelled at his boy's reverence. "Let's get your helmet sorted." He helped Toby to put it on and adjusted the straps, keeping the visor up for the moment. "You won't be able to talk to me as easily while we're riding, but if you want me to stop at any point, just tap my stomach three times. Okay?" Toby nodded, eyes wide.

Ollie opened the back door to take the bike out, grabbed the handlebars and took the bike off its stand. Pushing it through the door, he swung his leg over. He put his helmet on, started the bike and held it steady.

"Jump on," he told Toby.

His boy was hesitant, but he followed Ollie's instructions. Ollie grabbed his thighs and pulled him closer into him, then gripped his hands and tugged them around his waist.

"Slide your visor down unless you want to eat bugs, and hold tight. Remember, three taps if you want to stop." Ollie tapped his hands, then clasped the handlebar.

He took it easy as they moved out from behind the garage and through the streets. He didn't want to go so fast; he'd scare the life out of his boy. Maybe on the way back, he could take the long way and go a little faster if Toby wanted to see what it was like. They pulled into the shelter car park a few minutes later, and he held the bike steady as Toby climbed off. Ollie switched it off and settled it on its stand before climbing off himself. He wasn't sure what expression he expected to see on Toby's face, but the sheer exhilaration was surprising.

"That was amazing. Yes, I was scared stiff, to begin with, but wow. Can we go faster on the way back?"

Ollie chuckled. "I think I've created a monster. We can."

Toby fist-pumped the air. "Whoop!"

"Do you want to take the leathers off before we go in?" Toby's forehead creased, and he stared at Ollie. "What's wrong?"

"You can't take your leathers off!" he murmured. "You've got nothing on beneath them!"

Ollie laughed. "I meant just you. I'll be fine in my leathers. You might be warm, though. I'm not sure."

Toby lifted his legs one at a time. "I think I'll take the trousers off because they're so heavy! But I like the leather jacket." His mouth curved.

"I like it on you, too."

He helped Toby to remove the trousers, repeating their earlier actions, and threaded their fingers together as they wandered towards the entrance. He knew from his research that the shelter had several dogs in attendance, and they were open all day for visitors. A bell rang when they entered, and an older woman he knew from servicing her car greeted them.

"Good morning! Lovely to see you, Ollie. What brings you here?"

"Morning, Mrs Duffy. We're just here to look at the dogs if that's okay?"

She clasped her hands in front of her chest. "Are you looking at adopting?"

He hated to dash the hope in her voice, but he shook his head. "Not right now. Toby here loves dogs and works with them a lot. I wanted to show him what you have."

Mrs Duffy sighed but smiled. "Of course. Come this way. You never know, Ollie. I could persuade you to take one off my hands. Lord knows you need a companion." She eyed their clasped hands. "Although maybe not," she murmured, in what she probably thought was under her breath, but he'd heard it just fine.

"You might be right about persuading me, but not right now."

She laughed. "One day."

"Probably," he agreed.

She led them to the outdoor kennels, of which seven were occupied. "If you want to take any of them for a W-A-L-K, their leashes are hanging up over there, and the door to the field is at the back there. Make sure you lock it behind you from both sides, please."

"Thank you, Mrs Duffy," Ollie said.

"Thank you," Toby repeated distractedly.

Ollie let go of his hand and gave his lower back a little nudge. "Go say hello."

Toby moved to the first kennel and crouched, holding his hand against the side so the little Pomeranian could sniff his hand. "Hello, Choccy," he crooned. The dog yapped at him and ran around in a circle, and Toby giggled. "You sure are a cutie."

Ollie agreed, but not about the dog. He leaned against the wall while he watched Toby greet each of the dogs, loving the relaxed demeanour Toby showed. He was in his element there, and Ollie was privileged to see it.

Toby's laugh caught his attention again, and he focused on his words. "All right, all right! Hold on!" Toby stood and walked to the hooks, grabbing a leash and heading back to the kennel.

Ollie wandered closer as Toby unlatched the kennel and slipped inside, crouching to hook the leash to the dog's collar. When they exited the kennel, Toby had a sheepish expression.

"He's so excited. I thought he might like a bit of exercise."

Ollie held his hand out for the Border Collie to sniff, and then the dog tugged Toby towards the door. Ollie laughed and glanced at the name on the kennel before following. Flossie was a gorgeous name for the dog, and if they didn't both fall in love with her before the end of the visit, he'd eat his leathers.

They spent a very enjoyable two hours at the shelter, walking several of the dogs, and it tore at him to leave Flossie behind. He needed to because he had no way of looking after a dog at that moment. He spent too much time working. Although... No, he had to stay firm. Not the right time.

He took Toby the longer route home, increasing his speed on one open stretch before slowing down for the town roads again. He pulled the bike directly into the garage, having left the doors open for that reason. Once they were de-leathered again, and Ollie was redressed in his jeans, he led Toby to his apartment, where he already had a slow cooker meal bubbling away for dinner.

"I think it's lunchtime. Are you hungry?"

Toby nodded, staring around the place. "Do you want me to make a plate up for you, or would you like to do it with me so you can choose?"

Toby chewed his lip, and Ollie could see his mind going a hundred miles a minute. Ollie stepped closer and wrapped an arm around him, hooking a finger beneath his chin so Toby would look at him.

"We're learning, Toby. Don't force it. Listen to your instincts. Would you like me to help you relax?" Toby nodded. "I'm going to kiss you." Toby nodded again, this time more vigorously.

Ollie lowered his head, brushing his lips across Toby's before pressing harder. This was only their second kiss, but it was like he'd done it a million times and never all at the same time. He explored Toby's mouth when Toby opened for him with a small groan. Ollie slid his hand to the back of his head, holding him in place, and only pulled back when Toby's hands gripped his shirt hard enough that Ollie was concerned it would tear.

Toby's eyes were closed, and his mouth remained open. Ollie pecked another kiss on his lips and waited.

"Would you like me to make a plate up for you, or would you like to do it with me so you can choose?" he said, repeating his earlier question.

"Can you do it, please?"

Ollie nodded and smiled. "Sure. Feel free to wander around and look at stuff. I've nothing to hide." He winked. "Except in maybe the bottom drawer of my bedside table."

He left Toby gaping at him and headed for the kitchen. So far, so good.

9

TOBY

Toby's head was spinning from that kiss, and he shook his head and looked around. The place was far tidier than Toby's house. Ollie had some pictures on the shelves, and Toby studied them, noticing the similarities between some of the people. They were obviously his family, but who were the other guys? He might ask if he plucked up the courage.

He'd had a wonderful day so far. Ollie had been the perfect host, but something was missing, and Toby couldn't figure out what it was. It left him unsettled, though the kiss had gone a long way to relax him.

Ollie returned with lunch and put the plates and drinks on the coffee table. He sat on the floor, and Toby sat beside him, taking his initiative.

"I hope you like what I've put on there, but if you don't, just leave it. I don't know all your likes and dislikes yet."

"Thank you." He fell silent as he ate, happily munching away on the ham sandwich, crisps, apple and yoghurt—no vegetables in sight, which was a relief.

"I have a games console, but it's an older one. I can't remember what I have because I haven't used it for years. If you want, we can set it up after lunch, and you can see if there's anything you'd like to play," Ollie said.

Toby smiled. "That'd be cool. Thanks."

"I want you to relax here. I know we'll be swapping between here and your place, but I want the same sense of relaxation at both if that makes sense."

"It does. It's always nerve-wracking going somewhere new and not knowing what I can and can't do. The games might help me forget where I am, almost."

Ollie nodded. "We'll give it a try, then."

They cleared away the plates, and Ollie opened the cupboard beneath the TV. The console was older than what he was used to, but he'd had one when he was younger, so he knew how to use it. It was a little dusty, but it worked and was already hooked up to the TV. The games themselves weren't too bad, but he refused to go as low as playing a racing car game. Instead, he chose a classic he remembered having as a child: Abe's Oddysee. He set the game going and settled onto the floor, leaning back against the sofa as he started the first level.

Soon, he got lost in figuring out what he had to do, enjoying the blast from his past. Maybe he should see if he could get it on his console at home.

"Toby?"

Toby squinted at the screen, biting his lip as he took the character through the trials. He needed to get to the exit before he got killed again.

"Toby."

There it was! He manoeuvred the character to the bottom of the screen and exited, slumping back and sighing. He grinned. This was fun.

"Toby." The voice was low but hard, and he glanced to his side. Daddy sat perched on the edge of the armchair, fingers linked together and a frown on his face.

"Hey! Did you see me? I'm really enjoying this one. I'd forgotten how much fun it was, even though the graphics aren't brilliant. But it's great."

"I did see, but it's time to stop now. You need a break."

"But, Daddy, I've only been on here for a short time!" he whined.

Daddy raised his eyebrows, and Toby huffed. "You've been on here for over two hours already. Time for a break. Go to the toilet, and I'll have some food ready for when you're done."

Toby wanted to argue, but he knew he'd get nowhere. He stood and headed for the door when he remembered he didn't know where to go—and he really needed to go now!

"First door on the left, sweetheart."

"Thank you!" he called and raced to the door.

After he washed his hands, he found Daddy in the kitchen.

"Here you go." Daddy handed him a glass of orange juice and a plate with chopped-up fruit and a small bowl of cherry tomatoes with some sort of dressing on them. Toby frowned and glanced at Daddy. "Go to the table and just try it." He chuckled.

Toby sighed and sat at the small dining table. He sipped his drink and, realising how thirsty he was, drained the glass before eating anything. Daddy came to sit beside him, handing him another glass, this time of water.

"Thought you might be thirsty. Gaming seems like hard work."

"It is! My brain can hurt when I've been doing it for a while because it takes so much concentration." He chatted while he ate, telling Daddy about the game and how he'd forgotten it was so good.

"Well done, sweetheart. One more to go."

Toby stared at the plate and gaped. He'd eaten everything, including the tomatoes, except for one waiting for him. Now that he faced it, he wasn't sure. When he'd been talking, he was distracted. Was that why he'd eaten them? He'd not realised he was.

"You might be surprised. But if you don't like it, you can have a biscuit afterwards to get rid of the taste."

Toby scrunched his nose but put the tomato in his mouth. The acidic taste first hit him, then a mellow warmth from the dressing, he assumed. He chewed and frowned, but it tasted okay. He smiled when he swallowed. "It wasn't too bad."

"Glad to hear it."

Toby glanced to the side. "Do I still get my biscuit?"

Daddy laughed and brushed a thumb against Toby's cheek. "Yes, you can. Come and choose which you'd like."

They retreated to the kitchen, and Daddy showed him the different biscuits he had. The winner, which would happen until the end of time if they were available, was the chocolate digestive. He ate it, leaning his hip against the counter with Daddy watching him with a smile. When he finished, he hugged him, resting his cheek against his chest and listening to his heartbeat for a second.

"Thank you, Daddy."

"You're welcome, sweetheart."

Something between that second and the next hit Toby's brain, and he backed away, staring at Daddy—no, Ollie. He couldn't do this. It was wrong. He couldn't go down the same path he'd been down before. He'd barely come back from it last time. Toby spun around and raced down the stairs to the apartment door.

"Toby! Wait!"

He didn't. He ran for his car as if zombies were on his heels and fumbled with the keys he remembered Ollie had slid into his pocket earlier that day. The moment he clicked his seatbelt into place, he screeched out of the parking space and headed home. His hands clenched the steering wheel, and sweat dripped down his temple while his breaths see-sawed out of him. How could he have been so stupid to get so wrapped up in someone else? So quickly, too. He didn't know anything about Ollie. He could end up being exactly like his ex, so why was Toby risking it all?

He lost himself the last time he was in a relationship. When he came out of it, he had to learn who he was again. He couldn't go through that again.

Tears streamed down his face, and he had to pull over so he didn't have an accident. He hoped Ollie wasn't following him, and he kept checking in the rearview mirror to spot his car or bike. But Ollie didn't come. Was that a good thing? Or did it prove that Ollie didn't care about him at all?

Toby shouted and banged his hands against the steering wheel. Then he took several deep breaths and wiped his face.

"Stop it now. Go home," he told himself.

At home, he curled into the corner of the sofa and opened up the Daddy's Boy app. He clicked on Ollie's profile and opened the messaging section.

Oh2Bs3xy
I'm sorry, this was all a mistake.

He sent it and closed the app, dialling Ben instead.

"Hey, Toby. What's up? Are you having fun with Ollie?"

As soon as Ben finished speaking, Toby started crying again. What the hell was wrong with him? He hadn't cried this much since he'd left his ex.

"Toby? What the hell? What happened? Where are you? Are you safe?"

"Yes...I'm fine. I'm at home," he managed between breaths.

"Why are you at home? I thought you were spending time with Ollie."

Toby exhaled slowly, trying to regain control of his breathing. "It was a mistake, Ben. I can't do it. I can't lose myself again. I don't think I'd be able to find myself a second time."

"Did something happen for you to feel like this? Was Ollie mean to you?"

"No! No, he was great. I just...forgot where I was. Everything went away except me and Dad—Ollie. I was falling into the same situation as before. Giving everything of myself. I...can't."

Ben sighed. "I know it's difficult, Toby. I can't even begin to imagine what you went through. I had an unpleasant situation with my parents, which Dad—Gareth helped me out of, but it's nothing like that." Toby knew a bit about what Ben had been through, and it sounded awful. "Maybe you just need to take it slower. Don't rush into things until you get to know Ollie as a man before knowing him as a Daddy. What do you think?"

Toby blew out a breath, suddenly exhausted. "I don't know, Ben. I don't think I can."

"How did you leave things with Ollie? Does he know how you're feeling?" He didn't reply, and Ben cursed. "What did you say to him, Toby?"

"I ran," he murmured. "I didn't say anything and ran, but when I got home, I sent a message saying it was all a mistake."

"Do you think Ollie might be worried about you? He might be wondering what he did wrong to make you run away from him. He might think he's hurt you. That's not fair to him, is it, Toby? You need to explain. Give him...I don't know, something at least."

Toby closed his eyes, his heart hurting for knowing he caused Ollie pain. He hadn't thought about it until Ben brought it up, but of course, Ollie would be worried. Toby had run out of there as fast as his legs could carry him without saying a word of why.

"I can't talk to him."

"That's fine. Send him another message and let him know you're okay, and give him a little something to explain."

"I'm not sure I can."

"At least think about it. It's not fair to him, Toby."

"Okay."

Ben sighed again. "Just relax for the rest of today, okay? Go to bed or play your game or something. I'll call you later."

"All right." He was glad someone had given him guidance on what to do because his brain had gone on holiday.

When he ended the call, he took himself up the stairs and into his room. He stared at his computer but couldn't bring himself to turn it on. Instead, he slid under the covers of his chilled bed, with all his clothes on, and stared at the wall.

He must've fallen asleep at some point because he woke with an ache in his neck, and it was pitch black in his room. Fumbling for the lamp, he squinted against the bright light. His head pounded. He rubbed at it, and everything came rushing back to him, and he fell back against the headboard, groaning. He had to message Ollie because Ben was right. He'd be worried, and he'd think it was his fault. And it wasn't at all. Toby was faulty in some way.

He pulled his phone from where it had been in his jeans pocket all this time. He had two missed calls from Ben and another message from him saying he'd be pissed if Toby was anything other than asleep. It made him smile but didn't deter him from his task.

Opening the app, he hesitated over the keyboard, not sure where to start.

Oh2Bs3xy

I'm sorry for running. It's not your fault, Ollie. It's mine. I felt like I had lost myself for a minute, and I panicked. I can't do that again. I won't. I don't know what reassurance I can give you, but you are a wonderful person and Daddy, and anyone would be grateful to have you. It just can't be me. x

He sent the message and exhaled. There it was. The end. He ignored the ache in his chest and the overwhelming need to cry again and, instead, stripped and showered. He'd go back to the way things were before he met Ollie. He was happy like that, if a little empty, but he could manage with that. He had to. Because if he couldn't make it work with Ollie—who was everything he could ever want in a Daddy—then he could never make it with anyone. And a Daddy deserved someone who could throw everything in with them and receive everything back as well.

He dropped his head against the tiles, pretending his tears weren't mixing with the water. If he could pretend, everything would be okay. He would continue surviving. He had his dogs. That was enough.

10

OLLIE

When Ollie initially received the message that Toby thought it was a mistake, he sank to the floor in the kitchen and stared at his phone. He had no idea what had gone wrong, but something had. And he couldn't even speak to Toby to figure it out.

Enno and Denny had appeared at his door when the garage closed, and by that point, Ollie had come to terms with the idea that he just wasn't Daddy material. If he couldn't keep these boys happy, then it must be to do with him and not them. Why else would they leave him?

"I saw Toby flying out of here earlier but couldn't come up to check on you. What happened?"

Ollie sighed. "I'd like to know the answer to that as well. I've no idea. One minute we were talking and cuddling; the next, he flew out of the door and left." He shook his head. "I'm done. I can't keep doing this."

"Doing what?" Denny asked.

"Getting my hopes up that I'll have a boy to look after someday. When they leave, and I'm left crushed, it hurts more than when I'm alone. I can't do it anymore."

Neither of them said anything, but he caught the looks they

shared. To change the subject, he set about dishing up the slow cooker dinner for them all—no point letting it go to waste. He wished he could've made something that would take time because it would mean he had less time to dwell on what wasn't to be. Both men stayed in the kitchen with him, getting in his way, but for once, he didn't mind. He'd rather have company than be alone.

"Do you have plans tomorrow?" he asked them. "I was thinking of riding the roads for a bit. Do you want to come?"

Enno shook his head. "Sorry, man. I have plans with Rick and his parents. Apparently, it's been too long since we last took a walk around National Forest grounds." He rolled his eyes. "The only reason they want to go to a National Forest place is because they bought the membership and are worried they wasted their money."

"What is there to do at these places?" Denny asked, jumping up onto the only empty space on the counter.

"Not a lot. Don't get me wrong, the gardens are amazing at some of them, but I don't really want to look around an old house and be told about the people who used to live there."

Ollie chuckled. "It's why I choose the open road." He glanced at Denny. "What about you?"

He shrugged. "Why not? Maybe we can head towards Luton or something and watch the planes."

"Can do. I'm not standing at the end of a runway this time, though."

The last time Denny persuaded him to do that, the air blown back was breathtaking. Literally. Ollie was sure it had taken him nearly a day to get back to normal after that.

Denny laughed and lifted his beer into a toast. "Fun times."

They spent the evening chatting, eating and watching a movie before Enno called it a night. Denny hesitated in the doorway.

"Do you want me to stay over and keep you company?"

Ollie gave a small smile. "Nah. I'm good. I have a feeling I'm going to crash the minute my head hits the pillow," he lied.

Denny narrowed his eyes, but Ollie didn't retract his statement. "All right. Give me a bell if you need me. Otherwise, I'll see you at ten o'clock."

The silence wrapped around him the moment he closed the door, but he refused to let it win. He set about tidying up, loading the dishwasher, cleaning the counters, washing whatever pans either couldn't fit in the dishwasher or had to be hand washed, and when all that was done, he stared around him, not sure what to do. He doubted he'd sleep, but if he was going to ride in the morning, he at least had to try.

He showered using warm water, hoping to trick his body into relaxing enough to drop off, and then quickly climbed into bed. He checked his phone as he plugged it into the charger, his heart jumping when he saw a notification from Daddy's Boy. He clicked it, hovering over Toby's username. Would this be more of the same, or did he regret what he'd said?

Toby's words weren't the reassurance he probably meant them to be. How could Ollie not have seen that Toby was struggling? What kind of Daddy missed something so crucial? And what had he done to make Toby think he was anything like that ex of his? Ollie was nothing like him. Had he been too controlling? He didn't think so. Has he been too bossy? He hadn't done as much as he'd wanted to. He shook his head. It didn't clear anything up at all. It only made things more complicated. But Toby had reached out, and even if Ollie didn't get another reply, he had to respond. But what could he say?

He placed his phone back down on the bedside table and lay on his back, staring at the ceiling. The only true way to show Toby what Ollie was like was by showing him, but that was pretty much out of the window. Maybe he could enlist Ben and Gareth's help? They might have some advice for him, but he wasn't calling them after midnight for such information. It would have to wait until the morning. Could he wait that long to reply? Ollie blew out a breath. He could try. He didn't want to say the wrong thing and ruin everything again.

In that moment, he realised he was hoping they could pick up where they left off despite what he'd told his friends about having had enough. If Ollie could find the right words to show Toby who he was, maybe they could keep trying. Maybe they had a chance. But it would all depend on his next move.

He went over their conversations and interactions again and again, finally coming to the conclusion that Toby was scared. Scared of potentially losing himself in a relationship. Scared of turning into his past self. The truth was, Ollie didn't think Toby could lose himself or go back. He was too strong now. His running away showed that. And if Ollie continued to be truthful, *he* was scared too. Maybe that's why he'd been holding back. If he showed his true colours and Toby didn't like it, then he was back to square one. Again.

If he could let go of his fear that nobody could want him as he was, then just maybe he could find the person he was meant to be with. He wanted that person to be Toby.

D–Mad79

Thank you for explaining. I was worried I'd hurt you. In some ways, this is worse because you are hurt, and although it wasn't me who did it, I was the reminder. By the way, did Peppa ever go back to her owners? Or is she still getting the royal treatment from you?

He had no idea if Toby would ever reply, but he'd done what he could. He was hoping the question about Peppa the poodle would be enough to bridge the conversation between them again. Lingering on what had happened would only make things worse, so if he could veer them into nicer and funnier things, it might help.

The following morning, Toby still hadn't replied, but Ollie felt lighter. He was looking forward to the ride and even the plane spotting. When Denny arrived, they put in their earbuds so they could talk to each other during the ride and headed off. It was a fair drive, and they'd taken the more scenic but slightly longer route. There would be no full-throttle rides, but he didn't mind. Even riding at thirty miles per hour through towns felt good.

They stopped for breakfast on the way, filling up on greasy food and a couple of cups of tea, and continued, pulling into a layby close to the airport where they could watch the planes land and take off. Denny hadn't always been plane mad, but he'd once dated an air steward and had been bitten by the plane bug. Ollie could admit they were something to look at, but he wouldn't usually go out of his way to see them. It was the least he could do when Denny had agreed to ride with him, though.

"Toby messaged me yesterday." He explained the reason he gave. "I want to get him back. I'm *going* to get him back."

Denny clapped him on the shoulder. "'Them's fighting words,'" he quoted, though Ollie couldn't remember where they came from. Probably some cartoon or something similar. Denny had a quirky sense of humour. "Glad to hear it."

They didn't say any more about it, instead choosing other subjects until their stomachs lured them away from the planes and to a cafe for a late lunch and far too many cups of tea that would undoubtedly mean a toilet break stop on the journey home.

In all the time they'd been gone, he'd purposefully not checked his phone. He would've heard the chimes had someone messaged or called, but no one had, and if Toby had replied, he would've wanted to read it. However, he wanted to wait until he returned home before he put his only semi-made plan into action.

"Thank you for today," he said to Denny when they pulled up outside the garage.

"You don't need to thank me, Ollie."

Ollie clasped his shoulder. "I know, but I appreciate it nonetheless."

"You'll figure it out." Denny stared at him, the years they'd known each other showing in his eyes.

Ollie smiled, and Denny saluted and rode off. Ollie pushed his bike into the garage and sorted it out before heading up to his apartment. Once he was in joggers and a T-shirt, he settled on the sofa, flicked the TV on to something random as background noise and grabbed his phone. He had a notification from Daddy's Boy, and his heart jumped.

Oh2Bs3xy

Peppa is still with us. Bless her. We haven't heard from the owners in a week now, so we're not sure what's happening, but we'll keep hold of her for a little while longer before we decide what to do. I'm not sure of the protocol if the owners never show up again. Does she go to a rehoming centre? Does she stay with us? I've no idea. Please don't feel bad. It's not your fault.

Ollie needed to keep him focused on the dogs and not that he was talking to someone he had said he didn't want anything to do with. He knew it wasn't true. Toby was just scared.

D-Mad79

Is there such a thing as a foster home for dogs? Could someone look after her until something is sorted? I suppose, as long as the owners are paying for her lodgings with you, you could keep her there indefinitely, but that's not really a life for a dog, is it? I know you look after them well, but living in boarding kennels all the time can't be the best life. I don't know, though, so please tell me if I'm wrong.

He didn't want to wait around to see if Toby would reply, so he started cooking something he could put in the freezer. He'd eaten late enough that he didn't want dinner now, but he could still cook and distract himself for a little while. Going through the motions of making a lasagne, he focused on what he was doing and tried to blank his mind as much as possible. As Enno had recently told him, there was no point in borrowing trouble now. He wouldn't go back to being the grumpy asshole he was before unless his chances with Toby were one hundred percent over. Then all bets were off.

While the lasagne cooled, he checked his phone.

Oh2Bs3xy

There is! I never thought about that. It's definitely an option if they stop paying, or even if they continue paying, maybe. You're right, though. Staying in kennels, however good they are, is not good enough for dogs in the long term. It's not fair to them. I think the most we've ever had a dog before was three weeks when a family went on a holiday to America. After all, why not stay for as long as you can if you're going that far away?

Ollie smiled at the image of a wistful expression on Toby's face. Did he wish he could visit far-off places?

D-Mad79

If you're spending that long on a flight, it better be worth it, so I agree. Stay as long as you can manage. Is there somewhere you'd like to visit? I've always wanted to see what the Bora Bora fuss was all about.

It was still too early to go to bed, so Ollie took himself down to the garage to work on the Harley. He'd almost finished the modifications, so that would be another job off his list soon. While he worked, he considered his options. Should he contact Ben and Gareth so they can make sure Toby is okay or was that crossing an invisible line? He wiped his hands on a cloth and dialled the number Gareth had given him.

"Hello?"

"Gareth? It's Ollie." He put the phone on speaker and rested it on the toolbox next to where he sat.

"Hey! Were your ears burning? We were just talking about you."

Ollie snorted. "Should I be worried?"

"I don't know. Ben has plans afoot. I think we should *all* be worried." Gareth laughed. "Sorry, sweetheart. I couldn't resist."

"What plans might these be?"

There was a noise, and then Ben started talking. "Ollie, I want you to keep pursuing Toby. You're exactly what he needs. He just needs to realise it himself."

"I'm working on it."

Ben was quiet. "You are?"

"I'm still messaging him. I'm hoping to get him to open up again and let me visit him so we can talk. I'm only disappearing if I believe there's no hope. I was calling to ask you to check on him."

Ben sighed. "I have been. He's down in the dumps, but he didn't mention that he'd been talking with you." He hummed. "I wonder why?" he murmured. "Anyway, keep going. I'll work on him from my side because I'm not letting that asshole ex ruin Toby's future. I forbid it!"

Ollie chuckled. "I'm right there with you. I'm going to persuade him to let me visit by next Sunday at the latest."

"Definitely. I want you both at my Christmas party!"

Ollie paused at the new information. "Christmas party?"

"Yep, I'm having a Christmas party on Christmas Eve. I want you and Toby to be there."

"I can't promise anything, but I'll do my best."

"You better. Toby's worth that best and more."

"He truly is."

Ollie ended the call and shook his head. He could understand why Ben was the manager of a company because he was a force to be reckoned with when he had an idea in his head. Gareth certainly had his hands full.

Christmas Eve wasn't that far away. Ollie needed to get to work.

11

TOBY

Toby couldn't believe he'd agreed to Ollie visiting him. They'd been messaging almost non-stop for the past week, and when Ollie had asked if he could visit Toby so they could talk, he'd automatically said yes. He wasn't regretting the choice now, but he was nervous. What did he want to talk about? Toby had left in a rush the previous weekend, but he'd finally admitted to himself that it might have been a rash decision. He liked Ollie, and everything that had happened had been perfect until his freak-out.

He had been thinking a lot over the past week, and although he wasn't sure he could be in a relationship with anyone, he didn't want to lose Ollie's friendship. So that was what he was making today about. Friendship.

That went completely out of the window when Ollie pulled up outside his house. Toby flung the front door open, and when Ollie climbed out of the car, Toby ran to him. Ollie caught him, though Toby knocked him back a few steps.

"Good morning to you, too," Ollie murmured, and Toby could hear the smile on his face, even with his eyes closed.

He didn't want to let him go, but he was aware they were in the middle of the road in full view of his neighbours. Ollie must've come to the same conclusion because he disentangled himself, threaded their fingers together and tugged Toby towards the open front door.

"You'll waste all your heating if you leave this open too long." Ollie closed the door behind them.

Toby flushed. "Sorry."

"You don't need to be sorry. Would you show me around?"

"There's not much to see." He waved around. "This is the living room." They went through a door. "This is the dining room." He pointed to an archway. "That's the kitchen. Upstairs, there is a bedroom and a bathroom. It's small, but I don't need much."

"I think it's perfect for you. Shall I make us a cup of tea?"

"I can do it!" Toby went to leave, but Ollie wouldn't let go of his hand. Ollie tugged him to a stop in front of him.

"I'd like to do it. You've had a stressful week. Let me take care of you."

And just like that, Toby's tears started. Ollie pulled him into his chest and held him, soothing him with his words and his hands. Toby held on as tightly as he could. When he calmed, he sighed and pulled away.

"I didn't mean for that to happen." He sniffed.

"As I said, it's been stressful for you." Ollie pressed his lips to Toby's forehead. "Let me make us a drink."

Toby watched Ollie while he puttered around the kitchen, enjoying the play of his muscles in the T-shirt he wore. Did Toby need to let off steam? Was that why he was so emotional? Would it be wise to flirt a little and see if Ollie wanted something more than talking that day? Probably not.

Settling on the sofa with their drinks, they sat in silence for a short time before Ollie spoke. "I want to talk about what happened last weekend."

Toby sighed and curled his legs under him, resting his cup on his thigh. "The short version of the story, from what I've realised, is that I enjoyed it too much. I thought I was losing myself again. Falling into the same situation as before. It wasn't fair to you because you are nothing like *him*." He stressed the last words, staring at Ollie. "I know you're not, but at that moment, that's all I could see."

Ollie nodded. "It might happen again, too. I don't ever want you to think that I'm keeping you somewhere you don't want to be. If you need to run, you run. I promise, if we agree to try this again, I will be there when you want to come back."

Toby inhaled deeply, searching his feelings, but already knowing the answer. "I really would like to try again."

Ollie smiled. "Then we will. Would you like to start today?"

Toby straightened. "Can we?"

"Sure. I have someone covering the garage. I have all weekend if you like?"

"I have to go to my mum's for lunch tomorrow, but after that, I can." He bit his lip. "It's a lot of driving for you, though. You could..." He cleared his throat. "You could stay overnight?"

Ollie stared at him, and Toby fidgeted. "Let's see how today goes first."

The day went as great as their first day did. By the time they sat to watch a movie after they'd eaten the dinner that Ollie had cooked, Toby was feeling great. He had qualms, no doubt about it, but he couldn't help it. Teething problems was what Ollie called it. When Ollie put on *The Santa Clause*, Toby was in heaven. He snuggled up against Ollie's chest and sighed.

"Everything okay?"

"Perfect."

As the movie played, Toby smoothed his hands over Ollie's chest and stomach, slowly making the paths bigger until his little finger touched his waistband each time. He wanted to be brave and go further, but he didn't want to push too hard.

"If you want something, Toby, you need to ask for it," Ollie murmured.

"I want..." He swallowed, staring at a piece of lint on the floor. "I want you."

A hand cupped his cheek and brought his face around to meet Ollie's gaze. "What do you *want*, Toby?"

He inhaled shakily and took the leap. "I want you to hold me, to touch me, to be inside of me. I want to remember what it's like to be with someone who cares." He hadn't meant to add the end bit because he didn't want a pity fuck, but it was too late.

Ollie smiled. "Good boy. You're so brave." He ran a finger down Toby's nose, making it tickle. "Why don't we turn everything off down here, and you can show me your bedroom? But first..."

Ollie slid his hand to the back of Toby's head and lowered his mouth. The moment their lips touched, Toby's eyes closed, and he focused on the feel of the hair against his face. The scratch of his goatee wasn't as sharp as it would've been if Toby had been clean-shaven, but it was still there. When Ollie's tongue swiped against his own, he opened instinctively, and they duelled, exploring each other's mouths. Toby needed to be closer, and he crawled into Ollie's lap, straddling his legs, and slid his arms around his neck. The kiss deepened, and Toby thrust his hips, bumping his groin against Ollie.

Ollie pulled away, eyes glazed as he stared at him. "Let's turn everything off."

Toby whined, but Ollie lowered his chin and stared at him. He swallowed any more protests and climbed off his lap, adjusting himself. He turned off the TV, and Ollie disappeared into the other room. Toby followed and found him checking the oven was off and switching off the lights.

"Where's your room?" Ollie asked.

Toby spun around and climbed the stairs, with Ollie following. He hesitated, then grimaced. "I'm sorry about the mess."

Ollie chuckled. "Don't worry. It'll be tidy soon enough." Toby frowned and cocked his head, and Ollie laughed again. "It'll end up being one of your chores, I think."

Toby groaned and pushed the door open. He tried to see it from Ollie's point of view. There were clothes strewn across the floor, his bed was a mess because he never made it, and there were drink bottles and wrappers all over his desk from when he did remember to take some food and drink with him before he started playing. He glanced at Ollie, biting his lip.

Ollie raised his eyebrows. "Definitely a chore." He grinned. "But not today."

Toby rubbed his hands over his face. "As much as it pains me to say it, yes, I probably do need a chore list. And possibly a hundred alarms on my phone to remind me to do them."

"Noted." Ollie moved closer, sliding his arms around Toby's waist. "A problem for another day."

They resumed their kiss from earlier, and Toby lost himself in it, letting his body instinctively react but always needing more. He tugged at Ollie's T-shirt, wanting it off, but Ollie stilled his hands and pulled his mouth free.

"I'm in charge. Get on the bed."

"Yes, Daddy." Toby crawled onto the bed. "How do you want me?"

"On your back, sweetheart." When Toby lay down, Ollie settled beside him, his hands roaming across his stomach and chest. "What's your safe word?"

Toby's heart raced. He'd never used a safe word before, but he knew what he wanted to use. "The traffic lights. They're easy to remember."

"Good boy. And you're right. They are." Ollie pulled at the hem of Toby's T-shirt, slipping it up his body until it bunched under his arms. His fingers resumed their trek, this time on bare skin with goosebumps rising to meet him.

Toby's breathing increased, and his cock pressed harder

against his khakis. He could barely keep his hips still. Ollie leaned his head down and flicked his tongue over his nipple, and Toby gasped, arching into him when Ollie blew over the tip. He repeated the action on the other side, and Toby felt it all the way to his groin. He hadn't realised how sensitive they were—or how connected to his dick.

Ollie's hand skimmed down Toby's stomach, leaving fire in its wake, and covered his cock, his palm pressing against him while his fingers tightened against his balls.

"Oh!" Toby pushed his head into the pillow, panting while trying to get closer.

Removing his hand, Ollie grabbed Toby's T-shirt and yanked it over his head, dropping it to join the other clothes on the floor. He stared at Toby's jeans, his fingers playing with the button, and met Toby's gaze.

"Please."

Ollie licked his lips. "I didn't come here for this today. I just want you to know that. This isn't just about sex for me. This is about giving my boy what he needs."

Toby blinked a few times, trying to clear the tears filling his eyes, and nodded. "I know. He's not here with us, I promise."

"Good."

Ollie flicked open the button and lowered the zip, taking his time to remove the denim from his legs. He smoothed his hands up Toby's legs, pausing on his thighs before he slipped his fingertips into the waistband of his briefs. He played with the elastic, stretching it out and back over and over, while Toby tried his best not to fidget and beg for more. His cock was doing enough begging, being as hard as it was.

When Ollie stripped Toby completely naked, he paused, staring at him, and it was all Toby could do to stay still and let him look without covering himself with his hands. He loved the warmth that followed Ollie's gaze.

"You're beautiful, Toby. Inside and out." Ollie lowered himself, but Toby held out a hand to stop him.

"Please. I want to see you. Feel you against me," he whispered.

Ollie's mouth quirked as he lifted back up to his knees and then off the bed. "If you insist."

Ollie's hands grabbed the hem of his T-shirt and tugged it over his head slowly, revealing inch after inch of slightly tanned skin as if he'd been out in the sun without a shirt for a long time during the summer. Toby bit his lip when Ollie's fingers unfastened his jeans, already knowing what he'd find because his mind flicked back to when he'd stripped to dress in his leathers the previous weekend. Ollie hesitated at his briefs, but Toby begged him.

"Please, Daddy. I need you."

Ollie paused for a second longer, and Toby thought he wasn't going to remove them, but he did. Toby saw him in all his glory, and he wasn't disappointed at all. His Daddy crawled up the bed and covered Toby with his larger body, and as Toby wrapped his arms around Ollie's neck, he sighed, his eyelids fluttering.

Toby buried his face in Ollie's neck, unable to help, needing the comfort of being close to him. He spread his legs, letting Ollie settle between them, almost as close as anyone could get, and wrapped his legs around his back. They lay like that for several long minutes, with Toby breathing Ollie in and Ollie rubbing his skin, soothing him.

Ollie's lips skimmed across his shoulder and neck, along his jaw and to his mouth, where he proceeded to devour Toby's senses while Toby held on. When Ollie removed his mouth, Toby gasped and begged for more.

"Where are your supplies?"

Toby had to let the words sink in before he understood them, and he pointed to his bedside table. Where else did people keep their stuff? He didn't ask that, though. Ollie reached for the drawer, Toby barely letting him untangle himself enough to do it. He dropped the lube and a condom beside them and rested on his forearms, cradling Toby's head.

"You have to let me go, Toby. We can't go further without me prepping you, and I can't do that with you wrapped around me. I refuse to hurt you."

Toby stared into his Daddy's grey eyes and nodded, slowly letting his hands and legs drop to the bed. He instantly felt colder, but Ollie brushed a kiss across his mouth before moving.

"Good boy. Get comfortable for me. I won't rush this."

Oh, god. He might die from waiting.

Ollie lifted to his knees, taking the supplies with him, and Toby stared at Ollie's hands, so big and powerful, yet soft and gentle. He never would've believed such a large man being as careful as Ollie was. That was why it had taken him so long to find someone to share this with. Everyone reminded him of *him*, but Ollie threw all those preconceived notions out of the window. Toby was beginning to understand that Ollie was nothing like anyone else on the planet. It was as if he was made just for Toby.

He almost laughed at the thought. They were compatible; that's all it was. He shouldn't jump ahead and think of church bells and rings yet.

But it was difficult not to when Ollie took his time to prepare him as if Toby was the most precious thing he'd ever touched.

12

OLLIE

Toby was the most precious thing Ollie had ever touched. He didn't want even the most minute bit of pain to touch him any longer. His boy had experienced enough of that to last a lifetime—several lifetimes. Ollie wanted to make sure every minute of this was blissful, even at a detriment to his own arousal, because there was no way in hell he would come until his boy was satisfied.

He'd been truthful when he'd told Toby earlier that he hadn't visited with the plan to get him into bed. He'd dreamt about it, but he hadn't wanted to push. But he could see Toby was hanging on by a thread, and sometimes, a physical release helped with an emotional one. He wouldn't deny he wanted to feel Toby clench around him, but he'd happily have waited.

He squirted the lube onto his fingers and massaged it into Toby's pucker, pulling whimpers and moans from him. Pushing forward, his fingertip breached him, and Ollie knew he needed to take his time with how tight he was. He focused on every sound Toby made as he stretched him, making good on his promise to not hurt him. He lost count of how long he prepped him, but when Toby was easily taking three fingers and sobbing incoherently, Ollie deemed him ready.

As much as Ollie wanted to watch Toby come undone, he also wanted to touch him everywhere, so he settled to one side of his boy and nudged him over onto his side while he donned the condom and slicked it. Toby glanced at him over his shoulder with a furrowed brow.

"I want to see and touch you while we make love, Toby. Humour me." Ollie kissed him, and Toby reached up and around to hold Ollie's head. Ollie grabbed Toby's leg and lifted it, then nudged his cock against Toby's hole. Toby's mouth went lax, remaining open, and they just breathed into each other, eyes locked as Ollie slid inside. Going slowly was the only option because even with how much prep he'd done, he could still hurt him.

Ollie looked down Toby's body to where they were joined when he was finally deep inside. Toby exhaled heavily and gripped Ollie's hand, bringing it to his chest.

"Thank you, Daddy," he whispered.

Ollie kissed his shoulder and withdrew, garnering a groan from them both. He stilled when he was inside again and repositioned himself so they touched from head to hips. He wrapped his hand around Toby's cock as he started thrusting. For every forward movement, his hand slid down, and for every withdrawal, his hand stroked up and around the head.

"Oh, god! It's been too long! I'm...close. So close," Toby panted, gripping Ollie's forearm tightly enough that he would have marks afterwards.

"You like that, my boy? My cock sliding deep inside you? My hand stroking you?" Ollie kept up his rhythm as his words stuttered out of him.

"Please! Can I...? Can I...? Come?" Toby called.

"Come for Daddy, Toby," Ollie growled against Toby's ear, and half a second later, he obeyed. The sensation of Toby tightening around him sent Ollie over the edge, and he pumped his way through their releases.

When his body finally came down, he pressed his sweaty forehead against Toby's shoulder, kissing his salty skin. "Are you okay?" he asked.

"Mmhmm."

Ollie chuckled and shook his head. "Two minutes, then we're showering."

"Mmhmm."

It was more like ten minutes, but he hadn't minded having a sleepy boy in his arms, despite the feel of the rapidly cooling sweaty skin.

"Come on. Time to warm up again." Ollie coaxed a tired and unwilling Toby into his arms and into the bathroom, where he stayed until Ollie had turned on the shower for them. Ollie made Toby stand on his own two feet when they needed to get in, and though Toby grumbled, he did. But he wrapped himself around Ollie again the moment they were under the spray. Ollie chuckled but allowed it. For now.

He washed Toby's hair, scratching his fingers at his scalp when Toby made an adorable mewling sound. He could've been mistaken for a cat, but Ollie didn't say so with how much Toby loved dogs.

He set his boy away from him so he could wash him properly and repeated the actions for himself before switching off the shower and towel-drying Toby. He dried himself but didn't bother wrapping a towel around him. He set Toby in his gaming chair and stripped the sheets off the bed.

"Spare sheets?" he asked, trying to get some words from him. Toby pointed to a cupboard, and Ollie remade the bed. He dragged the towel from around Toby's shoulders, threw it in the direction of the bathroom—he'd need to sort it out later, or it would annoy him—and nudged Toby into the freshly made bed, slipping in beside him.

Once they were wrapped around each other, he kissed Toby's

forehead. "How are you feeling? You've been very quiet."

Toby didn't answer right away, but Ollie was content to let him think about his answer, even if he wanted to push him to say something.

"I keep waiting to feel...icky," he said, and Ollie frowned. But before he could ask, Toby continued. "I'd hoped it would be different with you, and it was—is. I feel happy, relaxed, cared for, which I've never had after sex before."

Ollie wished he knew who the guy was because he would punch his lights out. How could anyone have made Toby feel so unloved and useless when he was the brightest star Ollie had ever seen?

Ollie tightened his grip. "If you ever don't feel that way with me, you must tell me straight away. You deserve the world, Toby, and if I can, I'll give it to you."

Toby nuzzled his face closer to Ollie's neck. "Thank you, Daddy."

They stayed entwined for a long time before Ollie remembered something. "Don't you usually play with your friends at night?"

Toby yawned. "I do."

"Do you want to?"

"I do, but I'm super comfy here. I don't want to move." He yawned again.

Ollie chuckled. "Okay, sweetheart. Get some sleep. You can always play tomorrow."

"Okay, Daddy," he murmured, his voice trailing off at the end as if permission to sleep was what he'd been waiting for before he did.

Ollie stayed awake for a while afterwards. He never went to bed this early, but he couldn't bring himself to move and chance waking Toby, so he remained entangled with him. The sex had been amazing, but it was everything before, and after as well, that solidified how much he and Toby worked as a Daddy and boy. He was such a lucky son of a bitch that Toby was willing to take the chance with him. After everything he'd been through—of which

Ollie only had an inkling—he would've expected Toby to never trust a man again. Ever.

Toby snuffled in his sleep, rubbing his cheek against Ollie's chest, and he smiled down at him. How could Ollie be grumpy when his sunshine was right there? He just needed to not do something stupid and ruin it all.

⬥

"I don't want to leave you," Toby murmured, clinging to him as a koala would to a tree.

"It's only for a couple of hours," Ollie soothed, running his hand up and down his back and pressing his cheek into the top of his head. "You can manage that long to see your family."

"You could...come with me?" Toby glanced up at him, eyes wide.

Ollie brushed a finger down his nose. "You're not ready for that yet."

Toby sighed and snuggled into his chest again. "I know, but I don't want to leave you," he whined again.

"How about I bake you something special for when you get home? You can have lunch with your family, and I'll cook up a storm here. How does that sound?"

Toby sighed again. "Okay, I suppose."

A pouting Toby was adorable. "Good. Now, go on. You'll be late."

He huffed and let go of Ollie, sliding his hands into his khaki trousers and jingling his keys. "You won't leave, will you? I want to spend some time with you before you go home."

"I promise I'll be here."

He finally got Toby in the car and on the way to his parents' house, then stood in the centre of the small dining room, trying to decide what to make. It had been an impromptu offer, so now he had to come up with the goods.

It felt strange to be in someone else's house without them in it, but he had wanted to stay as much as Toby had wanted him to. Cooking would help make him feel easier about the situation. He didn't want to take any of the items from Toby's cupboards, so he grabbed the spare key his boy had told him about and searched for the closest supermarket.

As he perused the shelves, he thought about his mother's homemade cheesecake and grabbed the ingredients for that. It was simple enough to be ready by the time Toby got home but not complicated enough to take up too much time. Whether or not that was a bad thing was yet to be seen.

Ollie let his mind wander as he crushed the biscuits and made the base of the cheesecake. That morning, they had woken together, wrapped around each other, both hard as steel. Toby had bitten his lip, then shimmied down Ollie's body and taken his cock into his mouth. He'd sent Ollie crazy with that tongue of his, and he'd come much faster than he'd intended to. Ollie had wanted to return the favour, but his boy had attacked his lips and humped himself against him. Ollie had helped by stroking his shaft, leaving them with another mess to clean up.

After a shower, Toby seemed more content and less stressed than he had since Ollie had turned up the day before. He hoped, with time, he would lose the stress completely.

His phone rang, and he wiped his hands. He grinned. "Hello."

"I miss you already," Toby said, and Ollie shook his head at the pout in his voice.

"It's two hours, Toby. You'll be just fine."

"But we only get the weekends."

Ollie sighed. "I know, sweetheart. We'll figure something out. But right now, you need to concentrate on your family. I'm not going anywhere."

"All right." He huffed. "See you later."

"Bye."

He put the base into the fridge to set and headed for the bathroom. After its heavy use, he gave it a clean. Toby could have the chore of sorting his bedroom out, but Ollie didn't mind taking control of the bathroom duties. He gave everything a clean, and when he finished, he washed his hands thoroughly and continued with the cheesecake. Once he set the final product in the fridge to set, he pottered around the dining room and living room, cleaning a few bits here and there. He didn't want to go overboard because it wasn't his house, but he also wanted to help lower Toby's stress levels as much as possible, and from their talks, Toby had said he hated housework—like most people. Ollie was an anomaly.

The key in the front door was music to his ears, and he stood in the doorway of the living room when Toby hesitantly came in. The release of tension in Toby when he saw Ollie was immense, and Ollie barely caught him.

"Shh, I'm here. I'm here," he repeated, cupping the back of his head against his chest and holding him tight. "Did you have a good time?"

"It was good, but I wish you'd come with me."

"Maybe in a few weeks when you're ready to introduce me. We're only just starting, remember? We have plenty of time."

Toby tightened his hold. "I don't know how I'm going to survive the week without you."

"Think of it like a holiday. A chance to mess up your bedroom, then scramble to clean it on Friday." Ollie chuckled, trying to lighten the mood.

"I suppose." Toby paused and lifted his head. "Did you make something?"

Ollie grinned. "I told you I would." He threaded their fingers together and led Toby to the kitchen. He let go to grab his creation and slid it onto the counter. He'd left it in the cake tin he'd made it in to set, but now, he took it out.

"What is it?" Toby asked, craning his neck to see.

Ollie unpeeled the baking parchment, being careful not to take the sides of the cheesecake with him, and presented the white chocolate and strawberry cheesecake to his boy.

Toby gasped. "Cheesecake! I love cheesecake!" He bounced around on the balls of his feet. "Can I have some? Please? Please, Daddy?"

Ollie chuckled and rolled his eyes. "Yes, you can have a small slice now."

Toby fist-bumped the air. "Yes!"

"Wash your hands while I slice it."

Ollie was glad Toby liked cheesecake because not everyone did, and he'd taken a chance by making it. He was sure the future held many more cheesecake creations.

They sat facing each other on the sofa as they ate the creamy cake, and Toby told him all about the lunch. He spoke about his family, laughing about sisters who had turned his twin brothers down. Toby said they deserved it with all the broken hearts they'd left around town. It was their turn. His face lit up when he spoke about his family, and Ollie asked questions to keep that lightness there for as long as possible.

But when the time came for him to leave, he had no choice. "It's time, Toby."

"Can you not stay a little longer?"

"It's a long journey, sweetheart, and it's raining and dark. If I could've stayed longer, I would've tucked you into bed first. But not tonight, I'm afraid." He hugged Toby, holding him as tightly as he could to make it last until the following weekend. "Now, do you need any rules for this week while I'm not physically here?"

Toby sniffed, and Ollie's heart broke. "No. I'll be fine."

"What about a 'tidying your bedroom' chore?"

Toby groaned. "Do I have to?"

"How about fifteen minutes after work every day this week?

That should be enough." Ollie let go. "Let me have your phone." Toby passed it over, and Ollie set an alarm to ring at the start and end of fifteen minutes every day, then Toby wouldn't have to remember. "There we go. All set. You'll do great. And I'm on the other end of the phone if you need anything at all. In fact, I insist you call. And I will, too. The weekend will be here sooner than you can blink."

Toby stared up at him and blinked. "Is it the weekend?"

Ollie groaned and dropped his mouth for a kiss that turned far more passionate than he intended. When he pulled away, they were both breathing hard.

"It's just a few days."

13

TOBY

"I t's just a few days."

Toby growled into his pillow for the second night of not being able to sleep, no matter how tired he was. How had his life become so entrenched in Ollie's after such a short time? He'd be worried about it if he didn't know that Ollie was nothing like *him*. The sex between them had seemed to make things clearer in Toby's mind, which was a good thing, but it also meant his brain—or rather his heart—was calling all the shots now. He wanted his happily ever after *now*.

He gave up trying to sleep and settled into his gaming chair, switching his console on. While it loaded, he raced down the stairs into the kitchen and grabbed a few snacks, snagging a banana and a yoghurt as well as other unhealthier options. It was bad enough that he was extending his gaming time when Ollie asked him to be careful how much time he spent on it, but there was no way Toby would be able to sleep for at least a few more hours, so he might as well get some more time in.

The moment he logged on, two of his online friends asked what he was doing playing so late. They lived in America, so it wasn't as late over there. They didn't know his life story, and he didn't want to explain it. He told them he couldn't sleep. End of. He spent an enjoyable three hours creating havoc in the game and munching his way through his snacks before he called it quits. Exhaustion claimed him, and he fell asleep as soon as he lay down.

But waking up two hours later was not pleasant. He groaned and contemplated going back to sleep after calling in sick, but his phone rang.

"Ug," he said into the phone without checking to see who it was.

"Good morning, sweetheart. How are you today?"

"Tired," Toby mumbled, though he felt better now he'd heard his Daddy's voice.

"Did you not sleep well?"

Toby opened his mouth and snapped it shut again. "Not really," he hedged, not wanting to explain what had happened. Ollie would be upset with him.

"Hmm. I'm going to think about how to help you sleep while I'm not there. I can't have you not sleeping." Ollie sighed. "How much sleep did you get?"

"About two hours." Toby sat upright, sipping at the lukewarm water he'd put by his bed the previous night. "I'll be okay. The fresh air will help wake me up."

"When you get home later, I'd like you to try for a nap if you can."

"Won't that stop me from sleeping at bedtime?"

"It shouldn't. I'll hopefully have an idea of how to help by then."

Toby yawned and rubbed his eyes. "I suppose I better get ready. Thank you for calling, Daddy. I was contemplating going back to sleep."

Ollie chuckled in his ear. "I can imagine. It's why I rang. I wasn't sure if you'd get up if you'd had another terrible night's sleep like I know you've been having."

"Good call," he murmured.

"Have a good day, sweetheart. I'll speak to you later."

Toby smiled. "Definitely. Don't work too hard."

"I'll try. Plenty of work to keep me busy, though."

"Bye," Toby whispered.

Hearing his Daddy's voice had given him a boost of energy, but he doubted it would last long, so he got ready for work and walked, despite the weather being freezing. He needed the fresh air. That day, he was glad he had a job that kept him busy.

By the end of his shift, he wasn't as glad because his body felt like he'd been battered for hours. Clara even felt sorry for him and offered him a lift home, which he gratefully accepted without argument. Was he coming down with something as well as being tired? The moment he got home, he stripped and fell into bed.

As if on Groundhog Day, his phone woke him, and he fumbled for it. "Ug," he said in place of hello.

"Did I wake you?" Ollie's voice pierced through the sleep fog.

"Hmm." Toby tried to get his brain to fire. He rolled onto his back. "It's okay. What time is it?"

"Four o'clock. I was worried when you didn't call."

Toby reached for his drink and knocked it off the bedside table. "Oh, crap!" He dropped his phone and dived for the glass. Luckily, it landed on some clothes he hadn't yet put away, though they were now soaked. At least it hadn't been the carpet.

"Toby!" a muffled shout grabbed his attention.

"Shit!" He put the glass on the table again and rummaged around his bed covers to find his phone. "Sorry!" he said when he put it to his ear. "Sorry. I dropped my water glass, then my phone." He groaned and flopped back. "Is it tomorrow yet?"

Ollie chuckled. "Not quite, sweetheart. I'm sorry I woke you."

"It's okay. I didn't want to sleep too long, anyway. I forgot to set my alarm." He paused. "You make a good alarm."

"Glad to help. Have you eaten yet?"

Toby sighed. "No. I've done nothing but sleep." He climbed out of bed. "But I will now."

"Make sure you're properly awake before you attempt those stairs," Ollie cautioned.

"Don't worry. Dropping that glass scared me fully awake."

"Did it break?"

Toby shook his head, though Ollie couldn't see. "It landed on clothes."

"I suppose that's something." Ollie snorted. "What are you going to have for dinner?"

Toby sighed and opened the fridge, brightening. "Cheesecake!"

Ollie laughed. "Not for the main meal, no. Dessert, yes."

Toby pouted. "Meanie." He grabbed the leftover pasta he'd made the previous day and scooped it into a microwaveable bowl. Setting it to cook, he pulled out the cheesecake and plated a slice, telling his Daddy what he was doing as he did it.

"Good boy, Toby. I'm glad you're eating well."

He kept his mouth closed about what he'd eaten the night before—which reminded him he needed to clean up his desk to dispose of the evidence. The microwave beeped, and he pulled out his food. Taking the bowl and the plate to the sofa while he cradled the phone between his shoulder and ear, he settled into the corner and grabbed the remote for when he finished talking to Ollie.

"I'm eating," he said before stuffing a forkful in.

"Good. I'll leave you to it. Do you want to call me later? Or are you going to go back to bed?"

Toby considered his options as he finished his mouthful. "I don't think I'll be able to sleep anymore now, so I'll do my chore, then play for a bit."

"Glad to hear it. Don't play too long, remember? It won't help you sleep. Call me when you get into bed. I have an idea."

Heat blazed through him at the drop in Ollie's voice. What did he have planned? "Okay," he squeaked.

Ollie chuckled. "Enjoy your afternoon, sweetheart."

"You, too."

The silence permeating the house felt wrong after the warmth and laughter of the weekend, but he pushed the thought aside and switched on the TV. It wasn't the conversation he wanted, but it was all he could have for now. Only four more sleeps to go.

Five hours later, he snuggled beneath his covers with the phone held to his ear. "You want me to do what?"

"Masturbate, Toby. First, I think it will help you sleep, and second, I want to hear you." Ollie's voice growled through him, sending goosebumps along his skin, and Toby's breath caught.

"I've never..."

"Had phone sex? Well, it's a first for us both. I thought this might help us still be together, even though we're not physically within reach of each other."

Toby's eyelids fluttered closed, and he licked his lips. "Okay," he whispered.

He was naked already, and he slid his hand down his stomach, making himself shiver. When he wrapped his hand around his hardening cock, he gasped.

"Tell me what you're doing," Ollie ordered.

Toby swallowed. "I just wrapped my hand around me. I'm already hard."

"Close your eyes, sweetheart. Imagine it's my hand. My hand stroking up...and down." Toby followed his words. "And up, twisting at the head and rubbing my palm over you, then down again." Toby bit his lip as his breathing increased. "Keep going. Smear your precome around, make it slippery."

The phone slipped from his ear, but he pushed back, resting it against the pillow and rolling his head to the side to keep it in place. He wanted to fondle his balls, but Daddy hadn't said he could. Instead, he rested that hand on his stomach, stroking his skin.

"Use your other hand to rub your nipples. Get them nice and

hard."

Toby did, fire shooting down his spine. "Oh, god."

"Does that feel good?" Ollie growled.

"So good, Daddy. Please."

"Tug at your balls, sweetheart. Roll them in your hand while you stroke." Ollie's breath heaved down the phone. "Let me hear you."

"Ah, oh! Daddy! I'm so close. Can I come, Daddy? Can I?"

Ollie groaned. "Not yet. A little bit more, sweetheart. Stroke a bit faster now. Flick those nipples again."

"Please, Daddy! I'm right there." He panted. "I can't hold on."

"A few seconds more," Ollie ordered.

"Ah!"

"Now, Toby. Come for me. Now!" Ollie said.

Toby's back arched as he rode his climax, his release covering his heated skin. His mind misfired, and he lost himself in the swirling images of him and Ollie together. When he came back to himself, he blinked several times before his eyes would stay open. He grabbed the phone and put it back against his ear.

"Daddy?" he whispered.

"Yes, sweetheart?"

"I'm tired."

"Glad to hear it. Clean yourself up quickly and get back into bed. I'll wait."

Toby reached for a piece of clothing from beside his bed, realising too late it was a wet one he'd forgotten to tidy up earlier. It turned into a good thing because the damp fabric cleaned him off better than a dry one could. He dropped it back over the side of the bed, mentally reminding himself to clean them away in the morning, then grabbed the phone again.

"I'm back," he mumbled, snuggling back under the covers.

"Goodnight, sweetheart. I'll speak to you in the morning."

"Night, Daddy."

Toby barely remembered to put the phone on the bedside table before he closed his eyes.

He was awake before his alarm the following morning, staring at the ceiling with a small smile on his face. He couldn't remember the last time he'd felt so rested, and it had everything to do with his Daddy. Could they make this long-distance thing work? It wasn't long-distance in the grand scheme of things, but not being able to see Ollie during the week would get old quickly. Maybe he could drive over there during the week for one night a week. If he asked Clara, maybe she could change his shifts slightly so he had an early one on a Tuesday and a late one on a Wednesday, or a Wednesday and Thursday, so he could drive to Ollie's and spend the night. Should he ask Daddy first, or should he ask Clara first? He didn't want to get Ollie's hopes up if Clara said no. Maybe he could offer to do an extra long shift on a different day to appease her, though Daddy might not like that idea.

He was already showered and dressed by the time Ollie called. He'd even remembered to pick up the wet clothes and put them in the washing basket. They talked until Toby arrived at work, having walked again, then said goodbye. He went straight to Clara's office when he arrived and knocked on her door.

"Come in."

"Morning, Clara. I wondered if we could have a quick chat about my shifts, please?"

She lowered her eyebrows and nodded. "Okay," she said warily.

He settled down in the chair opposite her. "I know I mainly do the early shifts, but I wondered if I could swap one of those with a late shift on either a Wednesday or a Thursday?"

Clara exhaled. "I thought you were going to tell me you wanted fewer hours." She grabbed some paper from beside her. "You had me worried there." She scanned the paper in silence. "Usually, it's Sarah or Len who has the later shift on either of those days. Ask them first. If they agree, then it's fine with me." Toby raised his eyebrows, surprised she'd agreed so readily, and she snorted when she looked at him. "I'm not an ogre, Toby, despite what you all might think." She sighed. "I know I put a lot on you all—you especially—but I have a business to run. I can't always be the nice person in the room. I'm trying, though."

He couldn't believe what he'd heard. "Wow. What happened?"

She shook her head and huffed, staring down at her desk. "You did."

He frowned. "I did? How?"

"Yesterday. You looked so tired, so worn out. I was worried about you. After I dropped you at home, I went back over the three months of working." She glanced at him. "You've worked nearly double the hours of some people here. I put too much on you, and it's not fair. I'm sorry. I'll do better. I'll find more help."

Toby opened his mouth to tell her that his being tired was nothing to do with the job but stopped himself. This was a good realisation for her to come to, even if the reason for it was wrong. Instead, he said, "Thank you, Clara. I appreciate it. I have..." He bit his lip, then continued, "I have a boyfriend. That's why I wanted to change my hours. We only get to see each other on the weekends, so I wanted to visit him during the week for a night."

Clara raised her eyebrows and smiled. "I'm happy for you. If either Sarah or Len agrees, I'm happy to change it. If not, I'll see if I can find another person. We'll make it happen."

Toby left the office lighter than when he came in. When Sarah arrived for her later shift, he pounced. "Sarah," he singsonged. "Do you love me?"

She narrowed her eyes at him. "It depends. What do you want?"

Toby gasped. "So cruel to your best friend."

She slid an arm around his shoulders. "What do you want, munchkin?"

"Do you fancy swapping shifts on a Wednesday from next week?" He clasped his hands together, pleading with her with his eyes and pouting his lower lip.

Sarah rolled her eyes. "Fine. I hate mornings, but for you, fine."

Toby threw his arms around her. "Thank you! You're the best friend in the world!"

Sarah laughed. "So, why the change?"

"I'm going to spend the evening at Ollie's, then I don't have to rush back for an early shift." He shrugged. "It means we get to see each other for a night in the week and the weekends."

"How can I stand in the way of true love?" she said wistfully.

Toby coughed. "I don't know if it's true love," he hedged.

Sarah stared at him, and he squirmed. "I know you, Toby. You're in over your head already. It's not a bad thing. You deserve this."

"Thanks," he said, dropping his gaze and feeling his cheeks heat. "I'm just going to tell Clara."

"I can't believe she agreed to it."

Toby told her about the conversation with their boss, and it left Sarah speechless, which was a feat. He raced to Clara's office and explained that Sarah would swap from next week, and she amended the schedule before he raced back out again. He couldn't wait to tell his Daddy.

14

OLLIE

"You seem excitable today. Did something good happen?" Ollie asked his boy, who he could see was bouncing on the balls of his feet as he spoke on the video call.

"I have some good news. Well, I think it's good news. I hope you do. Maybe I should've asked you first, but I didn't want to get our hopes up in case she said no. But now, maybe I should've. I don't—"

"Toby, breathe." Ollie stared at him, watching the emotions play across his face as he did as Ollie asked. "Right. Now, tell me the good news. Don't worry about anything else."

Toby inhaled. "I changed one of my shifts at work. It means, from next week, I can come and visit you overnight on a Tuesday. If you'd like me to, that is." He bit his lip.

Ollie's stomach fluttered, and he grinned. "That would be fantastic. Are *you* sure?"

Toby nodded so much that Ollie thought his head would roll right off. "I am. I'll finish at two o'clock on Tuesday, and I don't have to be back at work until two o'clock the next day. I know you'll still have to work at the garage, but I could, maybe, just hang around, and we can chat while you work." He shrugged, looking unsure again.

"We'll figure it out, Toby. Thank you for doing that, sweetheart."

Toby beamed. Ollie was the luckiest man alive. After everything his boy had been through, he was still willing to throw everything into the pot and see what happened with them. He was beyond amazing.

"I have some other news, too."

"Will my heart survive these surprises?" Ollie joked, earning another smile.

"Ben is throwing a Christmas Eve party and wants us to come. Can you make it?"

Ollie nodded. "I don't have any plans for Christmas Eve, so of course, we can. I'll pick you up on the way."

"I don't mind driving us."

"Well, that depends. Do you want to go on the bike?" Ollie raised his eyebrows, smirking when Toby's face lit up again.

"Oh, my god! Yes! Can we go faster this time?"

Ollie laughed, garnering the attention of the men working the garage, even though he was in the office. He waved them off. "Yes. There will be open roads we can speed up on."

Toby danced around his kitchen, chanting, "Yes, yes, yes!"

"At the rate you're going, you'll be trading in your car for a bike," Ollie joked.

"Not quite. I don't think I'd like it when it rains."

Ollie agreed. "Yes. If it's raining on Christmas Eve, I'll bring the car. Nothing worse than being a lump of wet at a party." He changed the subject. "Have you done your chore?"

Toby's silence spoke volumes. Ollie shook his head and chuckled. "Come on. I'll stay on the phone while you do it."

⬩

It wasn't raining, or due to rain, on Christmas Eve, so Ollie took the chance and rode. If Toby had been more confident, he was sure the boy would've ridden all the way to Ben's house with his hands in the air with how much he laughed and cheered throughout the journey.

After they finished at the party, Ollie planned to spend the night at Toby's so they could celebrate Christmas morning together—with a few special gifts he'd bought for his boy—then he would return home to spend the afternoon with his family while Toby spent the time with his own family. They'd tentatively agreed to meet each other's families in the New Year.

When they pulled up to the address Ben had given them, Ollie was impressed with the spread. This screamed "family home," and it was something he would want if he ever had a family to look after. Did Toby want kids? He brushed the thought aside when Toby climbed off the bike. It was too early for those thoughts.

"Are we late?" Toby asked, removing his helmet.

Ollie shook his head. "No, we're on time. Don't worry."

They grabbed the present they'd bought for the hosts and headed up the path to the front door. Toby pressed the doorbell, fidgeting with his jacket.

"Hey," Gareth said when he opened the door. "Come on in." They took off their coats, and then Toby asked where Ben was. "He's in the kitchen. Better grab some cinnamon rolls before he eats them all."

Toby raced off, and Ollie and Gareth laughed. "He's eager. He's been so excited about this party," Ollie said.

"So has Ben."

They followed in Toby's wake, finding the boy hugging Ben and laughing. Ben smiled over at Ollie. "I'm glad you're both here," Ben said.

"Wouldn't miss it for the world. I have plenty to be grateful for this year," Ollie said, smiling at Toby, his heart lifting.

The front door opened, and someone shouted, "I found two

other people on the street. I thought I'd invite them in."

Ben gasped. "I might not have enough food for extra people." He disappeared into the hallway, and Gareth laughed.

"There's enough food to cater for another *three-dozen* people."

When Ben returned, he set them all eating and drinking and getting to know other people. It surprised Ollie that Toby went with it. He had expected him to be nervous. Conversation and laughter abounded, and Ollie was glad he'd agreed to come. It was great to meet new people.

Gareth's dad, Richard, cleared his throat. "I meant to ask how the app was going, Gareth. I know you said you had created one, but I never got the chance to ask what it was for."

Ben stared wide-eyed at Gareth, who stared at his father, and Ollie got the impression Richard knew nothing about their lifestyle.

Unfortunately, Toby shifted forward to the edge of his seat and started talking, "The app is absolutely brilliant. It helped me find my Daddy after waiting so long and having too many disastrous dates. I don't know how it works, but we're perfect for each other, aren't we?" He glanced at Ollie with a huge smile on his face.

Ollie slid his arm around Toby's shoulders and smiled back before glancing at Ben and Gareth with a small wince. "We are."

Richard tilted his head, forehead creased. "It's like a dating app?"

"Uh-huh, but for those who are struggling to find their Daddies or their boys. It happens a lot, I'm told," Toby continued, completely unaware of how much information he was sharing with someone who possibly didn't want to know so much about their child. "I'd been looking for a Daddy for five years with no luck. And for Ollie, I think it was longer."

"Eight years." He couldn't help but answer his boy's question, even if it meant digging a deeper hole for Gareth.

"I've been looking for eleven years," Victor mumbled. "And I'm still looking."

Richard glanced at Gareth. "And you're the Daddy in this relationship?" he asked his son. Gareth swallowed and nodded. "Makes sense. You always were the caretaker. I know I left you alone a lot, and you had a lot on your shoulders. It kind of makes sense." He peered at Ben. "Bet you have your hands full with him."

Everyone laughed at the acute description, breaking the tension. Ollie squeezed Toby's shoulder, and Toby smiled at him. Despite his boy having no idea what he'd just announced to the guests, Ollie couldn't help but think it was a good way of telling everyone without making a huge deal out of it. Whether Gareth and Ben agreed was a different matter.

They voted on what film to watch—*The Nightmare Before Christmas*—then played charades, eating more food afterwards and talking with so many people, Ollie was peopled out. When it was time to say their goodbyes, Toby protested, but Ollie had to be careful his boy didn't get too tired. He didn't want him falling off the bike on the journey home.

They arrived at Toby's unscathed, and Ollie locked his bike up outside before following Toby into the house.

He wrapped his arms around his boy and nuzzled his neck. "Did you have fun?"

Toby nodded into his shoulder. "I did, but I'm sooooooo tired now."

"Well, we need to get to sleep; otherwise, Santa won't come."

Toby giggled. "I wanted to sleep with you, but I don't have the energy."

Ollie snorted. "We have the morning, remember?"

"Okay," he murmured, and Ollie picked him up, Toby wrapping his legs around his waist, and carried him carefully up the stairs. "Let's get ready for bed."

It took a few tries, but he managed to get Toby out of his clothes and into bed with little to no help from his boy, especially when it came to the leather jacket. He'd probably sleep in it if he had the choice. If Ollie was to guess, he would've said Toby was asleep standing up by that point. Ollie crouched beside the bed, checking he was asleep before tiptoeing downstairs to fetch the small gifts he'd hidden in the back of the bottom cupboards the previous weekend. He knew Toby wouldn't look there because it seemed like nothing had been touched for months with how much dust had accumulated. Not that he was complaining. He wasn't at all. He had cupboards he barely used, too.

He placed the gifts on the sofa and filled the stocking he'd brought in his bag with yummy treats he'd have to be careful Toby didn't eat all of at once. Once he was satisfied, he crept back up the stairs, undressed and climbed into bed beside his boy. Toby immediately rolled over and wrapped himself around him, and Ollie smiled into the darkness. He had nowhere else he'd prefer to be.

Ollie woke to kisses being pressed all over his face and neck, and when he groaned, Toby whispered, "It's Christmas, Daddy! Merry Christmas!"

"Merry Christmas, sweetheart. What time is it?"

Toby fell silent, and Ollie opened one eye. Toby flushed. "Early," he mumbled.

"How early?"

Toby sighed. "Seven-thirty. I just couldn't stay asleep any longer. I only have you for a few more hours!"

Ollie pulled Toby against him. "I know. It's fine, but I think I need a cup of tea to wake up properly."

"I can do it!" Toby pushed against Ollie to get up, but Ollie pulled him back down again.

"We'll go together."

They got up and dressed, and then they aimed straight for the kitchen. Ollie was glad the living room was in the opposite direction, so their tea run didn't ruin the surprise. When they had mugs in their hands and a couple of croissants between them, they went to the living room. When Toby stopped, Ollie walked around him and smiled at the wide-eyed look on his face.

"Santa's been," Toby whispered, staring at the gifts.

Ollie put his drink and croissant down and reached for Toby's, then nudged him towards the sofa. "Let's see what he brought you."

Toby knelt beside the sofa and reached for the first gift. He slowly unwrapped it and touched the fluffy fabric.

"It's a weighted blanket," Ollie said. "I thought it might help you sleep at night."

"Thank you," Toby whispered, brushing his cheek against it. "It's so soft."

The second gift was a hoodie blanket so Toby could stay warm when he was playing his games. Toby almost screamed at the third gift, which was two tickets to a gaming convention taking place in a few months. Ollie'd had no idea if it was any good when he'd bought it, but if Toby's response was any indication, he'd done okay. The last gift was a gift card to the game store he thought Toby used.

"Thank you, Daddy. You didn't have to get me all this."

Ollie brushed his fingers against Toby's cheek. "I wanted to."

Toby stood, wringing his hands. "I have something for you, too. Wait here."

He disappeared, and Ollie drank his tea while he waited. When Toby returned, he held a small package. Toby settled in front of Ollie and clung to it.

"If you don't like it, you don't have to use it," he murmured.

Ollie took the offering and opened it. He held his breath while he ran his fingers over the palm-sized leather patch. It held the words "Toby's Daddy," and Ollie's heart pounded.

"You don't have to wear it, but I thought if anyone saw it, they might assume you had a son instead of me, and that would be okay. Kind of like a secret from the world. But you don't have to." Toby trailed off.

Ollie slid his hand to Toby's nape and squeezed. "I love it." He pressed his lips to Toby's. "I'll attach it when I get home."

Toby's smile lit up the room. "You like it?"

"Love it. I'd happily wear it and tell people it means you, not a son." Ollie brushed his thumb along Toby's cheek. "Thank you, sweetheart."

"You're welcome."

Toby climbed into his lap, and they traded kisses for a long while before Toby's stomach growled. Ollie laughed and pushed him off. "Eat your breakfast. I'll make you a fresh cup of tea."

After breakfast, he snuggled with Toby under the weighted blanket, trying to decide if he should buy one for himself, too. When the time came for him to leave, Toby clung to him.

"I'll see you on Tuesday, remember? Not long at all."

"Okay," Toby said, though his voice trembled.

Ollie lifted his chin and kissed him, slowly, reverently, until they needed to breathe and pulled away. "Call me tonight before you go to sleep."

"I will."

Ollie bit back the words that shouldn't come so easily to his lips because he knew neither of them was ready for them. He could feel them and acknowledge them, but he couldn't say them. Yet. He had to make sure he wouldn't hurt Toby before giving him those important words. But feel it, he did. Deeper and more painfully than with anyone else.

15

TOBY

A week later, Toby took Ollie to meet Sarah at a bar for a New Year's Eve party. His Daddy even wore his leather jacket, complete with the "Toby's Daddy" patch. His best friend and his boyfriend hit it off, which Toby was immensely grateful for. Sarah had never liked *him*, so to have her approval about Ollie was reassuring. Until she let the bomb drop that Toby had never been in a kink club.

Ollie glanced at him, eyebrow raised, and Toby's cheeks heated. "Will you tell me why?" Ollie murmured in his ear.

Toby sighed and turned his head to talk in Ollie's ear because the music was too loud for polite conversation. "Initially, I had *him*, so I didn't need to. Then I was too scared in case I saw him."

Ollie's jaw clenched, and Toby knew it was because Ollie was angry at the ex rather than Toby. "Would you like to visit one?"

Toby shook his head. "I wouldn't want to see him."

"What if we chose a different one? Somewhere else?"

Toby bit his lip, staring at Ollie. "Maybe. If we can check that he's not a member."

Ollie nodded. "We can ask. They might not tell us, but we can definitely ask."

He pushed the thought aside so he could enjoy the evening, and when the countdown happened, he spent several long minutes kissing his Daddy. The best New Year ever.

The following day, they visited Toby's parents. Toby was nervous, but not because he didn't want Ollie to meet them, but because he'd never introduced anyone but *him* to them before, and he wanted them to like him. Not that there was anything to dislike about his Daddy.

"Nice to meet you, Ollie," his mum said. "I hope you like roast dinners."

"My favourite meal," Ollie said, smiling. And that was all it took to win over his mother.

Toby's father, however, took Ollie outside to talk to, and Toby stayed inside, although he wanted to hear everything they talked about. When Ollie came back in, he didn't look worse for wear, so Toby assumed it went well.

"Are you okay?"

Ollie nodded. "Your father is a lot like my dad was."

"Did he threaten you?"

"Only once, but that was all that was needed."

Toby groaned and palmed his face. "Let's hope my brothers don't take after him."

All in all, the visit went well, although Nigel kept peppering Ollie with questions until Toby told him to stop. At least now they'd met each other, and Toby didn't have to worry about keeping things quiet anymore. Not that he wanted to, anyway.

He had wished Sarah had kept quiet about the club visit, though, because Ollie asked him again about the club a week later.

"I've been thinking about the club visit. Would you like to go to one near Ben and Gareth, and we can ask them to come as moral support, too? It might make it easier for you to have more people around. We can drive Sarah with us, so she gets to be there for you as well. What do you think?"

Toby's stomach swooped and dived, but he needed to be brave. "Can you still call and ask if he's a member? If there's even a slight chance he could be there, I don't want to go."

Ollie enfolded him in a hug. "Of course. I will do everything I can to find out if he's a member there. And if you're unsure at any point, we can leave. Going to a club is not essential for our relationship, Toby. I just think you'll enjoy it there. You'll get to meet other boys and have fun."

"Maybe Ben could invite Victor and Preston, too. They were nice when we met them on Christmas Eve." The more he thought about it, the happier he was becoming about attempting it. "Yes, okay. We can go."

Ollie kissed him. "You're such a brave boy. I don't know how I ever deserved you."

Toby scoffed. "It's taken me far too long to pluck up the courage to meet your friends and family. I wouldn't call that brave."

"That's a different type of bravery. Going to a club, if you don't like it you just won't go back again. Meeting family and friends, if you don't get along, you might still have to see them now and then."

"That's true." He sighed. "Are you sure they'll like me?"

"They'll love you." A knock sounded, and Toby froze. "Am I okay to let them in?"

Toby swallowed and stepped back before nodding. Ollie jogged down the steps to the door of his apartment, and conversation floated up. Ollie reappeared and immediately went to Toby's side, sliding an arm around his waist. Three men stopped at the top of the stairs.

"Toby, this is Enno, my best friend, and his boy, Rick." The two men waved. "And that is my other best friend, Denny."

"Other best friend, indeed. Nothing like being second place," Denny said with a huff, then strode forward with his hand outstretched. "Nice to meet you, Toby." He tilted his head. "Do you have a nickname?"

Toby opened his mouth, his face heating as he admitted it. "Toto. But only my brothers call me that."

Denny laughed. "Love it. Little Toto, it is." He clapped Ollie on the back. "Ollie and Toto. Perfect." He disappeared into the kitchen, and Toby heard the fridge open.

"Sorry about that. You can tell him to shove off if you don't want him to use the nickname," Ollie said.

Toby shrugged. "It's fine. I'm used to it."

Enno and Rick moved closer, Enno holding out his hand, too. "Nice to meet you. This is Rick."

Rick was the same height as Enno but more muscular. Toby had never seen a boy like him before, but he knew that what you saw on the outside didn't always match what someone was on the inside, so he didn't comment because that would be just plain rude.

"Hi, Rick."

"Hey."

"Ollie tells me you like video games?" Enno said. "Rick does, too, though he doesn't admit it often to new people."

Toby smiled at Rick. "Have you seen Ollie's ancient console?" Rick shook his head. "Come on." He pressed a kiss to Ollie's cheek and led Rick to the living area. "It's a PlayStation One, but it's in superb condition. He doesn't have many games, though. What types of games do you play?"

He got lost in the conversation and gaming with Rick, and it was only when Ollie kissed his head that he blinked and came out of the bubble he was in.

"Time to get ready," he said, and Toby's stomach rolled. Time to meet his family is what he meant.

"Thank you for the games," Rick said. "I really enjoyed it. We might need to upgrade if we want to play some of those others we spoke about."

Toby chuckled. "Definitely."

They said goodbye, and Ollie hugged him. "That wasn't too bad, was it?"

He smiled. "No. It was good. I like your friends."

"Good. I asked them if they wanted to come to the club with us, too. The more, the merrier."

"Good idea."

They got ready to go, and Toby twined his hands together as Ollie drove them over to his mother's house. He hoped she liked him.

"She'll love you."

Toby flushed. He must've said it aloud. He climbed from the car when Ollie rounded the front and opened his door, then clasped Ollie's hand as they headed for the door. It was a quaint little place from the front, but Ollie had mentioned that they'd extended out the back, making it much larger. Toby couldn't wait to see it.

The door opened before they could get to it, and a woman, the spitting image of Ollie, stood wiping her hand on her apron.

"Ollie!" She opened her arms, and Ollie leaned down to hug her and kiss her cheek.

"Hey, Mum." He tugged Toby forward. "This is Toby. Toby, my mother, Beatrice."

"Bea or Mum to you, my dear. We don't stand on ceremony."

"Nice to meet you, Bea." He wasn't touching the "Mum" with a bargepole right then. "You have a lovely home."

"Why, thank you. Ollie, why not take him on a brief tour while I finish up lunch?"

Ollie dragged him inside the house, and immediately, Toby's attention diverted to the walls, which were filled with photographs, haphazardly attached. He studied them, seeing Ollie, a female version of him, who Toby assumed was his sister, Bea and an older man, who he believed was Ollie's dad. He glanced at Ollie. A sad expression crossed Ollie's face as he stared at the pictures.

"I'm sorry. Let's go on the tour," Toby said, not wanting to upset him further.

Ollie shook his head and smiled. "No, it's okay. These are one of those things that have been here so long, I often don't 'see' them anymore, even though I pass them every time I come here." He pointed to one photo with the four of them on the beach. "I was seventeen in that photo, I think. We'd gone to the beach, and I hadn't wanted to go, but my parents insisted. It was one of the best holidays we'd had once I let myself enjoy it." He chuckled. "The joys of growing up."

"I don't envy our parents," Toby said.

"Do you want children?"

Toby swallowed at his words, glancing at him and finding his gaze on him. He inhaled, going for the truth. "Yes, I really do," he whispered.

Ollie smiled. "Me, too." Toby's heart missed a beat, and he grinned. "Come on. I want to show you the back garden."

They followed the hallway through to the back of the house, peeking into rooms as they passed. The garden was enormous but would've been bigger before the extension Ollie had mentioned. It would be the perfect place for dogs to run around. The image of them both throwing a ball for a dog and playing with small kids kept floating through his mind, and he tried to push it down. It was far too early for that.

"Lunch is ready!" Bea called through the back door.

They re-entered the house, and Ollie introduced him to his sister, Imogen.

"I was beginning to think he made you up," she said, a twinkle in her eye.

"Not that I'm aware of," he answered with a grin.

She winked at him. "You could be a robot?"

Toby nodded, affecting a serious expression. "I could be. I

wouldn't know it."

"Can you not search your brain and find commands or something? That would tell you the truth."

"Sorry, nothing there. I must be real."

"Damn it. I want a robot."

Toby chuckled. "Sorry to disappoint you."

Imogen waved him away. "One day, maybe."

"You could build one," he said, and Imogen's hands paused in cutting up her chicken, eyes wide.

Ollie groaned. "Now, you've done it."

Toby frowned, glancing between the two siblings. "Done what?"

Ollie pointed at his sister. "Can you see that glazed look? That's her plotting. You've given her an idea, and she won't let it go until she's figured out if it's possible or not. You get a similar expression when you're gaming." He smiled.

"Do I?" He studied Imogen. "It's scary."

"At least I can snap you out of it. Imogen, however, will stay like that for a while, even while going through the motions of everyday life. When she comes out of it, she'll not remember most of the past however long it's been. She's highly intellectual, scarily so."

Toby winced. "Sorry. I didn't know."

Bea chuckled. "Don't worry, Toby. We're used to it. I'm getting good at conversing with myself, even arguing opposite factors. It's highly entertaining."

Toby grinned at her wink, so similar to Imogen's. "Do you get the answers you want, though?"

Bea snorted. "No. It's irritating."

Toby relaxed after that, glad to have made a good impression, and when it was time to go, he received a hug from Ollie's mother, asking him to come back soon.

Ollie threaded their fingers together on the drive home. "Did you have fun?"

"I did. Thank you."

"I'm glad."

Ollie stayed quiet for the rest of the brief journey back to Ollie's apartment. When they climbed out, Toby squealed when Ollie grabbed him and threw him over his shoulder.

"Put me down!" Toby laughed.

"But I'm a big, strong man." He lowered his voice to a growl. "I caveman. I take man to cave."

Toby giggled for the entire journey up the stairs, even when he bounced on Ollie's sofa when the man threw him on it. "You're silly, Daddy."

Ollie gasped and crawled onto the sofa, covering Toby. "But you love it."

They froze, eyes locked as the words hung in the air. Toby inhaled and lifted his hands to cup Ollie's jaw. "I do," he whispered, his heart pounding with the potential implications.

"I do, too."

They didn't share the three words, but the moment felt just as profound. More so when Ollie leaned down a kissed him—as if sealing the deal.

"Do you want to play a game before you need to leave?" Ollie asked.

Toby shook his head. "Can we watch a movie or something and cuddle?"

Ollie smiled. "Of course. You choose a film, and I'll grab some snacks and drinks." He pecked Toby's lips. "And maybe set an alarm on my phone in case we fall asleep like we did last time."

Toby snorted as Ollie disappeared. The previous weekend, they'd watched a movie at Toby's house, and they'd fallen asleep. They'd not woken until nearly two o'clock in the morning, and Ollie had groaned at having to drive home that late, especially after only just waking. Instead, Toby had offered for him to stay the night and get up earlier. Ollie had agreed, but the following morning had said he couldn't do that again because getting up earlier hurt. Toby had agreed to the hurting bit, but waking to Ollie next to him had made it easier to bear.

"Okay, alarm ready, popcorn and chocolate drops set, and juice is a go. What are we watching?" Ollie put the bowl and cups on the coffee table, dragging it closer for them to reach, then slid in behind Toby again.

"*Speed.*"

"Good choice."

Toby rested his head on Ollie's arm when he slid it beneath him and stared at the screen as the movie played. Happiness flooded his body, and he never wanted to move. He wanted to freeze that moment in time and stay in it forever. Could he be lucky enough to keep Ollie for that long? He hoped so.

He closed his eyes and brought up the scene from earlier that day. They were throwing a ball for a couple of dogs, and Ollie was chasing two small kids around the garden. Ollie would be a wonderful dad, and the kids—and dogs—would be spoilt rotten. He blinked, tears escaping from his eyes. He tried not to show Ollie, but his finely tuned instincts must've realised something was up because he tightened his hold on Toby and pressed his lips to his neck and ear.

"I'm here," Ollie whispered.

"So am I."

16

OLLIE

The day of the club visit dawned, and Ollie could sense Toby's reticence, but he didn't complain once about it. He drove Toby and Sarah, and then they met Enno, Rick and Denny outside Gareth's house before heading over to the club. If they wanted to play, they weren't allowed to drink, which was why Ollie drove, but he wouldn't drink when Toby was with him, anyway.

The club itself was a nice place. Bound was located on an industrial estate on the outskirts of the town and unidentifiable unless you knew what it was. They parked and climbed out of the car, waiting at the front of the club for everyone. Ben and Gareth led the way, and they all signed up for the night. Ollie made sure to touch Toby all the time so he didn't worry.

"I've spoken to them, and he's not a member here," he reminded Toby.

Toby nodded but didn't reply. They entered the main area, and Ollie was impressed by the spaciousness. Gareth had been right when he'd said the place looked bigger on the inside. They continued through another set of double doors into another open-plan space, but this time, it was more niche. They had divided the space into rooms, ranging from nurseries to a teenage wet dream. The owners had covered every possible

Daddy and boy scenario from what Ollie could see and a few more he hadn't thought about.

"Welcome to the playground," Gareth said, waving his hands around. "It's a fairly recent addition. Before this, we all mingled in the previous room. But unbeknownst to the members, the owners were working on this behind the scenes. It opened last week."

"It's amazing," Denny said, wandering off to explore, but Ollie didn't miss the glance towards Preston. Interesting.

Ollie refocused on Toby's wide-eyed expression. "What do you think?"

"It's amazing. This must've taken them ages, but look at everything they've got!" Toby stepped closer to the teenage dream room, just like Ollie thought he would. "It's got a games console with loads of games."

"I see it." He kissed Toby's cheek. "Go for it. I'm right here."

Toby grinned. "Ben! Do you want a game?"

"Go on then."

The boys headed to the room, and Gareth stood beside Ollie. "Ben's not really into video games, but he plays because he likes the company. He's getting better at them, though, so a console is probably in our future."

Ollie chuckled. "I can imagine. Especially as they can play with each other online and talk at the same time. We'll never get them off it."

Gareth groaned and rubbed a hand over his face. "Maybe I should reconsider."

Ben dragged beanbags over in front of the enormous TV screen, and Toby handed him a controller before dropping into the soft chair. He sank into it, laughing.

"How is he doing?" Gareth asked.

Ollie blew out a breath. "He seems okay. He's been worried about coming here. I don't know what he or Ben has told you, but

Toby's ex was an asshole, and he's always worried about bumping into him, which was why he'd never been to a club before." Ollie snorted. "Although looking at this place, we may as well have stopped at home."

Gareth laughed. "Yeah, definitely a home-from-home situation. But the social aspect is worth it."

Ollie nodded and aimed for a sofa close to the room Toby was in. "How's the app going?"

Gareth settled beside him, crossing his ankle over his knee. "Really good. It's strange to think something so simple is already helping so many people."

"It was a great idea. There are too many people out there messing with others' heads, and it needs to stop. This app is a good way to have some control over who can sign up."

"Agreed." Gareth scratched his jaw. "We're thinking of opening up some events across the country."

"Events?" he asked when Gareth didn't continue.

"Social events, like parties and discos or whatever. But they'll only be open for those on the app and after another round of background checks."

"Sounds like a good idea. You seem hesitant, though."

Gareth exhaled. "I am. I'm thinking of the time constraints. Ben and I both work, and if we did this, we'd need to take on staff, which would take money. It's not just as simple as saying 'yes, let's do this,' unfortunately."

"Well, I can't offer much experience, but if you need anything, you only have to ask," Ollie offered.

"Thanks. We're still in the thinking stages, but I'll keep that in mind. No doubt Ben will tell Toby about it."

Ollie snorted. "They're thick as thieves, they are."

"Too right."

Ollie glanced around and raised his eyebrows when he spotted Denny sitting cross-legged at a small table with what looked like playdough while Preston hovered over him, hands tucked into his jeans. Denny looked up at Preston and said something, and Preston gave a small smile and sat opposite Denny, taking the playdough Denny offered. Was Denny a boy? He'd shown no sign of it. Or had Ollie been so blindsided by his own life that he hadn't seen what was right in front of him? Not that he wanted Denny—there was no attraction there—but was he blind to his best friend's needs?

"Preston's in between a rock and a hard place at the moment, though he's getting better," Gareth murmured. "A relationship went disastrously wrong, and he's still finding his feet. He's never shown an interest in a Daddy and boy relationship, but it might fit him. I don't know. I think he just needs to let things unfold and see what happens."

"Same with a lot of things in life. You can only control what you do, not what everyone else does."

"True."

Ollie focused back on Toby, his boy's eyes staring at the screen while his fingers flew over the controller. He needed to get him a drink and a snack.

"I'm going to get a drink for him. Do you want something for Ben?"

"Yeah. Could you grab some juice for him, please?"

Ollie wandered to the small bar in the centre of the room and requested drinks and snacks. When the tray was loaded up, he took it back to Gareth.

"I wasn't sure what everyone else would want, so I just got the same." He took Toby's drink and food over to him, touching his shoulder gently to let him know it was him before holding the refreshments in front of him. Toby smiled and took them, turning back to Ben after Gareth had done the same for him.

Ollie grabbed the tray and took it to Denny and Preston, placing two of each on a small table beside them without saying a word.

Then he went to each of the other couples that had paired off—Enno and Rick, and Victor and Sarah—to do the same. When he settled back next to Gareth, he chuckled.

"I feel like we're at a slumber party, and we're the only adults looking after a ton of kids."

Gareth laughed. "I hear you."

"I honestly didn't think this place would be like this. I expected more mundane amenities."

"The owners want to become the best of the best. To have one of the most sought-after memberships around. I think they're getting there. This goes a long way to making them in the upper echelons."

"Definitely. I wish this place wasn't so far away. It's not like we can just visit whenever we want."

"Yeah, not ideal. But it's good for a trip now and then. Plus, maybe if Toby likes this one, he'll be calmer at one closer to home."

"Only if his ex isn't a member. I don't know what I'll do if I ever go face-to-face with him."

"Probably the same as I would."

Ollie agreed. Toby glanced over at him and smiled, and Ollie got up to check in with him. He didn't want him to think Ollie was only there to chat with Gareth. After all, they'd come so they could experience the place together. He crouched at Toby's side, resting a hand on his knee.

"Are you okay, sweetheart?"

Toby nodded. "I'm more tired than I thought. My eyes are blurring." He leaned his head down to rest on Ollie's shoulder.

"Why don't you try something else instead of gaming? I know Denny and Preston were playing with the playdough. Or we could sit, and I could read to you? What do you want to do?"

"Can you read to me? It's not something I usually like, but I love the idea of cuddling up with you while you talk to me."

"Of course, we can." Ollie stood, holding out his hand. "Let's see if we can find a really comfortable chair to snuggle in."

Ben had already disappeared and climbed into Gareth's lap. Maybe everyone was tired. Ollie led Toby around the rooms until they found a library-style room with enormous chairs.

"How about this?" Ollie asked his boy.

Toby didn't say anything but detached himself from Ollie's arm and ran over to the biggest chair and jumped into it, bouncing slightly. Ollie laughed as he joined him, settling a lot gentler than his boy did.

"Would you like to choose a book?" Ollie pointed at the shelves, and Toby scrambled off the chair again.

Ollie pushed himself back into the soft chair, feeling so tiny in such a big chair. It reminded him of the oversized deckchairs and parasols they had at the beach that kids loved to climb on. He felt like a kid in this chair—his feet hung off the end, not even close to touching the floor.

"This one!" Toby said, climbing back on and dropping a book in Ollie's lap. He snuggled into Ollie's side, and Ollie lifted his arm around his shoulders.

Ollie picked up the book and read the title, then chuckled. "Dr Seuss, eh?"

Toby grinned. "I used to love him as a kid."

"He's one of Imogen's favourites, too."

Toby's face lit up. "Really? I'll have to ask her about it when I see her next."

Ollie's heart filled a little more at his words, but he cleared his throat and began reading. When he got to page five, he had another boy, Rick, settled at his feet, listening, while his Daddy looked on with a smile. By page eight, he had two more people at the base of the chair. Victor and Ben knelt with their arms resting on the chair and their chins on their arms, looking adorable. But what he loved the most was that Toby relaxed against him, bit by bit, until Ollie knew he was asleep. Ollie kept reading, though. He couldn't disappoint the others.

When he finished, the boys smiled and clapped gently, and Enno brought him a drink. "I thought you might need it," he whispered.

"Thanks," he replied, drinking the water all in one go. Enno took the bottle back. "I think I might be here a while." Ollie smiled, pressing a kiss to Toby's head when he snuffled and rubbed his cheek against Ollie's shoulder.

"We won't leave without you," Enno joked.

"I'd appreciate it."

The group left them alone, and Ollie closed his eyes. He couldn't believe how lucky he was. Despite the initial teething problems, which he'd told Toby were normal—and they were—they seemed to be finding their feet. He still needed to figure out how to help Toby during the week. He knew he struggled to sleep, and dirty talk only got them so far. He was also worried Toby was using his gaming to pass the time if he couldn't sleep, which wasn't good. If he could stay off that, he was more likely to fall asleep earlier than if he played a game and got lost in it, like he usually did.

And as for chores, Toby only had one so far, which was to tidy his room. Ollie hadn't put his foot down about it yet, but he needed to. Toby needed structure and routine to help him get the best out of life. And it was Ollie's job to ensure he had it.

Yes, he needed to put his foot down with things now. They had no plans for the following day, so he could put some plans into place.

He wasn't sure how long Toby dozed because he hadn't checked the time, but he inhaled suddenly and froze.

"I'm here, sweetheart. You're safe," Ollie murmured, hating that Toby's initial reaction was always fear.

Toby relaxed again and lifted his head. "Hi, Daddy."

Ollie pecked his lips. "Hi, sweetheart. Do you feel better?"

Toby nodded, though he yawned. "I don't like not sleeping with you, even though I've been sleeping alone for years. I don't understand it."

"Yes, it's something we need to figure out because you're exhausted, and I don't like it."

Toby fidgeted with Ollie's shirt. "I need to stop gaming."

"No, you don't. Maybe just finish earlier than you do." He paused. "Do you play during the night?"

Toby's fingers hesitated for a split second, and Ollie knew the answer before Toby opened his mouth. "Yes. That's why I need to stop gaming. I get lost in the game again, and before I know it, it's four in the morning."

Ollie sighed. "That's definitely not helping. We need some parental controls on that thing." He chuckled and shook his head. "We'll think of something."

"You could just help me sleep every night?"

"We can't do that indefinitely." Ollie huffed. "I don't know. Maybe we can ask Gareth for advice. After all, he's our DaddyG."

Toby laughed, the sound loud in the quiet room, and seconds later, Ben popped his head around the doorway.

"Toby! You're awake! Come and play!"

Toby waved and nodded. "Soon. I'm snuggling."

Ben rolled his eyes. "You can snuggle anytime. Come on!" He disappeared.

Toby's face was brighter than it had been for as long as Ollie could remember. Even with Ollie, Toby held something back, but in this moment, Toby was happy, and Ollie vowed to do everything in his power to make sure he smiled like that every day.

Ollie nudged him. "Go on. I'll snuggle you all you want when we get back to your house."

"Promise?" Toby held up his pinkie finger.

Ollie linked them together. "Promise." He kissed him, starting slowly, then deepening it when Toby straddled his lap. When they came up for air, Toby rested his forehead on Ollie's shoulder.

"I like this a lot," he whispered.

Ollie smiled, knowing what he meant. "I like this a lot, too."

He wasn't willing to voice the words he wanted to say, but it wouldn't be long before they spilled out of him. How could he hold them back when Toby was everything he'd ever hoped for? He'd realised shortly after Toby had run and told him it was a mistake that it truly wasn't. He knew it was the best thing for them both. The thing they'd both been missing. And now that it was here, Ollie wouldn't let it go without a fight, and he hoped Toby would fight too.

Fight for the love they wouldn't voice.

Fight for the life they wanted.

Fight for each other.

It was everything he wanted, and he refused to let it go.

17

TOBY

Toby fidgeted on the sofa, his cock pressing against his khakis as he waited for the lunch Daddy was making. They'd spent the morning in bed, snuggling, just like Ollie had promised him the previous evening, and Toby had even come twice. But he needed to come again. He wasn't sure why he was so horny all of a sudden, but he needed his Daddy as much as he could get him.

Was he saving it up for when Ollie wasn't there? Was he trying to fit in a week's worth of orgasms to keep him going during the few days he wasn't with him?

Probably, but he couldn't help it. He needed him. Again.

"Lunch is ready!" Ollie called, and Toby jumped off the sofa and raced to the dining room. "Woah, slow down!" Ollie said when Toby skidded on the wooden floor as he stopped to wash his hands.

"Sorry, Daddy."

"I don't want you hurting yourself." Ollie put a plate of pasta in front of him when he sat, and Toby wrinkled his nose at the small bowl of vegetables, his cock forgotten. "There's only a few, and it's something new for you to try. If you don't like them, you don't have to eat them." Ollie sat beside him.

Toby picked up his fork and inhaled, taking a scoop of the finely cut disgusting things and shoving them in his mouth. He chewed fast, but as the buttery flavour exploded over his taste buds, he paused and frowned. Why had he never had vegetables that tasted like that before? All the ones he'd had were soft and squishy and had no taste or were hard and crunchy. These were completely different.

"Okay?" Ollie asked.

Toby nodded and swallowed. "I've never tasted anything like that before."

"Do you like it, though?" Toby nodded. "Then that's great news. I bet it would taste just as nice if you added it to the pasta, too. Like mine." He pointed at his plate, where the vegetables were mixed in with the pasta and cheesy sauce. "Or if you're not sure, put a bit of everything on your fork and put it in your mouth to see if it would taste nice."

Toby did and found it tasted yummy. He tipped the small bowl onto his pasta and swirled it around to mix it. "Thank you, Daddy. I'm sorry to be a pain."

Ollie's hand rested on his nape. "You're not a pain. I'm glad I could help." He removed his hand, and Toby instantly missed it. "While we're eating, we can talk about your routines and chores."

Toby groaned and shoved another mouthful in. Ollie chuckled.

"No getting away from it, I'm afraid. We need to get you into a better routine, and that starts with sorting through your gaming time." Toby opened his mouth, but Ollie put up a hand. "I'm not stopping you from playing, but I would like you to have a bit of time after playing and before you sleep to relax a bit. Collapsing into bed after playing is not conducive to a good night's sleep."

Toby bit his lip. He didn't like disappointing Ollie.

"Hey, now." Ollie slid an arm around his shoulders. "I'm not upset. I promise. I'm trying to help. I want you healthy and happy."

Toby gazed at him, eyes filling. "But I am. Happy, I mean. And so scared I will lose it all."

Ollie pushed his chair back and dragged Toby onto his lap so that Toby straddled him. He nestled his face into Ollie's neck, inhaling. "You're not the only one, sweetheart. I'm happy and scared, too." He sighed. "Tell you what? Let's finish lunch, and then we can get comfortable while we talk. Together, we can plan, and you can tell me what you like and don't like about the plan, and we *might*—might—change things up. Sound good?"

Toby nodded and pressed his lips to Ollie's neck. "Okay."

When they settled onto the sofa with a notepad and a pen, Toby wrung his hands together. He had no idea what to expect from a routine from Ollie. His ex had been super strict. Would Ollie be the same?

Ollie rested his hands on top of Toby's and squeezed. "You've nothing to worry about." Toby nodded. "So, let's go through your day first." Toby told Ollie of a typical day during the week when he had to work an early shift and the slight difference when he had a late one, which wasn't often. "All right. So, here's what I think—and this is just my opinion. You can say no or ask for things to change within reason."

"Okay."

"I know you hate mornings, so have you ever thought of asking to change to afternoon shifts?"

Toby opened his mouth and then paused. He never had because no one wanted to do them, so he'd just accepted that it was his shift. Could they find someone else to do some mornings for him?

"I've never thought to ask," he admitted.

"That might be an option for you, then. And if not, you could maybe ask to change just one or two? I know you do the early shift on a Tuesday and the late one on a Wednesday, so you can visit me."

Toby nodded. "I don't want to change that. I enjoy seeing you in the week."

Ollie smiled and brushed his thumb over Toby's cheek. "I do, too."

"I'll ask Clara and see what she says."

"Good. That would make your evenings a little easier, and I think it might wear you out a bit and make it easier for you to sleep."

Toby frowned. "Why? I'm still doing the same hours."

Ollie nodded. "You are, but at the moment, when you finish, you do other stuff that needs doing or play your games. Basically, you're keeping your body going to reach bedtime, and that can make you overtired. When you're overtired, it makes it even harder to fall asleep. However, if you do your chores and jobs in the morning, then work, then game for a bit, maybe read a book for half an hour, I think you'll find you sleep much better." He held up his hand. "You might not, but you might."

Toby tilted his head, thinking about what he'd said. "It makes sense. I know I often feel tired before I've even played my game, but I still do it. Habit, maybe?"

Ollie shrugged. "Possibly. But if you enjoy it, then we want to keep it." He flipped to a clean page in the notepad. "As for chores, you need to keep on top of tidying your bedroom. If you can change your shifts, you can sleep in later in the morning, and when you wake, you can get your chores out of the way before work. If you can't change your shifts, then you will need to do them as soon as you get home."

"What chores?" Toby groaned.

"So, tidying your bedroom so we don't trip over your clothes is the main one." Ollie held up two fingers. "You need to keep your desk tidy, or you'll end up with some unwanted guests."

Toby frowned. "What?"

Ollie chuckled. "Spiders, mice, rats, even. If you leave stuff around like that, they'll attract pests."

"Never thought of that." Toby shuddered. "Anything else?"

"Finally, I'd like you to finish your gaming an hour earlier than you usually do, please."

"Do you mean I need to reduce the hours I'm on it, or just that you want me to finish earlier?"

Ollie smiled and shook his head. "Trust you to think of loopholes. You should be a lawyer. Either. If you still want to play for however many hours you play, then do but start it earlier. I want you to read in bed to relax your brain and help you sleep."

"They don't sound too difficult." He pulled out his phone and opened the clock.

"What are you doing?"

"Putting alarms on my phone to remind me to do things." He set up new alarms for the chores and changed the one for his gaming to an hour earlier. "Okay." He showed Ollie.

"Good boy." Ollie put down the notepad. "Now, a quick talk about punishments." Toby pouted. "In a past conversation, you said you liked the sound of a cock cage."

Toby flushed, remembering he'd brought it up after he and Ben had been talking about it on the phone. He liked the idea behind it—not being able to touch what belonged to his Daddy—but he wasn't sure about the "being unable to get it off if he needed to" aspect. He told Ollie of his concerns.

"Okay, how about we try it where I have the key, but there is a spare here in case of an emergency?"

"What do you consider an emergency?"

Ollie's mouth curved. "Should've been a lawyer," he mumbled. "I think if you can try to call me before you take it off, I might be able to calm you down. But if I can't or if you can't get hold of me, you can take it off if you panic or get scared or anything like that. How does that sound?"

Toby nodded. "I don't think I'll need it, though, will I?"

"You're usually a good boy, so I don't think so, but it's there in case we need it."

"When would I need a punishment?"

"If you don't do your chores. If you don't look after yourself when Daddy's asked you to. If you game for longer than you should and make yourself too tired." Ollie narrowed his eyes. "I'm sure we'll think of more as we continue, won't we?"

Toby swallowed. They probably would. He held up his phone. "I have my alarms, though." He smiled, pretending it would be enough. He didn't believe it himself.

"You do. And there will be times when that's enough, but some days, you won't want to do what you need to look after yourself. We can try the cock cage, but if that doesn't work, we can find something else. Maybe spanking?"

He didn't enjoy impact play, but a hand spanking would certainly deter him. "Probably would be more of a deterrent than the cock cage," he muttered.

"Good to know." Ollie stood. "Should we do something about that erection, sweetheart?"

Toby glanced down at himself, having not even noticed his shaft was rock hard again. It was a regular occurrence around his Daddy. He grinned up at Ollie. "Yes, please!" He raced to the stairs, with Ollie's words following him, "Slow down! Maybe that should be one of your rules."

Toby giggled and climbed the stairs, already half undressed by the time Ollie entered the room. He threw his clothes on the floor and crawled onto the bed, laying on his back with his legs spread, his cock bobbing against his stomach.

"Hmm. Beautiful sight, Toby." Ollie grabbed Toby's ankles and dragged him down the bed until his ass was near the edge. His Daddy dropped to his knees on the floor, and Toby gasped. "Will you taste as good as you look?"

Ollie encircled Toby's cock and lifted it to his mouth. His tongue snaked out and flicked against the head, and Toby wanted to thrust into his mouth, but he kept his hips down by gripping the sheets with his hands.

"Please, Daddy!"

Ollie licked off a pearl of precome, then sucked Toby into his mouth. He sank down until Toby's dick was in his throat and pulled off again.

"How quickly can you come for me?" Ollie winked and sucked him again.

"Very quickly, Daddy!" Toby panted, unable to stop his hips from bucking. He could already feel the tingling down his spine, which meant he was seconds away from release. "Can I come, Daddy? Can I? Please?"

He held back as long as he could, thoroughly grateful when his Daddy pulled off. "Come for me, sweetheart." Down onto him again, and Toby groaned his release, his body tensing and releasing so hard he ached when he finally relaxed. He closed his eyes, hands unclenching, body limp as a bedraggled dog.

Daddy pulled him into his arms, and Toby sighed when he dragged a cover over him too. "Thank you, Daddy," he whispered.

How could he have ever thought Ollie was anything like *him*? There were so many glaring differences that Toby felt like smacking himself upside the head for waiting so long to listen to his heart. As he dozed, he imagined their future. A wedding, children, dogs, a bigger house, maybe next to Ollie's garage. It was everything he had ever wanted.

Why was he scared again?

He blinked and lifted his head, staring right into Ollie's eyes. "I love you, Daddy."

Ollie's eyes widened, and then a smile stretched across his face. He pulled Toby up so he could kiss him, holding him steady as he ravished his mouth. Toby straddled his lap, wrapping his arms around his neck and holding on. When Ollie pulled away, Toby whimpered and followed, but Ollie cradled his cheeks, keeping him close.

"I love you, Toby. So much. You are such a brave, brave boy. I cannot even explain to you how proud I am of you. You blow me away."

Tears trickled down Toby's cheeks, being wiped away by Ollie's thumbs. "I'm not scared anymore, Daddy. You've helped me to realise who I am and who I can be. I won't be perfect. I'm sure I will worry at times when I don't need to or get scared when I think you're upset, but I know that will go with time." He swallowed and said words that were even harder than the three little words. "I trust you."

"I will never, ever let you down. I promise."

Ollie kissed him again, slow and languorous, sending Toby's arousal through the ceiling once more. They spent the afternoon talking, laughing and planning before it was time for Ollie to go home. And though it was difficult because Ollie wouldn't hold him for two days, it was also a little easier because his heart clung to his Daddy and wouldn't let him go.

As he closed the door and the silence descended, Toby smiled. He could do this. He had his alarms to remind him. He had Ollie on the other end of the phone. He had friends if he needed advice. But most of all, he had himself and the strength he'd found just that afternoon. It still buzzed inside him. That strength he thought had been beaten from him. It had come roaring back to life, and he refused to push it down again.

Four days later, he called upon that strength again when his cock erupted over his hands and the cock cage, and he froze, waiting for the shouting to begin. That strength reminded him that Ollie wasn't *him*, and he lifted his sweaty face to Ollie's on the video call.

"I'm sorry," he panted, trembling as he tried to push back the worry and, instead, trust in their relationship.

"You don't need to be sorry. I wondered if the exercise of

putting the cock cage on yourself would be more teasing than you could handle. You did well to hang on as long as you did."

"I thought the whole point was for me not to come, though."

"That's true, but it's the first time, Toby. I'll let that one slide. But...you need to clean yourself up and try again. You're still getting punished for staying on your game longer than you should have."

Toby sighed. "Yes, Daddy." He pouted at the camera and headed for the bathroom.

18

OLLIE

Ollie waited for Toby to return, holding back a smile. His boy had broken the rules the previous evening, and when Ollie had called him before his bedtime, Toby had answered the phone with bloodshot eyes and rumpled clothing instead of freshly showered and in his pyjamas. It hadn't taken Ollie long to get the truth from him. He had been a little cruel, though. Asking Toby to put the cock cage on himself was a task of torturous proportions for some people—as Toby had found out.

He hated that Toby still doubted him, but shaking off those ingrained responses would take time. It hurt his heart every time he saw the worry in his boy's eyes.

"I'm back," Toby said, appearing on screen again.

"Hey, sweetheart. Ready to try again?" Ollie asked.

Toby nodded, fiddling with the cage. "It's not easy, but I think I've figured it out now."

"That's great. I know you can do it."

Toby knelt on the bed, in view of the camera, and inhaled. As he exhaled, he slid his cock into the cage, nostrils flaring while he attached it, and inhaled again when he finished. He grinned at Ollie. "I did it!"

"You did! Well done." He paused and added, "Remember, no

taking it off until I say you can." Toby bit his lip. "Or there's an emergency," Ollie said with a smile. "Let's see if this is enough of a deterrent to playing your game too long."

Ollie chuckled at Toby's expression. Toby didn't believe it would help, but Ollie thought it would because every time Toby moved, he would feel it caging his cock. Time would tell, though.

"You need to get ready for work now," Ollie said. "You'll be late."

"One more day," Toby whispered.

Ollie smiled. "One more day, sweetheart. I'll talk to you later. I love you."

Toby beamed. "Love you, Daddy."

Ollie ended the call and leant back, smiling at nothing in general. He was trying to put his foot down with Toby, but it was difficult. Mainly because he preferred to spoil the boy, but also because he couldn't be there with him all the time. Their situation wasn't ideal, but they were managing.

He descended the stairs and opened the garage, smiling at the customers already waiting to drop their cars off for the services and whatever else they needed doing. He stepped behind the desk and took keys and booked them in so they could disappear for the day. His staff had arrived by the time the last customer had left, so he handed out work to them all and set about fixing the car he'd allocated himself. Today was his day for the shitty jobs. None of them enjoyed all jobs, so whenever the shitty ones came in, they took turns—unless there was no other option.

He lost himself in the work, only surfacing when someone needed to ask something or when his stomach growled hard enough to hurt. When that happened, he washed his hands and climbed the stairs to get his lunch. He checked his phone as he settled at the table, smiling when he saw a selfie from Toby. His boy had his arm around a cute poodle, which Ollie assumed was Peppa. Why weren't the owners nicer towards their dog?

That thought reminded him of the dog he and Toby had taken

for a walk at the shelter there. Had Flossie found a forever family now? He hoped she had. As lunch continued, he couldn't concentrate and ended up calling the shelter.

"Mrs Duffy, it's Ollie."

"Hello, Ollie. How can I help you?"

"I was wondering if Flossie had been adopted yet?" Why was he worried about the dog?

"Oh, yes! She has. She went to a couple who were looking for a dog like her." She paused. "Why? Were you looking for a dog?"

Ollie swallowed against the lump in his throat. "No, no. I was just hoping she had been. She was lovely."

"Yes, she was. Such a gorgeous soul, that one."

"Okay. Thanks, Mrs Duffy."

"You're welcome, Ollie. Come visit again soon, okay?"

Ollie ended the call and frowned. He hadn't planned on adopting a dog, but if he had, Flossie would've been perfect for him. But never mind. She had a home now, which was good news.

He finished his lunch and returned to the garage, getting lost in the work again until his name roused him again. He glanced around, mouth gaping when he saw Toby standing at the entrance to the garage, wringing his hands.

"Hey," he said when he reached him. "What are you doing here? I wasn't expecting to see you until tomorrow."

Toby flushed. "I couldn't wait." He frowned. "Is that okay?"

Ollie smiled. "Of course, it's okay. I would hug you, but I'm filthy."

"I don't mind," Toby murmured, his eyes darting around the garage at the undoubtedly nosey staff.

"Hang on a second." Ollie tugged him to the side and stripped off his coveralls, then grabbed Toby in a bear hug. "I'm so glad you're here." Toby held on to him, and Ollie pulled back a little, cupping his face. "I've missed you."

"Can I kiss you, Da—?" Toby cut off the end of his whisper.

"Anytime, anyplace, anywhere."

Toby lifted to his toes and slotted their mouths together. Ollie tightened his hold and licked into his mouth, not having had nearly enough of him. Wolf whistles and cheers echoed around the garage, and Ollie lifted a hand and pointed his middle finger at them all. Toby pulled back and blushed, hiding his face in Ollie's chest.

"Ignore them. They're a group of heathens."

Toby chuckled. "They seem nice enough."

"Would you like to meet them?" Ollie asked.

Toby hesitated but nodded. Ollie pecked his lips and threaded their fingers, tugging him to the middle of the garage.

"As you can't keep your noses out, I'd like you to meet Toby. Toby, this is," he pointed at each person in turn, "Rio, Landon, Jen and you already know Enno."

"How come Enno got to meet him first?" Rio yelled.

"Because he's better looking than you," Landon replied, flicking a rag over at Rio.

"Nice to meet you, Toby," Jen said. "Ignore these guys. They've no manners."

Toby smiled. "Nice to meet you."

Ollie turned to him. "I still have some work to do. Are you okay to wait for me?"

"Of course. Can I sit in the office like I usually do?"

Ollie nodded, loving the idea of having him close. "If you get bored or tired, though, head upstairs."

"Yes, Da—" He bit his lip.

Ollie led him over to the office but leaned down and whispered, "Are you still wearing it?" Toby nodded, his breath catching. "Good."

He kissed him, then pulled on his coveralls, headed back to the car and continued with the issue. He didn't care what job he had to do that day as long as he finished it quickly enough to spend some decent time with his boy.

Two hours later, he was done. He put the keys in the office and shouted for Enno. When he popped his head in the door, Ollie said, "You okay to close up for me?"

Enno grinned. "Always." He disappeared again.

Ollie disrobed again and grabbed Toby's hand, leading him to his apartment door. When he closed the door behind them, he pushed Toby against it and kissed the ever-loving hell out of him. He lost all track of time as he pillaged Toby's mouth, stealing his air and offering his own. He finally pulled away when Toby sagged against him, both gasping for air.

He rested his forehead against Toby's and rubbed their lips together, though he didn't kiss him. Then he grabbed Toby's thighs and lifted him, carrying him up the stairs to the apartment proper. He continued through to the bathroom and finally set him down.

"I need a shower. Join me?" he asked.

"Definitely."

Toby immediately yanked his T-shirt over his head and dropped it on the floor. His eyes widened, and he picked it up again, resting it on the counter. Ollie grinned.

"You're learning," he murmured.

"Trying," Toby amended.

"That's all I can ask of you." Ollie kissed him again. "I'm going to take you to the edge but make you wait to come. We'll keep that cage on for now and see how crazy it makes you."

Toby's breath hitched. "Okay, Daddy."

"Undress for me," he ordered, and while Toby fumbled with his trousers and briefs, Ollie undressed, throwing his clothes into the washing basket just outside the door. He switched on the shower and held out a hand for Toby, helping him in first before joining him. He quickly cleaned himself as best he could, then he backed Toby into the spray and dropped to his knees, his hands smoothing over his thighs as his eyes caught on the cock cage. It looked divine on him, and he knew it wouldn't be the only time he used it, even if it wasn't needed as a punishment.

"Daddy?" Toby said, and Ollie glanced up, squinting against the little drops of spray bouncing off Toby's body. "I need you."

"I know, sweet boy. Put your leg up on the edge."

Toby opened himself up, and Ollie ran a finger behind his balls to his pucker. Toby whimpered as Ollie massaged against it. He didn't press in yet, needing the special lube he stashed on the shelf behind him. He reached for it and squirted some onto his fingers, then returned to Toby's hole. This time, he massaged and applied pressure, receiving Toby's gasp as he pushed through the tight ring. Toby circled his hips as Ollie slid his finger deeper, slicking his insides and readying him for Ollie later.

"More, please!" Toby moaned, gripping Ollie's shoulders.

Ollie complied, slipping two fingers into him and curling them to hit the spot most men loved.

"Oh! Yes!" Toby's nails bit into him, but Ollie didn't care. He withdrew his fingers and pushed back in with three, stretching Toby so he wouldn't hurt him when he took him. "Please, Daddy!" Toby's hips increased their movement, and he could tell he was close, but the cage wouldn't let him fall over the edge. All it would do was frustrate his boy.

Ollie removed his fingers, and Toby whimpered. Ollie rose and helped Toby to stand while he washed him, bringing his boy's arousal down a bit. When they were both clean, Ollie switched off the water and dried them both. He pulled Toby towards the bedroom and nudged him onto the bed.

"Spread your legs for me, sweetheart." Ollie crawled up the bed between his legs and reached for a condom. Sliding it down his length, he positioned himself at Toby's hole. "You ready for me?"

"Yes, please, Daddy."

Ollie pushed against the ring wanting to keep him out, but

he made it through and slid deeper and deeper until his groin touched Toby's. He exhaled. "Are you okay?"

Toby smiled. "Perfect." His eyelids fluttered closed when Ollie withdrew and slid back in again. He kept up the slow pace until his arousal pushed him too far, and he slammed forward. "Oh, god, yes!"

Taking a breath, he paused, sweat trickling down his temple. He unfastened Toby's cock cage, and his shaft lengthened, quickly filling after being confined for so long.

"Oh, Daddy! Oh, my god. I'm... I'm..." Toby blew out a breath.

"Good boy. Let go now."

He started a fast rhythm, their skin slapping together as Ollie took them higher and higher, Toby's fingernails digging into Ollie's sides.

"That's it, sweetheart. Come on." He wrapped a hand around Toby's cock and stroked, and Toby fell over the edge immediately. He watched Toby's expressions, listened to his sounds, and committed them to memory, wanting to bring them up whenever he needed them. Only then did he follow him over.

After cleaning up, they snuggled on the bed and dozed but were woken when the apartment shook and a crash sounded, followed by shouting. Ollie darted out of bed and pulled some clothes on, Toby copying, and they raced down the stairs to the garage. The shouting got louder as they got nearer, and Toby gripped tightly to the back of Ollie's shirt.

When they entered the garage, it was in chaos.

"What happened?" he yelled at Landon, who held a phone to his ear.

"The car slipped off the fucking lift!"

"Is anyone hurt?"

Landon stared at him. "Rio was beneath it. He's pinned but alive."

Toby gasped, covering his mouth with his hand. Ollie turned to him. "Stay with Landon, okay? You don't need to see this."

Toby nodded, and Ollie raced over to where his staff converged. He slipped through, dropping to his knees beside Rio.

"Hey, man. How're things?" he said, eyeing the car, which appeared to be crushing Rio's legs.

"Been better," Rio gasped, his face pale. He shook his head. "It was my fault, Ollie. I didn't check I'd secured it. I was too busy laughing with Jen."

Ollie rested a hand on Rio's shoulder. "It's all good, man. All good. Let's get you sorted."

"Ambulance is on its way!" Landon called.

Ollie moved around, trying to see anything, but the car was on its side, partially still hooked up to the lift.

"Jen, Enno, get some chains around the car but *do not* move it. Just get the chains around it, and we'll wait to see what paramedics say before we do anything. All right?"

They nodded and raced off. When he turned back, Toby was beside Rio, holding his hand, but with his back to the car. Ollie didn't like him being so close to the precarious vehicle, but he didn't say anything because Toby was talking quietly with Rio.

Bloody hell. What a fucking nightmare! He settled beside Rio and Toby until the paramedics arrived, then watched helplessly as they worked on him. Ollie asked them if he should get the car moved, but the paramedics told him to wait until the second ambulance arrived. They needed all hands on deck.

19

TOBY

Toby couldn't look behind him because if he did, he'd probably be sick, so instead, he concentrated on Rio, talking to him and asking him questions about his life. He had an ex-wife and a teenage daughter, who were going to kick his ass for getting hurt.

"Maybe, but it'll be because they're scared for you," Toby said with a smile.

Rio nodded, white lines appearing around his mouth. "Sasha appears brave, but she's only a kid."

"I'm sure she's stronger than you want to believe. I bet she takes after her father."

"In more ways than one." He coughed and grimaced.

Toby's heart raced, but he relaxed a little when Ollie settled beside him, a hand on his shoulder. He continued talking with Rio, asking him about his daughter until the paramedics arrived, then he stood on shaky legs and stepped away to give them room. Ollie slid an arm around him, and he turned into him, trying to breathe through his stress.

"He'll be fine, sweetheart."

Toby couldn't reply and, instead, inhaled Ollie's scent. At least until Ollie kissed his temple and pulled away to listen to the

169

paramedics. Toby moved further back, stopping when his back hit the wall. He could still see everything, but he wasn't in the way. Ollie spoke with two paramedics who'd just arrived, and afterwards, he spoke with his mechanics, pointing and directing them before they got to work securing the car. He couldn't hear the conversations, but he could see from their actions what they were trying to do.

Toby wasn't sure how long he stayed there—how long it took—but then a paramedic counted down, and when they reached one, Ollie pressed a button, and the car began lifting.

In all his years to come, he'd not forget the sound Rio made when he was free, and it wasn't a pleasant one. Despite the pain relief they'd most likely given him, he still hurt.

After that, it was a whirlwind of movement while the paramedics rushed to get Rio into the ambulance and to the hospital. Toby jolted when someone stopped in front of him, but he couldn't peel his eyes off the ambulance until it roared away. He lifted his blurry gaze to Ollie, then fell into his arms and sobbed.

"I know, sweetheart. You've been so brave." Ollie mumbled to him and led him out of the garage and up the stairs to his apartment.

They settled on the sofa, and Toby crawled into Ollie's lap, tears drying on his face. He closed his eyes and sighed, resting his cheek against Ollie's shoulder. Ollie's hands rubbed his back, soothing him with his hands as much as his voice.

"Is he going to be able to walk?" Toby asked, unable to keep the question in.

Ollie sighed. "I don't know."

"Do you need to go back downstairs?"

"No. I've closed the garage for today. I'll see what the police say before I decide if to open tomorrow."

Toby bit his lip, not knowing how to help Ollie with the sadness in his voice until he realised he had the perfect way—by being his boy. He felt a little selfish because he didn't want to make it about him, but he didn't know any other way to distract Ollie. It worked, thankfully. Even when Ollie made a call to the hospital to check on Rio, he came right back to Toby afterwards.

That night, they spent themselves several times, trying to get as close as they could. Neither of them said so much in words, but Toby could feel it in their actions, their furious couplings throughout the night, their slightly over-tight grip on each other.

Life was too short to leave everything hanging in the balance, and Toby needed to decide what he wanted because he wasn't sure he could do this long-distance thing much longer.

When Ollie went down to speak with his employees the following morning, Toby called Ben.

"Oh, I'm so sorry to hear that," Ben said once Toby had explained everything that had happened, along with a few more tears of his own.

"I'm worried about Ollie. I don't know how to help him."

Ben huffed. "It sounds like you're doing fine. Sometimes distraction is all you can do to get through each hour. There's not much else to do until you have more news, either from the hospital or the investigators, but I doubt they'll visit until Monday at the earliest. Nothing's going to be fixed in the next few days."

Toby leaned back on the sofa and stared at the swirls on the ceiling. "That's the worst thing about it. He's going to have to deal with this while I go back home. I'll have to leave him by himself."

Silence reigned for a moment before Ben said, "Long distance is never easy, Toby, but you need to communicate. Talk about what you want. It might seem like the wrong time, but I guarantee you, it'll make you both feel better. Decide together what the best options are for you as a couple. Don't make decisions for him, and don't let him make decisions for you. If you already know what you want from this, fight for it, even if he thinks it's not the best choice."

"You sound like you know what's coming."

Ben chuckled. "I've got to know you, Toby. I consider you one of my closest friends. Yes, I do think I know what your choice is going to be, and I believe you'll be right."

Toby snorted. "Not cryptic or anything, are you?"

"I've never advertised myself as anything other than I am."

Talking to Ben had helped, but Toby used the time he had when Ollie disappeared for a couple of hours on Saturday afternoon, when he was allowed to visit Rio, to figure out exactly what he wanted. His Daddy was haggard by the time he arrived back. Toby distracted him again, this time with sex. As they lay cuddled up on the bed afterwards, Toby broached the subject he'd finally made a decision on.

"Daddy, I don't want to keep going like this. I want more," he added quickly before Ollie got the wrong idea. "What do you want from our relationship?"

Toby's head lifted and fell with Ollie's sigh, and Ollie tightened his hold around his waist. "I want everything," Ollie whispered into Toby's hair.

"Everything?" Toby lifted his chin to stare at him. "What's everything?"

Ollie's eyes glistened in the weak light of the room. "I want everything you're willing to give me. Sharing a home, sharing a life, sharing a family. I want it all."

A tear trickled down Toby's cheek as he smiled. "So do I. We need to talk about how to make that happen."

Ollie nodded, though his expression tightened. "I don't know how. I don't want you to give up everything you have at home, but I also don't know if I can give up what I have here. I can't see a solution."

Toby inhaled. "I do." Ollie's eyes widened. "I want to move here." He flapped his hand. "I don't mean *here* here, just in town. I don't want you to give up the garage; it means too much to you. Yes, my family and friends are in Milton Keynes, but it's not like I can't drive to visit them. I see them less than I see you, and I make the journey here, or you make the journey to me every week. It makes sense."

"But what about your job?"

Toby shrugged. "There'll be something around here, I'm sure. Maybe even the shelter. Mrs Duffy might need some help."

Toby shrieked as Ollie grabbed his waist and hoisted him up and over Ollie's lap until they were both sitting upright, facing each other. "You're serious?" Toby swallowed the lump in his throat, unable to decipher Ollie's expression, and nodded. Ollie pulled him into a hug, and Toby held onto him. "Move in with me?" Ollie whispered into his ear. "I want you here. With me. Always." He pulled back, cupping Toby's face. "If you want to, that is?"

Toby's grin made his cheeks ache. "I'd love to."

A single tear trickled down Ollie's face, and Toby wiped it away with his thumb. "I love you," Ollie said and pressed their lips together.

Toby didn't reply, too overwhelmed by their decision. He'd done it. He'd taken the leap, and it had worked out. He couldn't deny there was still a tiny part of him that was unsure about giving his complete trust to Ollie, but it was easily squashed, especially when he thought of how well Ollie had been taking care of him over the past weeks. If he could give Ollie even a fraction of what Ollie gave him, then he'd do it. Ollie was worth everything to him. And wasn't that a surprising notion for someone who had never believed he could trust again?

Toby shoved his hands into his pockets to hide his nerves as they climbed out of the car at Ollie's mother's house. Ollie had invited him for Sunday dinner with his family, and Toby couldn't deny him anything. Ollie grabbed his wrist, pulled his hand from his pocket, and tangled their fingers together. He smiled.

"Ready?"

"No," Toby squeaked and cleared his throat. "Yes." He nodded decisively.

Ollie chuckled and tilted his chin up so he could drop a kiss on his lips. "You've met them before. It'll be fantastic. I promise."

"Only once!"

His Daddy had been reassuring him since they'd got up that morning and Ollie had asked, but he wouldn't settle until the initial introductions were done, and even then, probably wouldn't relax until they'd left. They were important to Ollie, and that was exactly why it was nerve-wracking. He wanted them to like him. It didn't matter that their first meeting had gone well.

"Are you going to tell them what we decided last night?" he whispered as they closed in on the front door.

"If that's okay with you?"

Toby nodded. He just hoped they were as happy about it as he and Ollie were.

Ollie knocked on the door and opened it. "Mum! We're here!"

They took off their coats and shoes, and Ollie took his hand again, leading him deeper into the house. Toby swallowed hard, eyes darting everywhere to take in everything for the second time. The decoration was inherently plain, but it worked with all the busyness of the knick-knacks that covered all the shelves and spaces. Photographs adorned the walls in all the rooms they passed, including up the stairs from what Toby could see. He made a note to check them out again if he had the chance. Seeing pictures of a mini-Ollie was adorable.

They entered the kitchen, and a woman stood in front of the cooker, stirring something.

"Ollie, Toby, so glad you could make it. Sorry, I can't greet you properly at the moment. I'm in the middle of making the gravy. If I stop stirring now, it'll go lumpy."

Ollie leaned down and kissed her cheek, and Toby smiled at her—he hoped it was a smile, anyway. "Good morning, Mum." He let go of Toby's hand and slid his arm around his waist instead.

"Hi...Bea."

Bea beamed at him. "Help yourself to drinks. Imogen won't be here today. She had to help a friend. Some boy trouble, I believe."

"And Imogen's helping?" Ollie sounded surprised.

"They're friends. Of course, she's helping," Bea said.

Ollie settled Toby at the table and moved to the fridge while Toby twined his fingers together on the tabletop. Ollie placed a drink in front of him with a smile, and Toby smiled back, relaxing a little. They made small talk—getting Bea up to date with news on Rio—until lunch was ready, then as they sat to eat, Ollie brought up their news.

"Mum, we have something to tell you."

Bea put her hand on her chest. "You're pregnant!" She gasped.

Toby choked and sipped his drink. Ollie stared at her and sighed. "Yes, Mum. I'm pregnant," he deadpanned.

Bea laughed. "Sorry, I couldn't resist." She patted her son's cheek. "What do you have to tell me?"

"Toby has agreed to move in with me."

Bea clasped her hands together. "Oh, I'm so happy for you." She picked up her knife and fork. "I must admit to being a bit concerned about the long-distance thing. I know it's only an hour, but I was worried about the 'out of sight, out of mind' aspect."

Ollie chuckled and placed his hand over Toby's, gazing at him. "There's no 'out of mind' with Toby. He's always there." A small smile graced his lips, and Toby smiled back, relaxing more now they had Bea's blessing.

"Glad to hear it." She clicked her tongue. "I'll be hearing wedding bells or the pitter-patter of tiny feet soon."

Toby's smile froze, but Ollie rolled his eyes, reassuring him. "Not yet. But hopefully, one day."

The rest of the visit was uneventful, but Toby got the opportunity to explore the photographs in more detail again, and Ollie was still just as cute as a child as Toby had remembered. Arms came around his waist as he stared at one picture that had caught his attention. Ollie chuckled in his ear.

"I was eight in that photo. It was my first night at boy scouts, and I was so excited. Hated every minute, though, and never went again."

Toby laughed. "I never even tried it. I knew it wouldn't be for me."

"Life has a way of making some people see things clearly enough without experiencing it first. I'm not like that. I need to experience it first before deciding if it's for me. When I met you—or rather, messaged you—there was something in your messages that had me hooked from the first word. I knew I would do everything in my power to be what you needed."

Toby leaned his head back against Ollie's chest and closed his eyes. That last piece of him that had been holding back broke free. All he felt was a deep connection, and there was no denying he trusted Ollie with everything he was. He twisted in Ollie's arm and sought his mouth.

"I love you," Toby said, staring into his eyes. "With everything I am and all that I have."

"That almost sounds like wedding vows," Ollie teased, but Toby could see the pleasure in his expression.

"Almost, but not quite."

Ollie laughed, and their mouths met once more.

When Toby handed his notice to Clara, she sighed but smiled. "I had hoped you would never leave, but I wish you all the best. You deserve it."

"Thank you, Clara."

He exited the office and bumped into Jem on the way out. "What's this I hear about you leaving, my lad?"

"Sarah has a big mouth." He chuckled. "Yes, Jem. Two weeks, and I'm done."

"She also said you have a boyfriend." Jem winked at him, and he laughed again.

"I do. I'm moving in with him. He lives in Milton Keynes. Not too far away."

Jem tutted. "We need a leaving party, then. I'll tell Sarah to set it up," she said as she walked away.

"No, I really don't!" he called after her, but Jem waved her hand as if she hadn't heard him. He sighed. "I really don't," he said to himself.

20

OLLIE

As much as Ollie was ecstatic that Toby was moving in with him, the pall of Rio's accident hung over them. The investigation lasted a few days, but the result showed that it was user error. The lift was solid and still useable, but Rio hadn't secured the car properly. In some ways, that was good news because it meant Ollie and the garage weren't responsible, but in other ways, he hated that the fault lay with Rio.

The man had been in and out of surgery since the accident, but the doctors had finally told him it was unlikely he'd walk again. Knowing Rio as he did, Ollie would be surprised if the man let those words stop him from doing what he wanted. Knowing Rio, he would be back on his feet quicker than anyone else in the same situation.

Ollie had decided to set aside some money from the garage's profits to send to Rio to help with the cost of living. The man would get some benefits to help him, but not enough, Ollie was sure. It was the least he could do when Rio had given so much to the garage over the years.

The days passed, and faster than he could've hoped, he turned up for Toby's leaving party, which was the day before he moved.

"Ollie! You're here!" Sarah shouted, clearly already tipsy.

"I am. So are you."

"Of course I am. I'm the...the...person who the party is for's best friend. I ornagised it." She frowned. "Ornagised... Ornagised..."

"Organised?" he supplied.

"Yes, that!" She smiled. "Did a good job if I say so myself."

"Looks good, Sarah. Enjoy yourself."

"You, too!"

She wandered off, and he grinned as he made his way through the throng to the bar, where he hoped he'd find his boy.

"Ollie!"

He turned just in time to catch Toby in his arms rather than with his body. "Hello, sweetheart."

Toby gazed up at him with bleary eyes. "Sarah gave me a drink."

"Only one?" Ollie chuckled.

Toby nodded like his head was like a bobblehead character from the dashboard of a car. He held up his finger. "Juss one. I don't jink a lot."

"I can see why."

He stayed by his boy's side for the remainder of the evening, meeting several of his ex-colleagues as they said goodbye, and then helped him into bed at the end of the evening. He might hate the morning, despite only having that one drink. Ollie would have to be ready with paracetamol and water, just in case.

The following morning, Toby jumped out of bed with no problems, much to Ollie's surprise.

"It's moving day!" Toby shouted.

They spent the day packing the small van they'd hired to move his boy into his home.

"Is that everything?" he asked.

Toby nodded slowly, staring at the house. Ollie slid his arms around his waist and leaned down to rest his head on Toby's shoulder.

"Is it weird that I don't feel sad about leaving here?"

"You can feel however you want to feel."

Toby sighed. "I feel like I should be sad because of the memories this place holds, but I'm happier about moving on."

"Maybe look at it as a temporary placement. Somewhere you stayed until you were strong on your own feet."

"Maybe." Toby glanced up at him. "No matter what, I'm glad to be moving in with you."

Ollie smiled and kissed him, though he kept it quick. "I'm glad too." He pecked his lips again. "Shall we get going?"

"Let me do one quick run around to make sure I've not forgotten anything."

Toby disappeared, and Ollie double-checked that the contents of the van were secure enough to stay in place as they drove home before closing the doors. He met up with Toby by the front door.

"All empty," Toby said.

"Let's go then. We can drop the keys off with the landlord and head home."

Toby paused and stared at him before a beautiful smile spread across his face. "Home!"

Ollie chuckled. "Yes, sweetheart. Home."

Barely able to contain his excitement, Toby spent the entire trip fidgeting in his seat, playing with the radio and talking non-stop. And Ollie let him. He knew his boy would be exhausted by the time they'd finished unloading the van, but he would have time to sleep afterwards and for as long as he wanted. Toby didn't have a job lined up, but that didn't matter straight away. Ollie had enough funds to cover looking after him, although he knew Toby wouldn't be happy about that for long.

When they pulled into the car park of the garage, Toby had quietened a little.

"You okay?" Ollie asked.

Toby smiled at him. "It's really happening, isn't it?"

Ollie chuckled. "Yes. This is now yours, too."

Toby's eyes glistened, but he wiped them quickly when his door flew open.

"Come on! We have work to do, then pizza!" Denny said.

Toby laughed and climbed out, followed by Ollie. He'd enlisted the help of his friends and employees to help them unload, knowing they would both be exhausted from having to empty Toby's house alone.

Two hours later, everything was piled in the living room and the spare bedroom, ready for them to sort out whenever they had the energy. Ollie ordered pizza for everyone and then told Toby to put on a movie. By the time the movie was over, Toby was fast asleep with his head on Ollie's lap, and Denny was asleep with his head next to Toby's stomach.

"Enno," he whispered, and once he had his attention, he pointed at Denny. "Can you move him while I get Toby up? Then he can sleep on the sofa."

Enno nodded and slipped from beside Rick. He slid his arm beneath Denny's head, who murmured and readjusted but stayed asleep. Ollie slid from beneath Toby and picked him up, smiling when his boy snuggled in closer to his chest. Enno lifted Denny and settled him on the sofa, throwing a blanket over him.

"Thanks. I'll be back out in a minute."

Ollie took Toby into his room and laid him on the bed. He carefully undressed him down to his briefs, then pulled the covers over his sleeping boy. Pressing his lips to his forehead, he left and closed the door behind him. Landon, Jen, Enno and Rick were waiting by the door.

"Thanks for the food," Landon said.

"Thanks for the help," Ollie countered.

"See you Monday." Landon and Jen waved before descending the stairs.

"Thanks, you two. I appreciate it," he told Enno and Rick.

Rick smiled. "You're welcome. I'm glad you found him."

"Me, too."

Enno hesitated after Rick went down the stairs. "I'm always here. You know that, right?"

Ollie frowned but nodded. "Of course. Why?"

Enno sighed and shook his head. "I don't know. I just felt like I had to say it."

Ollie hugged him for slightly longer than he normally would have. "Thank you."

After they left, Ollie checked the windows and doors were locked and that Denny was settled before heading back to the bedroom. Toby had rolled to his other side but had not woken. Ollie had a quick shower and slid in beside him. Straight away, Toby shifted to rest his head against Ollie's chest. He pressed his lips to Toby's hair and closed his eyes.

"I don't know where else to look," Toby said, his head in his hand as he scoured the job listings a week later.

"There's no rush, sweetheart."

"But I don't want you to have to pay for everything all the time."

Ollie slipped into the seat beside him. "I know, but I would prefer you find a job you'd enjoy rather than taking just any job out there."

Unfortunately, the dog shelter wasn't hiring, and there didn't seem to be any pet-related jobs in the area, from what Toby said. It was purely by chance that Ollie found something that Toby might enjoy when he visited the supermarket a few days later. He took a photo of the advert and, as soon as he got home, showed it to Toby.

"Dog walker wanted for small, growing business. Fifteen hours a week with the potential for more." Toby glanced at him, and Ollie could see the excitement in his eyes.

"Ring them," he encouraged.

"Now?"

Ollie shrugged. "Why not? It's not too late, and I still have to make dinner."

Toby bit his lip, then nodded. "Okay."

He wandered out of the kitchen, and as Ollie put away the food, he heard Toby talking. He got out a pan to cook the chicken when Toby came back in, beaming.

"She said she wants to meet me tomorrow! It sounds really good. I'll have certain dogs that I'd walk each day, and then there would be the ones who are just as and when needed. She's the only dog walker she has at the moment, but her waiting list has grown enough that she could employ someone now."

Ollie smiled. "That sounds great."

"She said if it goes well tomorrow, I can start the next day."

"Fantastic news!"

Toby jumped into Ollie's arm and squealed under his breath. Ollie laughed and hugged him tightly.

"Why don't you play your game for a little longer until dinner is ready?"

"Okay!"

Toby pecked him on the lips and bounded out of the kitchen. Ollie huffed a laugh and continued cooking, allowing the scent of meat and sauces to relax him. He was glad Toby had found something, but he'd also had another thought that had been nibbling his brain, and while Toby was distracted, he called Gareth.

"Hey, how are you?" Gareth said.

"Good, thanks. How's business?"

Gareth chuckled. "Booming. Which I really shouldn't be as surprised about as I am."

"Well, that's what happens when you find a niche and fill the gap," he teased.

"True. How's Rio?"

Ollie had told Gareth and Ben all about the accident, and they had helped support Toby when he needed it, as well as Ollie, in moments of feeling low.

"He's doing good. It's a long road to recovery, but he has a good attitude about it."

"Glad to hear it. I don't need to ask how Toby is because he was talking to Ben earlier. Any luck on the job front?"

"Actually, yes. I saw an advert for a dog walker while I was at the supermarket. Toby's meeting with her tomorrow to see what it's about."

"Great news."

"Yeah. There was something I wanted to ask you, but I haven't mentioned anything to Toby about it yet. It's just something that came to mind, but I don't know if it's possible."

Gareth paused. "Well, unless you tell me what it is, I can't give you my opinion on it."

Ollie snorted. "Sorry, yes, that would help, wouldn't it?" He pushed the chicken around as it browned. "I wondered if there was anything Toby could do to help with the event planning or the app? He's always talking about how it's such a great idea, but I have no idea if he's even interested in it as a job. I wanted to get your thoughts first before I approach him about asking either of you."

"Hmm. I bet there are plenty of things he would be able to help with. I'll speak to Ben about it, as he's the one organising it with Lindsey. He won't let me touch it with a bargepole."

"I wonder why that is?" Ollie teased. "Have you decided on a date for the event yet?"

"Not yet, although we're hoping for some time closer to the summer. We think it would help with attendance if the weather wasn't atrocious."

"Good call. Although I bet, most men would arrive even if there were ten feet of snow."

"Maybe, but we want to try to make it as accessible as possible."

Ollie poured the sauce into the pan with the chicken and left it to simmer. "You know where we are if you need anything."

"I do. Thanks. I'll talk to Ben and get back to you."

"If you decide there is something he can do, just go direct to Toby. I don't need to be the middleman."

"Okay."

He ended the call after a little more small talk and then called through to Toby. He got no answer, which was not unusual. He rinsed the rice and left it on the side while he fetched Toby, bringing his boy out of his game-daze, as Ollie had started to call it.

"Hey, sweetheart. Dinner's ready. Go wash up."

"Okay, Daddy."

Ollie could tell from his response that Toby was already getting tired. He might have a fight on his hands after dinner because if Toby was too tired, Ollie would put his foot down and stop him from playing any longer and get an early night instead. He might be able to dampen the argument by playing the "potential new job" card.

They sat at the table and ate while Toby talked about the job and what it might be like. When he'd exhausted that topic, Ollie asked about his online friend, and if he'd spoken to him recently.

Toby shook his head. "He's not been online for weeks. I don't know what's happened, but I hope he's okay."

"And you don't have any information about who he is?"

"No. That's both a blessing and a curse about online friends."

"True." Ollie put his knife and fork on his plate, his meal finished. "Hopefully, he'll come back online soon."

Toby finished his dinner and helped tidy away, putting

everything in the dishwasher and turning it on. Ollie braced himself.

"Right, time for bed."

Toby snapped his head around. "What? No!"

"Yes, sweetheart. You're tired. I'm tired. It's time for bed."

"But I want to play a little longer!" he whined.

"You also need your sleep so you can meet this woman tomorrow." Toby opened his mouth to argue, and Ollie said, "Do we need to use the cage again?"

Toby snapped his mouth shut, his shoulders lowering. "You're right. As always."

Ollie hid his smile. If Toby thought the cock cage wasn't a deterrent, he was wrong. "If it helps, I'll give you a goodnight gift before you go to sleep."

Toby's eyes sparkled, and he beamed. "A gift?"

Ollie nodded. "I think you'll like it."

"Okay!" Toby shouted as he raced out of the kitchen.

Ollie laughed and followed at a more sedate pace. The gift would be something that would help his boy sleep because orgasms always did that. He visited the bathroom before Toby did, and when he reached the bedroom, Toby was already undressed and on his way to the bathroom. Ollie slapped his ass cheek as he passed, and Toby yelped and jumped.

"I've never seen you get ready so quickly," Ollie said.

"Gift!" Toby called back.

Ollie shook his head and undressed until he was completely naked. He waited under the covers for Toby to return, lifting them when he did. Toby removed his briefs and climbed in, snuggling into Ollie's side.

"Gift?" he asked.

Ollie pressed his lips to Toby's, tasting the mint of freshly brushed teeth. He started slowly, licking Toby's lips, tangling their tongues, exploring his mouth until he had to deepen it. Their bodies fit nicely against each other, but finally, Ollie pulled back, sliding down Toby's body and pressing kisses to his skin. He straddled Toby's legs but flipped his boy over to his stomach. He dragged Toby to his knees and spread his cheeks. His pink pucker clenched even though nothing touched it. At least until Ollie lowered his mouth to it.

Toby's gasp was music to his ears, and Ollie sucked against the rosebud, using his tongue to loosen him and spear inside him. He had no plans to fuck him with his cock, but he was going to make him delirious by only using his mouth and fingers.

"Oh, god!" Toby gasped.

Ollie held his hips still as he licked, sucked and bit, knowing exactly when Toby was nearing his climax. What could be better than feeling his boy clenching around him? Ollie slipped his tongue inside his channel again and fastened his mouth around the pucker.

"Fuck! Yes!" Toby shouted and contracted around his tongue.

When Toby slumped, Ollie removed his tongue, working his jaw where it ached, and rolled Toby to his side. He tucked him in as best he could while avoiding the wet patch, then cleaned the mess. He couldn't be bothered to change the sheets right then. He wanted nothing more than to pull his boy into his arms and fall asleep.

So he did.

21

TOBY

Toby rubbed his hand against his khaki trousers as he wandered towards the park Aster had asked him to meet her at for his interview. It made sense to him for it to be in a park because she still had a job to do, after all. The area was extensive and had plenty of grassy areas but also a path around the perimeter and an area for kids to play. It was the type of place Toby would like to bring his kids one day.

He smiled to himself and stared at the ground. He'd been with Ollie for three months and had already moved in. But he'd never felt happier or more certain of something than he was of them. And this was coming from a guy who didn't trust easily after *him*.

He heard a bark and lifted his head, seeing a woman walking towards him holding the leads of two dogs. If Aster hadn't told him she would be wearing a pink armband around her upper arm, he wasn't sure he'd ever figure out which one was her with how many dog walkers there were. It was a popular place.

"Hi, I'm Toby," he said as he neared, waving his hand a bit.

Aster's smile lit up her face, and he instantly felt at ease. "Toby! Hi! I'm so glad to meet you." She stopped and held out her hand. "You mentioned having just moved here. What do you think of the place?"

Toby huffed a laugh. "I like it. Not so different from St Neots, but it's going to take some time to get used to where things are."

She chuckled. "You'll soon figure it out. Especially if you start working with me. I have clients all over Milton Keynes and a couple further afield. But you don't need to worry about those." She started walking again, and Toby fell into step beside her. "So, tell me what experience you have and why you want to do this job."

Toby explained his work with the kennels and his love of dogs themselves. It was so easy to talk to her, and he found himself telling her about wanting a dog of his own one day.

Aster pulled the dogs to a stop again and faced Toby. "Job's yours if you want it?"

Toby gaped. "Really?"

Aster laughed. "Yes, really. I can't say no to someone as passionate about dogs as you are. I can hear it in your voice and the way you didn't hesitate to clean up after Milo without me even asking it of you. I'd be a fool to say no."

"Wow. Thank you."

They talked some more about wages and the clients he might take on, then arranged another meeting at Aster's house for the following Monday to go through the contract and discuss which clients would be the best fit for him. Especially as he was just learning to navigate the town.

Toby had a pep in his walk as he headed back home, eager to tell Ollie all about the job. As he drove back, Ben called, and he answered it through his car speakers.

"Hey!" Ben said. "Look, I wanted to ask if you wanted to help with the event we're planning. I know you've just moved and are waiting for things to settle, but if you want to, I could do with the help."

He pulled into the garage car park and drove around the back, where he usually parked his car. "I don't know if I'd be any good meeting new people. You know how quiet I am."

"You wouldn't have to meet people. Just help me out with the organising of it. You know, making sure I have everything in place."

"Isn't that what Lindsey's for?" He switched off the engine and put the phone to his ear when it disconnected from the car.

"She is. I just..."

Toby had never heard Ben so unsure. "I'd love to help if you think I can. I won't have as much time as I did when I first got here, though."

"How come?"

Toby smiled, though Ben couldn't see him. "I have a new job."

"That's fantastic! What is it?"

Toby snorted. "A dog walker, funnily enough."

"Woohoo! Go you, Toby! I'm so happy for you. You honestly don't have to worry about my offer. I—"

"No, I want to help. Send me a list of things you're struggling with, or call me later, and we can discuss it more. If I can help at all, I will."

"Thanks, Toby. Organising this event has just got real."

"I understand. It'll be fantastic, though."

Ben exhaled. "Yes, it will." He sounded more upbeat when they finished the call.

Toby wandered into the garage, keeping away from the cars, and waved at Ollie. His Daddy wandered over to him, wiping his hands on a cloth. There was something sexy about seeing him so dirty, and the look in his eyes cemented the thought. Maybe he could persuade him to dirty Toby up one day when everyone had gone home.

"How did it go?"

Toby blinked away the images. "I got the job."

Ollie grinned. "I knew you would. She would've been crazy to turn you down."

"I'm meeting her on Monday to sign the contract and discuss my hours and everything." He frowned. "I also had a call from Ben."

Ollie's eyebrows rose. "Yeah. What did he have to say?"

"He asked me to help him with the event."

"And what did you say?"

"I told him to send me what he needed help with, and we'd see. It depends on what he needs, I suppose. I'm not up for meeting people—" A blaring ringing sounded through the garage, and Toby winced, but it ended just as quickly when someone answered the phone. He continued, "I'm not up for meeting people and talking to them, but if there are things behind the scenes I can do, I will. He seems stressed."

Ollie nodded. "I can imagine it's a lot of work to organise something like this."

"Boss?" Ollie glanced up at the office door where Jen stood. "Phone call for you. Lawyers."

Ollie groaned. "Thanks, Jen."

"I'll leave you to it," Toby said.

"No. Will you come with me?"

It wasn't often that Ollie sounded fed up, but Toby knew the lawyers were taking forever to sort out the ownership of the garage. It wasn't exactly rocket science, especially as Ollie's father had stipulated it in his will, but for some reason, the lawyers were dragging it out.

"Of course."

They traipsed to the office, and Toby shut the door. He settled onto Ollie's lap and cuddled into his chest when Ollie patted his thighs, then Ollie inhaled and picked up the phone.

"Hello." Toby held onto his Daddy when he tensed. "Are you sure? What I mean is that this has been going on for so long. I don't want you to say it's done, then turn around, and I have another hoop to jump through. No offence." Toby heard the murmuring on the other end of the phone but couldn't understand the words. "Okay. Thank you. I'll be there. Bye."

Ollie exhaled and fastened his arms around Toby's body. "It's over. I just need to sign the final forms, and the garage is mine," he whispered.

Toby tightened his hold. "I'm so glad. One less thing hanging over your head."

"Hmm."

Toby lifted his head. "What's wrong?"

"Rio."

Toby sighed and snuggled in again. "He's in excellent hands. Whether he walks again is up to his body and, to some degree, Rio's determination. From what I know of him, which granted isn't much, I can see the strength inside him. He'll be fine."

"I know. I still feel bad, though."

"We'll keep him involved with the garage if he wants to be. Maybe he can do your paperwork for you when he's feeling up to it?"

"Huh. I never thought of that." Ollie kissed Toby's head. "Thank you. I'll ask him. It'll probably make him feel better about taking my money if he's doing something to 'earn' it."

"It'll also stop him from feeling like he can't do anything. I've heard that's something people in his situation often feel. When they've been torn away from life as they knew it, finding a new normal isn't easy. This way, he's still with the people he knows, even if he can't do exactly what he was before."

"Sounds perfect. I'll see what he says." He cupped Toby's chin. "Two job offers in one day. Who's a lucky boy?"

Toby chuckled. "Ben's wasn't a job offer. I'm just helping a friend."

"Regardless, it's your lucky day, it seems."

"You make me feel lucky, Daddy," Toby whispered, sliding his hand around Ollie's neck and leaning closer to fuse their lips.

Clanks of metal against metal and cheering had them pulling

apart, and Toby laughed, hiding his face in Ollie's neck. The mechanics were merciless with their teasing, but it was the good-natured kind, so he took it well.

"I better let you get back to work."

"We'll celebrate tonight. We can invite Enno, Rick and Denny."

Toby's face heated. "I'd rather it just be us."

Ollie's pupils dilated, and his hands tightened on Toby's thigh and hip. "Even better."

Toby scrambled off Ollie's lap before they could do what was in Ollie's expression. He cleared his throat. "See you after work."

"Maybe."

Toby grinned and raced out of the room and to the apartment, closing the door behind him. He panted and stared at his cock tenting his khakis. He blew out a breath, knowing he couldn't—no, wouldn't—do anything about it when Ollie wasn't with him. He wanted to share his orgasms now he had someone who cared about them. Instead, he wandered into the living room and bit his lip. He hated his chores, but he set around tidying up the mess he left. He knew it was his mess because Ollie always tidied his things straight away. The mug and bowl left from Toby's breakfast were still on the dining table, and some wrappers were on the coffee table from when he had a biscuit packet before he'd headed out to meet Aster.

He worked steadily for half an hour or so until he was happy with the place—he'd even tidied his clothes away from where Ollie had put them after being washed. Once he'd finished, he settled on the sofa and logged on to his game. He'd finally set up his gaming console and the two screens in the living room after Ollie had vetoed putting them in the spare room. Ollie had argued that he wanted to be able to spend the time with Toby, even if Toby was engrossed in his game. Plus, it meant Ollie could keep an eye on how long he was on it. Win-win situation, according to his Daddy.

His phone alarm went off, and he blinked a few times before silencing it. He put the controller down and rubbed his face, then headed for the kitchen to grab a large glass of water and some tomatoes drenched in that dressing Ollie had made especially for him. It was the only way he could eat them unless they were mixed in with Ollie's cooking creations. And knowing the proud smile Ollie would have on his face when Toby told him he ate them was worth the occasional mouthful of something he wasn't hugely fond of. Although that could be completely psychological at that point.

That smile arrived a couple of hours later when Ollie entered the apartment just as Toby's alarm reminded him to stop for a break again. Toby jumped up and ran to him, climbing his body and kissing him.

"I ate the tomatoes, Daddy!"

That smile. "Good boy. I'm so glad you like them." Ollie helped him slide down his body. "How about we order in tonight, and I can spend the extra time worshipping my boy?"

"Sounds good to me."

Toby started his dog walking job the day after signing the contract with Aster. He loved everything about her business and what she planned to do to expand it. The wages were on par with what he'd been earning at the kennels, so he wouldn't have to worry about money, even though it wasn't quite as many hours as he'd had before. Aster had told him more hours would be available as more clients came on board, which was understandable.

What he'd been surprised about was that Ben had hired him to be the Daddy's Boy message replier—that was Ben's official job title for him. Toby wasn't sure it was real, but he could hardly decline when it meant he helped the men who had brought him and Ollie together. He'd argued with Ben about being paid, but Ben had refused to let him do it for nothing, and in the end, Ollie had persuaded him to take the money by saying he could always keep it to spend on gifts for his friends or nights out if he didn't feel right spending it on himself.

He and Ollie had also had their first argument that week. Now Toby had a job, he wanted to pay towards the bills, but Ollie had refused, saying it was his job to look after Toby. Even when their voices rose, Toby wasn't scared of Ollie, not like he had been with *him*. Ollie wouldn't hurt him.

In the end, Ollie agreed to let Toby pay for food when they went shopping, and Toby had thrown himself into Ollie's arms and sobbed his thanks. As much as he was a boy and loved being looked after, he didn't want to feel like a burden and paying his way, even a small amount like that, would help him feel more in control.

Make-up sex was fantastic, though. He would remember that for the future.

His life was becoming better and better, and although he couldn't see his family whenever he wanted, he could still make it over to see them every other weekend with Ollie in tow. The opposite weekends they spent at Bea's house. Sometimes with Imogen, sometimes without, depending on what she'd focused on that week. He'd also gone with Ollie and Bea to the final lawyer meeting to sign over the garage to Ollie fully. The moment Bea and Ollie signed the forms, Ollie slumped back in his chair, tears in his eyes. Knowing he had a part of his father always with him was something Ollie had whispered to Toby in the middle of the night a few days before the meeting. When it had been up in the air, he hadn't wanted to believe it. But now he could. The garage—and his father's legacy—was now Ollie's.

And Toby loved the idea of passing the garage down the line to their kids.

There it was again. The idea of kids and weddings and dogs. One day. Soon, hopefully.

22

OLLIE

"**A**re you ready?" Ollie asked, taking Toby's hand and squeezing.

Toby inhaled and blew the air out again. "As I'll ever be."

They headed into the club, The Vault, and Ollie checked them in. He'd signed them up for a membership after speaking with the owners to check Toby's ex wasn't a member. The membership was to help Toby find some other friends in the lifestyle. Ben was too far away to have playdates, and Rick wasn't always available when Toby was because of his job. Ollie wanted Toby to find someone he could interact with outside of Ollie's friends. He hoped this would be a suitable compromise. And besides, it wouldn't hurt for Ollie to find some Daddy friends, too. This wasn't the club he usually visited, but whether he bumped into anyone he knew was another thing.

It wasn't in the league of Bound, but it wasn't bad either. The Daddy and boy areas weren't separated from the rest of the club, but there were rooms they could use for privacy which had themes if they wanted them—or even if they wanted some peace and quiet. They wandered around, looking at everything that was available, and Toby clung to his side quietly.

Despite the noise, Ollie heard the small gasp Toby gave and

focused on him. He followed Toby's stare and smiled, seeing a boy sitting at a table with a hand-held console.

"Shall we move closer?"

Toby licked his lips and frowned but followed Ollie as he led the way. Ollie glanced around, trying to find the boy's Daddy—if he had one. A man wearing a suit and thick black glasses stepped forward, and Ollie smiled, holding out his hand.

"Hi, I'm Ollie, and this is my boy, Toby."

The man smiled and shook his hand. "Nice to meet you. I'm Jon, and this is Lyle." He nodded towards the boy playing the game. "I've not seen you around before."

"First time we've been here. We're trying to find some like-minded people."

Jon nodded. "You'll find plenty here. Not all of them are...decent, but most are."

Toby's hand trembled in his, and Ollie squeezed harder, not wanting the reminder of the less nice ones to make Toby want to leave. "Does your boy like gaming? Lyle is obsessed. It's a feat to get him off them at home."

Ollie glanced at Toby with a grin. "He does, yes. I've had to create a routine for him; otherwise, he'd never eat."

Jon chuckled. "Well, I don't have any problem with Lyle eating, that's for sure. But stopping the games is another matter." He tapped Lyle on the shoulder. "Lyle, come meet Ollie and Toby."

"Let me just finish this," Lyle said, concentrating on the screen.

Toby peered closer, then said, "He's coming! Jump! Now!"

Lyle didn't make any outward movement to show he had heard, but he followed Toby's words. Toby leaned closer to Ollie again when Lyle put the console on the table and peered at him.

"Have you played this game before?" Lyle asked. Toby swallowed and nodded. "This is the first time I've passed this level." He narrowed his eyes. "Would you help me?"

Toby smiled and nodded. "I'd like that."

Ollie squeezed his hand, and Toby let go, settling beside Lyle, and immediately started talking about stuff that went straight over Ollie's head.

"I doubt we'll hear from either of them for the next however long. Do you want to sit?"

Jon pointed to a couple of small armchairs nearby, and Ollie brushed his fingers over Toby's shoulder to get his attention.

"I'll be over there."

Toby glanced at the chairs and nodded, then went back to Lyle. Ollie huffed a laugh. Forgotten already.

"Do you live locally?" he asked Jon when they'd ordered drinks for all four of them.

Jon sipped his water. "Yeah. Well, on the outskirts of town, anyway. The opposite side to this one. You?"

"Right in the centre of town. I own a garage." The pleasure of those words warmed his chest.

"Ah, always good to know a mechanic." Jon chuckled.

Ollie smiled, glancing at Toby, who had taken control of the console with Lyle peering over his shoulder.

"How long have you been together?" Jon asked.

"Just over four months now." It felt like so much longer. "What about you?"

"Two years. We've been in Milton Keynes for about a year. I moved with a new job, and Lyle came with me. Best decision we ever made."

"Sounds like it. What do you do—"

"Get away from him!"

Ollie's gaze snapped to where Lyle's voice rose above the music, and blood froze in his veins at a man gripping Toby's wrist and trying to pull him away from Lyle, who was clinging onto Toby. He raced over, getting between the man and Toby, and grabbed the man's wrist, tightening his hold.

"Get the fuck away from my boy," he said, anger tinting his voice to a growl.

"*Your* boy? I don't think so. This...*boy* is mine. He lost his way, but he's finally found me again."

The man's voice grated on Ollie, but his words had fire burning through him. "He is nothing to you. He's mine. Remove your hand before I remove it for you."

Toby's whimper met his ears, but he couldn't be distracted right now.

"Benson, let's go," another man said, resting his hand on the guy's shoulder.

"No," Benson said, gaze searing into Ollie. "Not without my boy."

Ollie tightened his hold on Benson's wrist and twisted slowly. Enough that Benson wouldn't hurt Toby too much as his arm moved. Benson winced as his wrist rotated, and with a growl, he let go of Toby and pulled his arm away, though Ollie refused to let go. Instead, Ollie stepped closer, getting into Benson's face.

"Stay the fuck away from us. He's nothing to do with you anymore." Yes, Ollie knew exactly who this asshole was.

Benson chuckled, but his eyes were hard. "You know who I am?"

"I know who you *were*, and I don't think you want me to voice that to the room, do you?"

Benson's jaw clenched, but then he peered over Ollie's shoulder. "I'll be seeing you," he sneered at Toby.

Ollie intercepted his view and stepped forward. "Not if I have anything to do about it."

Benson stared at him, and Ollie expected him to lash out and punch him, but the man from earlier pulled him away, murmuring in his ear. The moment the crowd swallowed him up, Toby's sobs met his ears, and he swung around, finding his boy in Lyle's arms, eyes screwed shut. Not wanting to scare him further, Ollie crouched beside him.

"Hey, sweetheart. He's gone. It's just me now. Can I take you home?"

He got no response, and Lyle's eyebrows lowered. Ollie took a chance and thumbed away some tears from Toby's cheek. His boy flinched, and Ollie's heart broke. He was supposed to protect him, and he hadn't. He didn't blame Toby for not wanting him near him. Ollie glanced at Jon, who nodded and spun his finger as if to tell him to keep going.

"Toby, sweetheart. It's time to go. We need to get some rest now."

Inhaling, Ollie rubbed a hand on Toby's thigh, and this time, Toby didn't respond to his touch. His eyes flickered open, though, and Ollie had never been more grateful to meet his gaze.

"Time to go, sweetheart." He held out his arms, and Toby's eyes darted from Ollie's face to his arms and back again before Toby flew into them. Ollie held him in his arms, murmuring soothing words and rubbing his back. He could feel the heat of Toby's tears as they soaked into Ollie's T-shirt.

Ollie picked Toby up, and Toby wrapped his legs around his waist. No matter how awkward it was to walk, he wouldn't make him get down. If Toby needed to be that close to him, Ollie would make it work.

"We'll walk you out," Jon murmured, stepping in front of him with Lyle at his side.

They headed for the door, and a man stopped them before they could leave. "The manager would like a word."

Ollie saw red. "The manager can fucking wait. I'm taking my boy home. The manager can call me tomorrow."

The man blanched, then nodded and stepped aside. Ollie slipped through the door Jon held open and carried Toby to the car. He fumbled for the keys, which were in his jeans pocket—not as easy to reach when Toby didn't want to get down, but he managed. When he unlocked the door, he crouched, trying to encourage Toby to get into the seat.

"He's gone, sweetheart. There's only me, Jon and Lyle. I promise he's gone."

Toby exhaled and slowly loosened his hold. Bloodshot eyes met his, and Ollie wanted to bring Benson back and truly fuck him up, but he shoved the need down in case Toby mistook the direction of Ollie's anger. He cupped Toby's cheek.

"Are you okay?"

Toby swallowed and opened his mouth. "You said he wouldn't be here."

The words, though whispered, were like a shotgun through Ollie's heart, and he felt his own tears building at the mess he'd made.

"I checked with them, and they didn't recognise his name. I don't know how he was here. I'm so sorry. So sorry."

Toby looked away and slipped into the car seat properly, facing forward, his hands covered by the cuffs of his long-sleeved T-shirt. Ollie's heart broke all over again. Toby might never forgive him for this, and it was exactly what Ollie deserved. He had promised to protect his boy, but he hadn't.

He stood and pivoted to face Jon and Lyle. "Thank you. I appreciate your help."

Lyle stepped around him and crouched beside Toby, murmuring too quietly for Ollie to hear. Jon clasped Ollie's shoulder.

"You're welcome. Look, here's my number. If you need anything, even if it's just a witness statement or something, call me. But I'm here if you need to talk, too." He squeezed. "He'll forgive you, Ollie."

Ollie shook his head. "You don't know what that asshole did to him. I wouldn't be surprised if Toby left and never looked back."

"That boy worships you, Ollie. It might take him some time to figure out how he feels about it all, but he won't leave you. I can promise you that."

Ollie didn't reply. "Thanks for your number." He rounded the front of the car and climbed in beside a quiet Toby.

Lyle let go of Toby's hand and stepped away from the car, closing the door and making Toby flinch again. Ollie gritted his teeth, barely keeping his anger and sadness in check. He'd fucked up, and now he had to fix it, but he had no idea how.

He waved at Jon and Lyle as he pulled out of the car park. He couldn't bring himself to say anything during the journey home, not wanting to scare Toby. When they arrived home, Ollie turned off the car but didn't make a move to get out straight away.

Keeping his voice low, he said, "Are you okay staying with me, or would you prefer to stay with someone else?"

Toby didn't say anything, but he did climb out of the car and head for the door. Ollie scrambled to follow, trying to keep his movements easy and soft. He unlocked the door and opened it for Toby to enter. Toby went up the stairs and stopped at the top, his hands fidgeting with the cuffs.

"Denny," Toby said without looking at him.

Ollie frowned, not understanding. "Denny?"

"I want Denny here. Or Imogen."

Ollie kept his hurt inside, knowing he deserved it all. "Okay." He pulled his phone out and dialled Denny. "Hey, Denny. Are you free?"

"Sure thing. What do you need?"

"Um, something happened. Can you...can you come over?"

"I'll be there in five." Denny ended the call.

"Denny will be here in a few minutes."

Toby nodded and headed for the bedroom. Ollie was glad to see him enter it rather than the spare room, which was where he'd expected him to go. He couldn't move. Just stared down the hallway to where Toby had disappeared, but the knock on the door roused him enough to let Denny in.

"What happened?" Denny asked straight away.

"Shh," Ollie said. "We met Toby's ex, unfortunately. Asshole grabbed Toby. He doesn't..." Ollie glanced away, biting his lip. "He doesn't want me near him and asked for you. Could you...look after him for me?"

Denny moved to pull Ollie into his arms, but Ollie held out his hands. "I can't right now. Please. Just...help him."

Denny nodded. "Where is he?"

"Bedroom."

Denny disappeared, and Ollie heard the bedroom door close behind him. Only then did he allow himself to walk away. He took himself to the furthest corner of the apartment and sat down, burying his head in his knees and, finally, letting the tears come.

He'd failed his boy. Again. Why was he so bad at doing something that seemed so natural to him? Why couldn't he be the Daddy Toby deserved? All he wanted to do was shower Toby with love and affection and give him everything he could to make him happy, but what did he do? He put in a viper's nest instead. How Toby could ever trust him again was beyond Ollie's comprehension because Ollie certainly would never trust himself again.

Maybe he could help Toby move back to St Neots, where his friends were. His friends who hadn't let him down and who were always there for him.

Ollie sniffed when his tears dried and rested his head back against the wall, staring at the ceiling. No matter what Toby wanted to do, Ollie would do it. Even if it broke Ollie's heart, he would do it. All that mattered now was Toby, and Ollie doubted if Toby would ever forgive him.

But he made one promise to the universe. No matter what happened between him and Toby, Ollie would find Benson and make him pay. He'd make sure the man was banned from as many clubs as Ollie could find to ensure he didn't hurt another boy like he had Toby. Maybe then Toby could relax enough to lead a normal life without being scared the asshole would turn up unannounced one day. Living in fear was not living, and Ollie refused to let Toby go through that any more than he had already done so. It was the least he could do.

Now, he just had to find the fucker. And he knew just the man to help him.

23

TOBY

Toby curled onto his side on the bed, his back to the door. Denny had settled on the bed beside him, his legs stretched out in front of him, his hands linked in his lap. Or they had been before Toby closed his eyes.

He was so tired, but he couldn't sleep.

"You want to tell me what happened?" Denny asked.

"Tonight?" Toby asked quietly.

"Or before. Whichever you want."

Why did he feel so at ease with Denny? Was it because there was no pressure with him? Was it because he wasn't a Daddy? He didn't know, but he found it easy to let the words pour out of him. Everything from what *he* had done for years to what Toby had been through afterwards—the therapy and the therapy dogs and his reason for being obsessed with them—to what happened that night. Denny didn't interrupt. He didn't ask questions. He just let Toby talk, holding a bottle of water out when his voice went hoarse.

When he fell silent, having run out of words to say, Denny chuckled. "You are the strongest person I've ever met."

Toby's eyes snapped open, and he focused on Denny. "What?"

"If I'd been through everything you have, I wouldn't have even taken the chance with Ollie. I would've sworn off relationships forever. And you? You threw yourself into this relationship with barely a wobble." Denny held up a finger. "Okay, one wobble, but still. How are you even standing?"

Toby bit his lip, but he couldn't stop his retort. "I'm not. I'm lying down."

That startled a laugh out of Denny, and Toby joined in. "See? That right there." He pointed at Toby. "You're laughing. After everything that's happened, you're laughing. You're still finding joy in life when a dog has shit on you."

"Hey, leave the dogs out of this." Toby sighed and pulled himself upright. His sleeve pulled up, and he froze, staring at the evidence of what had happened that night. The bruise around his wrist was already forming. "I used to look at these bruises and believe they were handcuffs," he murmured. "Something locking me to him."

"But you got free," Denny reminded him. "Physically, at least. Emotionally, I believe so. Mentally, however, I think those handcuffs need to be broken. I know someone who can help you with that, but it'll take time."

"Who? A therapist?"

Denny shook his head. "Ollie."

Toby's eyes widened. "Ollie!" He scrambled from the bed and slammed open the door. "Ollie!" He stood in the doorway of the living room. Where was he? "Daddy!" he called, turning to face Denny. "Where is he? He'll be frantic."

Denny pointed behind Toby, and he spun around again. Ollie stood in the corner by the windows on the far side of the room. Toby raced across the space and flung his arms around his Daddy.

"I love you," Toby said. "I love you. I love you. It's not your fault."

Ollie held him, but not as tightly as he usually would have, and his voice, when he spoke, was not as strong as it had been before. "Yes, it is. I was meant to protect you, and I didn't. You were right to ask for Denny."

Toby pulled back, cupping his jaw. "I asked for Denny because I didn't want to put any more weight on your shoulders. You've been through so much with me already; I wanted to ease that burden. I don't blame you for any of it."

"You should."

Toby shook his head. "No, I shouldn't. You did everything you could to make me feel at ease. Calling the club, checking he wasn't a member, pandering to my crazy worries." He wiped a tear trickling down Ollie's cheek. "You saved me when he was there. You got him away from me."

Ollie glanced down at Toby's wrist. "That shows otherwise."

"*That* proves I'm alive. *That* proves you got me away. *That* reminds me of how much you love me. Because *you* don't do that." He sniffed. "I'm sorry I asked for Denny. I was wrong. We need to get through this together. And I know exactly how." Toby gave him a smile.

"How?"

"A dog. Or two."

Ollie blinked at him, then frowned. "A dog?"

Toby nodded. He grabbed Ollie's hand and pulled him towards the sofa. "I told you about the dog I saw when I was in therapy before, didn't I?" Ollie nodded. "We should get another one. Or maybe two. One for each of us. There's nothing more helpful than a dog when you're feeling down or need to work through things. They don't have to be trained as therapy dogs. Just dogs, in general, are cute and cuddly—"

Ollie snorted. "You just want a dog."

"That too." Toby smiled.

Ollie sighed and rubbed at his face. "I don't know if I can be what you need."

Toby climbed into his Daddy's lap. "You already are what I need. Nothing needs to change." He tilted his head. "Apart from maybe a dog."

Ollie laughed, shaking his head. "How are you brushing this aside so easily? I expected you to hate me. To need comfort from someone. Not to be comforting *me*."

"It's okay to need comforting sometimes. And I'm not brushing it aside. It will come back and haunt me at times I don't expect. I'll flinch when I don't mean to. I'll pull away for a second. I might have nightmares. Probably more stuff, too. But we'll work through it together. We have to work through it together."

"With a dog."

Toby smiled. "With a dog. Or two." He leaned further down. "Kiss me, Daddy. Show me I'm yours."

Ollie brushed his thumb across Toby's jaw and bottom lip while sliding his hand into Toby's hair and pulling him closer. "I don't deserve you," Ollie whispered before closing the gap. Toby couldn't reply because he was immediately lost in the kiss. They started slowly, their mouths slightly open, sharing air, until Toby licked Ollie's lower lip. Ollie pressed in harder, sliding his tongue into Toby's mouth. Toby inhaled through his nose as their mouths sealed, their tongues duelling and twining as they tried to get closer and closer. Toby wrapped his arms around Ollie's neck and deepened the already deep kiss. He wanted more. He wanted everything.

Eventually, he pulled away, the need to breathe making his body ignore his mental command to stay as close to his Daddy as he could. He pressed his forehead against Ollie's, panting.

"I'm yours," he murmured.

"And I'm yours." Ollie kissed him again, chastely this time.

Toby snuggled into Ollie's chest. "It'll take time to find ourselves again. At least, that's what my therapist always told me. Each setback is another excuse for my brain to ignore what I'm capable of. Or something like that, anyway. He won't win. I have you, and I'm not letting you go."

Ollie didn't reply, but he held him a little tighter, and Toby sighed and closed his eyes. They would be okay. He had to believe they would.

A few days later, Ollie hummed down at his phone as it rang, then answered and put it on speaker. "Hello, Mrs Duffy. Is everything okay with your car?"

"Oh, yes, dear. It's working wonderfully. No, I was just ringing because...I don't know if I was reading into anything before, but..." She paused, and Toby raised his eyebrows at Ollie, who shrugged. "Okay, what I mean is the dog you asked about before, Flossie, she's been returned." Toby pouted. That was always hard, both on the shelter and the dog. "I wondered if you were interested in adopting her?"

Ollie blinked at him, but Toby's smile stretched. "Serendipity," Toby whispered.

Ollie rolled his eyes and leaned his elbows on his knees. "Mrs Duffy, we'll be there this afternoon to have a look, okay?"

"Oh, that's wonderful, Ollie. Thank you so much! See you later."

She hung up before Ollie could say anything else, and Toby beamed at him. "We're getting a dog?" he asked hopefully.

Ollie exhaled and palmed his face. "We're getting a dog."

Toby jumped off the sofa and danced around the room. Then stopped. "We need to go shopping."

"That's why I told her we'd be there this afternoon. Gives us the morning to buy what we need." He and Ollie had taken a couple of days off work after the events of the weekend.

Toby fisted the air. "Yes!" He settled beside Ollie again. "She's gorgeous, though, isn't she?"

Ollie nodded. "She is. I called about her a while back to check up after we'd been to visit, but she'd been adopted."

"Were you planning to adopt her?"

Ollie shook his head, then stopped. "Not consciously, but maybe." He shrugged. "I don't know."

"She's been waiting for us," Toby said. "Come on. Let's shop!"

They spent the hours visiting several pet stores to make sure they had exactly what they needed to look after a border collie. Thankfully, Toby had spent plenty of time around the breed, so he knew what food was good for them and what they needed for equipment and toys. Toby used the money he'd been saving from what Ben paid him, knowing it was a good use for it, though Ollie tried to argue.

Once they'd set everything up at home, Toby bounced around until Ollie pointed to the door with a grumbled, "Let's go."

Toby squealed and raced down the stairs, barely stopping himself from falling through the door.

"Careful!" Ollie shouted. "We won't be able to get a dog if you hurt yourself."

Toby slowed but couldn't contain his excitement as they drove to the shelter. Ollie held his hand on the walk to the building, possibly to stop him from floating away. Mrs Duffy clapped her hands when she saw them.

"I'm so glad you're here. Let's go back."

She whirled around and disappeared, and they had to rush to catch up. They entered the kennel area and slowed in front of Flossie's cage.

Toby lowered to a crouch, reaching a hand out to the metal so Flossie could sniff him first. "Hey, sweetie. Do you remember me?"

Flossie whined as if answering, and Toby beamed up at Ollie. Ollie sighed. "We'll take her, Mrs Duffy."

"Oh, wonderful! I'll just get all the paperwork for you. You won't regret it, you'll see."

Toby opened the door and slid inside, crouching down so

Flossie could greet him properly. "Come in, Daddy. She'll want to meet you again."

Ollie stepped inside and closed the door behind him. He knelt beside Toby, stroking down Flossie's back. "Hello, Flossie. How about a forever home with us, huh?"

Flossie lifted her head and nudged her wet nose against Ollie's cheek, and Toby giggled. "I think that's answer enough."

Toby's gaze caught on the dog next to Flossie's kennel, and his heart skipped a beat. He hadn't looked at any of the other dogs when they'd arrived, too excited to see Flossie, but there sat a gorgeous grey Great Dane. He must've made some sort of noise because Ollie asked him what was wrong. Toby pointed, and Ollie groaned.

"We've only bought enough for one dog, sweetheart. We can't take two."

Toby pouted at Ollie. "But it's my favourite breed."

Ollie sighed. "We won't have enough room—" His shoulders lowered, and he closed his eyes before opening them to stare across at the other dog while ruffling Flossie's ears. "Oh, fuck it! Mrs Duffy? We'll need two sets of adoption papers!"

Toby held in his squeal, but he couldn't stop the smile that spread across his face. "I'll look after them both! You don't have to do anything!"

Ollie smiled and cupped his face. "We can both look after them. They'll be part of our family."

Toby leaned forward and kissed him. "Thank you."

"Right, what's this I hear about a second adoption?" Mrs Duffy said.

Ollie pointed at the Great Dane. "We'll take this one, too."

Mrs Duffy frowned, and for a moment, Toby wondered if the dog had already been reserved. "Yes, okay. I can see them working well together. I have to be careful, you see. I need to make sure their personalities and behaviours won't clash, but I think those two would be fine together. Ghost, here, is a very laid-back dog."

"Ghost? Aww," Toby said. "That's such a cute name."

"All right. Come and finish the paperwork, then you can take them home."

"Don't you need to check our apartment or anything?" Toby asked.

Mrs Duffy shook her head. "Usually, yes. But I know Ollie's mother and Ollie, and I trust them. The apartment will be fine for them. I will come and check on them in a couple of weeks, though."

"Okay."

The paperwork took them around fifteen minutes, then they paid, and Toby took Ghost's lead and Ollie took Flossie's lead and led them to the car.

"I think we need to lay the back seats down," Ollie said, handing Toby Flossie's lead. "You hold them, and I'll sort it."

Toby crouched down and fussed over the dogs while Ollie got the car ready. Ghost was easy-going, resting against Toby, whereas Flossie wanted to explore, pulling on her lead. At least until Toby told her to sit. They would both need training to make sure they were safe in their new home, but Toby could see to that. He'd speak to Aster, but maybe he could even take them for walks with the other dogs sometimes.

He pulled out his phone and took a selfie of himself with the two dogs, and sent it to Ben. Within seconds, Ben called, and Toby answered with a smile.

"Who are those gorgeous creatures?"

"Our dogs."

"Sorry, what?"

"Our dogs. The Great Dane is called Ghost, and the border collie is called Flossie. We've just adopted them."

Ben gasped. "Oh, my god! I'm so happy for you. You've always wanted dogs of your own. How did you persuade Ollie to go for it?"

"Well, funny story actually..."

While he explained, he watched Ollie finish arranging the car, then handed Flossie's lead to him. He stood and led Ghost over to the car and helped her to settle down while he talked. They would need a better solution for transporting two dogs in the future, but it would be fine for the brief journey ahead of them.

When they pulled up to the garage, and after he'd finished bending Ben's ear, they walked around the space and let the dogs explore and sniff their new surroundings.

"What have you got there, boss?" Landon said from the doorway.

Ollie huffed a laugh. "Additions to the family."

"Seriously?" Enno said. He glanced at Toby. "You managed to persuade him?"

Toby grinned. "Sure did. Though he would've probably caved himself, anyway. We're going to introduce them to Rio soon, too."

24

OLLIE

Ollie sighed and led Flossie over to his mechanics, letting her sniff at them. Toby did the same with Ghost. After introductions were made, they took the dogs up the back stairs to the apartment. Toby knew just as much about Great Danes, so he told Ollie what other items they needed to buy to ensure she stayed healthy. Once they were settled, Ollie offered to fetch the items they needed while Toby settled down on the floor and let both dogs rest beside him while he watched the TV. His boy was so happy, and he couldn't wait to tell Sarah and his family. He was hoping his parents would let him take the dogs to Sunday dinner next weekend. It was a long journey, though, so they'd have to see how the dogs settled in first.

When Ollie returned with the equipment, they set it up. Then Ollie washed up and started dinner. Toby, on the other hand, logged on to his game and caught up with his online friends. Ollie couldn't believe they'd started the day with zero dogs and ended it with two. How the hell had that happened? Getting two dogs after being together for a few months was barmy.

"Dinner's ready," Ollie called, and he heard the scrabble of paws on the floor and laughed when Flossie and Ghost heeded his call. "Not for you two! Go sit down."

Both dogs sat but watched Ollie's movements with keen eyes, undoubtedly waiting for him to drop something. They wouldn't be allowed to eat anything off the floor because they had to be careful it didn't become a habit, but he wanted to see their initial reactions if it happened. When he purposefully dropped a piece of pasta, Flossie's muscles bunched, but she didn't move. Ghost, however, snapped forward and gobbled it up.

Good to know who needed the most training. When a second piece fell, Ollie held out his hand, and Toby grabbed her collar. "No," he said in a firm voice, and Toby tugged her gently back to sitting. It would take more than one command for her to learn, but she would eventually.

He picked up the pasta and threw it away, and Toby poured out some dinner for the dogs. He left it on the counter until Ollie said their food was ready and then put it on the floor. "Wait," Toby said, standing and stepping away. "Go," he said once he was out of reach. He was glad to see that Ghost had listened, so she maybe had some training already.

Toby washed his hands and joined Ollie at the dining table. "Only time will tell how quickly they'll learn."

Ollie smiled. "I have no doubt it won't take them long with you as their daddy."

Toby stared at him. "I'm a daddy," he whispered.

Ollie chuckled. "You're a doggy daddy."

"If they love me as much as I love you, I'll be a happy doggy daddy." He leaned forward and kissed Ollie. "Thank you."

"You're welcome. Thank you for wanting to share your life with me."

"How could I not? We're meant to be."

✦

Ollie had been certain that the trouble with Toby's ex had only just started, but they hadn't heard anything from him. He had spoken to the manager and explained the situation and found out that the manager had wanted no trouble and had lied about whether Benson was a member. At that moment, Ollie saw red and ordered the man to refund their membership. They wouldn't be visiting that club any longer. The only club they would ever go to again is Bound, and only when there were plenty of friends to go with them. He didn't trust anyone else anymore.

The sound of alarms was a daily occurrence for them now. For Toby to keep track of his chores as well as his role as chief of messages for the Daddy's Boy app and the Boys, Daddies, Snuggles & More blog, he needed his alarms to remind him what he was to do. Ollie often heard them when he was in the garage if it wasn't too busy because Toby needed them loud enough to pierce his concentration.

When the day of the event arrived—seven months after Ollie and Toby had met—Toby was both excited and nervous, but Ollie knew he would be amazing. They weren't there as employees; Ben had insisted on them being guests, but Toby still wanted everything to go well for them.

The app itself had been an immense success, pairing many boys and Daddies and finding genuine success with the matches. Some of those couples were attending, but most members were single and looking for their match with someone at the event itself.

Gareth and Ben greeted them when they arrived and gave them a glass of bubbly to celebrate before they both disappeared to start the event. Ben made a speech, having been designated the face of Daddy's Boy, while Gareth stood in the shadows, content to watch from the sidelines. Ollie stared across the sea of blue and red T-shirts. The organisers had decided that Daddies should wear blue and boys should wear red, so they were easily identifiable. Couples were told to stay away from those colours, and the stewards were decked in white shirts and black waistcoats to differentiate them, too. All in all, it seemed a well-thought-out event.

Throughout the night, they mingled with Daddies and boys, many of them gushing over meeting Toby, who had given more than one of them advice over the last few months. Towards the end of the night, Ben introduced them to a boy called Andy, who was just as nervous and shy as Toby had been at their first meeting. It gave him hope Andy would find his confidence with the right person, just as Toby had. And it might just be the person by his side, Scott. Though Ollie couldn't account for taste—he wore purple Dr Martens.

That reminded him of the college reunion Denny had been pestering him about. It was coming up in a couple of months, and he'd still yet to RSVP his answer. He wasn't sure what to do because, although he didn't want to go, he'd love to show Toby off. Wasn't that the point of reunions? To show that you had something worthy in the intervening years? He kept going back and forth about his answer, but he still couldn't stick with one.

As they entered the lift to send them to their room—compliments of Ben and Gareth—Ollie broached the subject again.

"Okay, I need to decide once and for all about this reunion. What do you think?"

Toby slid into his arms and rested his cheek against his chest. "I think you should go. For no other reason than Denny wants to. I don't like the idea of him going alone."

"Would you come with me?"

Toby gazed up at him. "If you want me there."

"Of course I do. I always want you with me."

"Let's do it, then."

Ollie groaned. "I'll never hear the end of it from Denny now."

"At least it's only a couple of months away. Not too long to put up with his excitement." Toby paused. "Has he mentioned much about Preston to you?"

Ollie shook his head and frowned. "No. Why?"

"He mentioned him a few times when we've been talking. I couldn't get a read on whether Denny saw himself as a Daddy or a boy or neither, but there's definitely something there, I think."

They'd met up a couple of times at Bound since the disastrous visit to the club that would no longer be voiced in name. It had taken all of them to convince Toby to try Bound again, but with all his friends there, he managed the first visit with barely any issues, and since then, they'd visited once a month—or planned to.

Ollie unlocked the hotel door and added the do not disturb sign on the outside before locking it behind them. He grabbed Toby and lifted him, his legs immediately wrapping around Ollie's waist. He carried his boy to the bed and laid him down, covering him and delving in for a kiss. His fingers worked nimbly on the buttons of Toby's shirt until he could touch bare skin. His mouth kissed down his neck, across his chest and fastened around a nipple, causing Toby to arch and groan.

"Please, Daddy. I need you."

Ollie didn't answer, instead licking and sucking across his skin to the other nipple and giving it the same attention while pulling Toby's shirt from his waistband. He removed his mouth and pulled the shirt off, following it quickly with his own. Toby's legs wrapped around Ollie's waist again, his hips thrusting up to nudge their cocks together. Both moaned into each other's mouths, and Ollie reached down to unbutton and unzip Toby's trousers, pulling his dick free.

Ollie stroked fervently, wanting to send Toby soaring as quickly as he could, but Toby's hands fumbled with Ollie's trousers until their shafts were pressed together. Ollie wrapped his hand around them both and continued to kiss Toby as he sent them higher.

"Yes! Please!"

"Come on, sweetheart. Come for me. Show me what you've got. Come for Daddy," Ollie growled.

"I..." Toby's head pressed into the bed as his back arched and his cock spurted across their skin and clothes.

Ollie watched Toby's face while pleasure washed over him, and he followed suit, gasping as his dick released all over his boy. When he jerked in sensitivity, he let go and braced himself over his boy, resting his forehead on Toby's shoulder.

"I'm tired, Daddy," Toby murmured.

Ollie chuckled. "Me, too, sweetheart."

Gathering his energy, he pushed upright and stumbled to the bathroom, shedding his dirty clothes as he went. He wet a flannel with warm water and took it back to the bed, wiping his sleepy boy clean, then himself. He put the flannel on the floor beside the bed and lifted Toby further up the bed, pulling the covers from beneath him, then over the top of him. Once his boy snuggled down, Ollie climbed in on the opposite side and spooned him, resting a hand over Toby's heart.

"Sleep, sweetheart. I'll be here."

As tired as Ollie was, he couldn't sleep. He listened to Toby's even breathing, felt his heartbeat beneath his palm and inhaled his scent, all of which reminded him how lucky he was. He'd spent most of his adult life looking for Toby without knowing it was Toby he was looking for. He didn't want to imagine his life without Toby in it.

Ollie froze. It was too early to ask him. They'd barely been together for seven months, but he knew, deep inside, it was the right choice. He just had to choose his time. He wanted the uncertainty that Toby's asshole ex had left them with to be fully washed away. It helped that Ollie, Gareth and Enno had been actively and systematically shutting down Benson's club options. Several clubs had already known about him—and the name he often used to *hide* his behaviour—and were grateful for the excuse to put him on the non-entry list. Others refused point blank, and those were marked as "never to visit" on their list. It wasn't foolproof, but it was better than nothing. He doubted Toby would visit any club except Bound now, especially as the owners had personally spoken to them and added Benson's photo to their computers to ensure, no matter what name he used, he wouldn't be allowed access.

After everything that had happened, Ollie had booked them a week away in Wales for Toby's birthday—not that his boy had any idea about it yet. They left the following weekend, and Ollie wanted to keep it a secret for as long as possible. He wasn't entirely sure how Toby would cope without his gaming, but he was sure they could figure something out if it became a problem.

Toby snuffled in his sleep and rolled in Ollie's arm until his face pressed against Ollie's chest. He rooted around a bit, then sighed and settled. "Love you, Daddy," he murmured, the words barely audible.

Ollie's heart expanded further. He hadn't thought he could love his boy any more than he already did, but every day, every hour, every minute he spent in his company made him fall harder. When he thought back to what he'd believed he'd had with his previous partners, it was so obvious that they paled in comparison. If someone had told him that what he now felt for Toby had been possible, he'd have laughed in their face. He now understood what Enno meant when he said they weren't the right boys for Ollie. Never had truer words been spoken.

He pressed his lips to Toby's head. He would never tire of holding and loving his boy.

"Uh, Daddy?"

The whispered words pierced his sleep-fogged brain, and Ollie blinked heavy eyelids to see Toby. "Yes, sweetheart?" At least that's what he tried to say, but his tongue was stuck to the roof of his mouth.

"Will you fuck me?"

Ollie continued to blink blearily for a few seconds before the words finally registered. He squinted at his boy. "Huh?"

"I'm horny, Daddy. Will you fuck me?" Toby squirmed beside him, and Ollie woke properly.

He pushed his boy to his back, raising his eyebrows at Toby's grin. "You woke me for a fuck?"

Toby bit his lip, trying to hide his grin, but it didn't work. "No?" Looking innocent didn't work for him.

Ollie's fingers dug into Toby's side, a place he'd recently found was amazingly ticklish. Toby squealed and squirmed beneath him.

"No! Daddy! Stop! No!" Each word was punctuated with giggles.

Ollie finally stopped, bracing himself over Toby. "I'll always wake for you, sweetheart. No matter what it is you want."

Toby beamed and pulled his legs from between Ollie's legs, spreading them wide. "I'm ready, Daddy."

Ollie shook his head. "I have to prep you first, sweetheart."

"No, you don't," Toby whispered. "I've already done it."

Ollie lifted his legs, bending Toby in half as he stared at his boy's pucker, shiny with lube and flexing for him. "Hmm. Who's a naughty boy?"

Toby rolled his lips inwards but didn't reply. Ollie reached for a condom from the bedside table, where he'd stashed them the night before. He rolled it on, keeping eye contact with his boy as he rested his head against his hole. Pushing forward, there was a slight second of resistance before Toby opened for him without hesitation.

"Fuck, baby. You never cease to amaze me." Ollie lowered his head, joining their lips while he slid deep.

"Oh, yes, please, Daddy. Can I have it harder today?"

"Anything my boy wants."

Ollie spoilt his boy, that went without saying, but he didn't regret a second. Watching the happiness, the pleasure, the satisfaction, and every other emotion cross Toby's face during their time together was more than he could ever have hoped for. And he'd spend every future moment making sure he was worthy of receiving it.

25

TOBY

Toby was excited about his birthday. He'd turned thirty-nine—only one more year until it was all downhill, so his brothers said. Not that they'd know. Ollie made it look easy, though, so he wasn't taking his brothers' word for it. He had no idea what Ollie had planned for them other than they were going to visit his parents that afternoon. He'd felt bad taking another day off dog walking, but Aster had wished him a good birthday with no qualms.

"Ready?" Ollie said from the kitchen.

Toby closed his eyes and leaned back on the sofa as he'd been told to do. "Ready!"

He heard Ollie's footsteps and the wagging of Flossie's and Ghost's tails, but nothing else until a slight clink, then a rustle of something plastic.

"Okay. Open your eyes."

The first thing Toby saw was his Daddy, which was the best present anyone could've given him. Then he glanced in front of him and gasped. There were four bags by his feet and a large metal travel mug on the coffee table.

Ollie settled beside him and reached for the mug. "I made you a cup of tea while I was in there."

Toby grinned and sipped it, then replaced it on the table and pointed at the bags. "You spoilt me."

Ollie tilted his hand back and forth. "Maybe. A little." He smiled. "You're worth it."

Toby leaned to the side and kissed the corner of his mouth. "Thank you."

"You haven't opened anything yet!"

"I'll love it, no matter what they are." But he reached for the first bag. He pulled out a long, wrapped box and set about tearing the paper off. He unveiled a sound bar and bounced on the sofa. "Oh, wow. You might regret that later."

"I regretted it the moment I bought it, but I knew you'd love it."

"You haven't heard anything until you've heard it through this." Toby grinned.

Ollie sighed. "I'm sure my ears will love it."

Toby continued opening gifts. His Daddy *had* spoilt him. He got some cuddly dogs—which would sit on a shelf so their actual dogs didn't get to them—a box of chocolates, a snowglobe, plus some gaming gifts. He was overwhelmed by how much he'd received.

"One last present," Ollie said, reaching to the side of the sofa and bringing out a bag Toby hadn't seen.

Toby took it and rested it between his feet. It was heavy. He pulled the tissue paper out of the way and gasped. He stared at Ollie. "You didn't."

Ollie just smiled.

Toby pulled the black material from the bag and held it up. "I can't believe you bought me a leather jacket!"

"You said you liked them, and the ones I have downstairs are too big for you. If this one doesn't fit, we can take it back and change the size."

Toby stood and slipped his arms into the jacket. He pulled it over his shoulders, burying his nose in the collar and inhaling the new leather smell. Sliding his hands down the fabric, he bit his lip to contain his smile. He zipped it up and put his hands in his pockets.

"What do you think?" he asked.

Ollie's eyes had darkened, and Toby wasn't ignorant enough to mistake that expression for anything but lust. But Ollie cleared his throat and said, "It looks good on you."

"Fits perfectly."

"I agree." Ollie stood and wrapped his arms around Toby's waist, burying his head in his neck. "Happy birthday, sweetheart."

Toby slid his arms around Ollie's neck. "Thank you, Daddy."

"You deserve everything."

Toby closed his eyes and hung on, trying to stop the tears of happiness from falling because Ollie would worry. They stayed entwined until someone—or rather some *dog*—nudged them. Toby laughed and glanced down at the canines waiting impatiently at their feet. He rubbed his hand over Ghost's head.

"Shall we—" He was cut off when someone pounded on the door.

Ollie dropped a kiss on his lips and disappeared. Toby frowned. They weren't expecting anyone, and it was too early for the post. Voices drifted up the stairs, but he couldn't hear what they were saying. More feet climbed the stairs than had descended them, and Toby grinned when Enno, Rick and Denny came into view.

"Happy birthday!" they shouted.

Toby laughed. "Hey! Thanks. I wasn't expecting to see you guys today."

"Is that your new jacket?" Denny said.

Toby nodded. "I love it."

"Looks good on you, Toto."

"We couldn't not see you on your birthday," Rick said, answering Toby's earlier statement and holding out a wrapped box.

"Thank you." He unwrapped the present and grinned at the

controller covers. He'd mentioned to Rick once that there were some unique rainbow covers he liked the look of, but he hadn't planned on buying them for himself, not being able to excuse the expense. "You didn't have to, but thank you." He hugged his friend.

"I have one, too!" Denny said, thrusting a package into Toby's hands.

It wasn't the best-wrapped present he'd ever seen, but he was grateful that Denny had taken the time to wrap it himself. He opened it and laughed, even as his cheeks heated. It was a dildo with a tail, and Toby covered his face.

"Oh, my god. Um, thank you, Denny."

"I thought it might come in handy." Denny winked.

Toby snorted and re-wrapped it, burying it in a bag. He didn't think it would ever get used, but he wouldn't get rid of it when Denny had bought it for him.

Ollie clapped. "Okay. The plan is for you, sweetheart, to relax and have fun for a couple of hours. I'm going to make pizza for lunch before we have to leave."

Toby slid into Ollie's arms. "Sounds wonderful."

"You might want to take the leather jacket off. You'll get too warm."

Toby shook his head, stepping away and putting his hands over the zip. "Not happening. It's mine. It's staying on."

Ollie held up his hands. "Okay, okay! Just don't get too hot. It's not exactly a winter's day today."

Toby pouted. "I'll take it off *if* I get warm."

"Good." Ollie dropped a kiss on his lips and headed for the kitchen.

Toby spent an hour playing with Rick, and then Ollie called them for lunch. He'd made five pizzas, one for each of them, and some garlic bread. Discussion was lively as always, and Toby couldn't remember the last time he'd had so much fun on his birthday. His family was amazing, and he never felt like he'd been without, but there was something about being surrounded by friends. Now, if he had his family *and* his friends, it would be the best birthday ever.

"Are you ready to go?" Ollie asked him once their friends had left.

Toby glanced around, patting his pockets. "I need my phone and wallet. Oh, and my jacket!" He moved to the shelf he usually left them on and whirled around. "Ooh, are we going on the bike?"

Ollie chuckled and shook his head. "No, not this time." Toby frowned. "Next time, we can."

Toby slid his jacket back on, having had to take it off while he'd been eating, and slipped his phone and wallet into his pockets. "All ready."

"Let's go."

They filled the journey with plenty of chatter. Ollie had made the right choice of taking the car because it meant Toby could talk to him properly. It didn't take long to get there, and he raced to the door once they'd parked, his mother waiting for him.

"Happy birthday, darling," she said, hugging him.

"Thank you, Mum."

He pulled away, but she ran her hands down his jacket. "I like this."

Toby grinned. "Da—Ollie gave it to me." He just caught himself before his slip, but his mum's eyes twinkled at him, and he was sure she knew what he had almost said.

"It's gorgeous."

"Yo, Toto! Will you get in here so we can have cake!" Nigel shouted from somewhere deep in the house.

Sally huffed. "Wait!" she called back. "Sorry, boys. They're impatient as always, but I would suggest going straight through because you might not get to see the design if they're left in there alone for much longer."

Ollie chuckled as they wandered down the hall, and Toby

gasped when he saw some of his friends from the kennels, including Sarah, waiting for him.

"Surprise!"

"Happy birthday!"

Toby's eyes filled, and he couldn't say anything. He'd known he had friends, but to see them there with his family reminded him of his earlier thoughts. Friends and family were the best of everything. Ollie slipped his arms around his waist and rested his head on his shoulder.

"Are you okay?" he whispered.

Toby nodded and swallowed. "Hey, everyone," he croaked, leaning heavily on his Daddy for support.

Sally brushed past them and busied around the kitchen, making sure everyone had something, and Ollie herded him towards the table, where Nigel and Fletcher waited to pounce on the cake his mother had made. Toby's heart melted at the controller-shaped cake. Everyone who was there knew him. He didn't feel uncomfortable at all. And although these were people who were in his life before Ollie was, it was undoubtedly Ollie who brought them all together because his mother would've never invited his friends without speaking to him first—not that he minded.

"You'll have to wait a few minutes more, boys," Sally said, clipping the backs of Nigel's and Fletcher's heads.

The doorbell sounded, and his father shouted, "I'll get it," from wherever he had been. Toby frowned, glancing around. Was someone else coming? He thought everyone was here.

But he was wrong.

"I'm so sorry. There was an accident on the way here, and we had to detour. Took us forever!"

Toby squealed when Ben came through the door and ran to him, hugging him. "I can't believe you're here."

Ben chuckled and squeezed him harder. "We wouldn't miss this for the world."

Gareth smiled at him over Ben's shoulder. "Happy birthday, Toby."

"Can we do the cake now?" Nigel whined.

"I think your brother might need a Daddy," Ben whispered with a giggle, pulling back.

Toby groaned. "Please don't say things like that."

"Right, come on. Let's get this cake done before my boys have an aneurysm," Sally said.

Toby moved to the table and stood before the cake. Sally lit the matches—two large ones in the shape of a three and a nine—and Toby closed his eyes and made a wish. He wished for nothing to change because he was happier than he had ever been. Asking for more would just make him greedy. He leaned down and blew the candles out, and the guests sang happy birthday to him, even though the candles relit themselves. Toby laughed, and his brothers groaned. Toby licked his finger and thumb and pressed the wick between them, ending the flame on both.

"Speech! Speech! Speech!"

Toby blew out a breath and reached for Ollie's hand. "I don't really know what to say," he said after everyone fell silent. "Thank you so much for being here. It means more to me than you could ever realise. I have never been happier than I am at this moment, and it's because of all of you." He squeezed Ollie's hand, glancing at him and sharing a smile. "Thank you."

Everyone clapped, and he hid his face in Ollie's chest, feeling a little overcome.

"Are you okay, sweetheart?" Ollie asked, rubbing his back.

"Mmhmm." He sniffed and lifted his head. "Thank you."

Ollie smiled. "You're welcome."

Sally had cut into the cake by the time he turned around, and his brothers were already demolishing a slice. She handed him and Ollie a small plate each, and he wandered around talking to everyone while Ollie sat with Toby's dad.

The party went on for several hours, although people left gradually until there was only his family, Sarah, Ben and Gareth left.

Ben stepped closer. "We're going to be leaving soon. We don't want to hit the Friday traffic."

Toby nodded. "It's okay. Thank you for coming."

"Wouldn't miss it for the world, as I said."

"Toby?" Ollie said, garnering his attention. "Could you come here a moment, please?"

Toby stepped over to his Daddy, smiling. "What's up?" Ollie handed him an envelope, and Toby frowned. "What's this?"

"Open it and find out."

Toby rolled his eyes and slipped open the flap, pulling out a piece of paper. He unfolded it and frowned again, reading. Then his eyebrows rose, and his stomach fluttered. He glanced at Ollie.

"We're going on holiday?"

Ollie nodded. "A week in Wales. Fresh air. Walking. Climbing. Views to die for."

"When?" Ollie pointed to the top of the paper. "Today? But what about work?"

"I'd already spoken to Aster about it, and she's fine with you taking the time off. And Enno is taking over the garage for me. Enno and Rick are also looking after the dogs for us."

"We could've brought them with us."

Ollie nodded. "We could've, but I wanted this first trip to be for just us."

Toby flung his arms around Ollie's neck. "Thank you, Daddy," he whispered. He pulled back in a panic. "But I haven't packed anything!"

Ollie chuckled. "I have everything under control. Our suitcases are in the car."

"Now I know why you said we couldn't take the bike." Toby

wagged his finger at him. He turned to his guests. "We're going to Wales!"

Ben clapped. "Woohoo!"

Toby narrowed his eyes at him and pointed at him. "You already knew, didn't you?"

Ben waggled his head back and forth. "Maybe," he said with a grin.

Toby shook his head and laughed. "Everyone's keeping secrets. Tut, tut, tut."

"Good secrets, sweetheart," Ollie said.

"True."

They spent half an hour longer with everyone before Ollie said they had to go. They had a long journey ahead of them.

Toby sighed. He was getting tired, and he knew he'd probably crash the moment he sat in the car. "Do you want me to drive first?"

Ollie shook his head as they headed for the car. "You sleep. I'll be fine."

He tucked Toby into the car, fastened his seat belt and dragged a blanket over him. Toby waved to his family and friends as Ollie climbed in and drove off. He watched the scenery pass him and smiled, his eyes fluttering closed, lulled into a doze by the vibration of the car.

His birthday had been wonderful. He promised himself he wouldn't take any of his friends or family for granted. He'd make sure they understood how important they were to him. And as for Ollie, his Daddy needed the most amazing gift Toby could think of for his birthday. He just had to figure out what.

26

OLLIE

Two days later, Ollie's palms sweated, and his stomach rolled, neither having anything to do with the mountain they were climbing. He had a plan for when they reached a certain spot, the view apparently as breath-taking as the man beside him. His reason for why they hadn't brought the dogs had been true, but there was another reason, too. He wasn't sure how the plan would end, so he hadn't wanted to be distracted by making sure the dogs weren't wandering off.

"Everything okay?" Toby asked, his voice quiet.

Ollie smiled at him. "Perfect."

"At least we're not going right to the top." Toby's nose scrunched up as he looked up to where they couldn't see the summit for the cloud cover.

Ollie chuckled at his expression. "Maybe another day," he teased. "We're nearly there, I think." He pointed across to the left. "If we follow that path, it'll take us to our destination."

"You're so mean not telling me where we're going."

"You'll like the view. That's all you need to know."

Toby huffed, but he followed Ollie's instructions, and when they reached the lip of where they were headed, he gasped.

"Told you," Ollie said, his voice shaking.

He stared across the space. They stood on the edge of a crater-like area with a blue-green body of water at the bottom. The colour was mesmerising, not quite teal, not quite turquoise. Almost a mixture of them both, depending on how he looked at it.

"This is beautiful," Toby murmured.

Ollie blew out a breath and reached for the box he'd stored in his zipped pocket, not wanting it to fall out. He licked his lips and called Toby's name. As his boy turned around, Ollie dropped to one knee, and Toby's hands covered his mouth as he stared at him.

"Toby, sweetheart. I love you so much, and I want to spend as much time with you as possible. I know it's fast, but I wanted to show you how important you are to me and how much I love you. Will you consider marrying me?" Ollie paused, having never felt so nervous in his life but knowing he couldn't leave it at that with how Toby's past had affected him. "I understand if you're not ready. And if you aren't, would you instead accept this as a promise ring of how I feel about you?"

Tears slipped down Toby's cheeks, and Ollie didn't know which way he would go. Toby sniffed and wiped his face, stepping closer. "We've not even been together for a year yet." He blanched and shook his head. "No, that's not what I meant. Everything seems too good to be true. I know I want to get married, but I'm scared, Daddy."

Ollie had known this was what he'd probably answer, but his stomach still churned, so he continued. "I know you're scared. Will you accept it as a promise instead? I can put it on your right hand, and if or when you're ready, you can move it to your left." Toby licked his lips, staring into Ollie's eyes. "But don't feel pressured to do either."

Toby smiled. "It's just like you. Giving me a way out." He inhaled. "I'll accept your promise."

Ollie's shoulder loosened, and he stood, slipping the ring onto Toby's right ring finger and pressing his lips to it. "I'm sorry for surprising you with this, but I couldn't help but ask."

"I'm sorry, I can't say yes yet. It doesn't mean I don't love you. It doesn't mean I don't want this. I just need my brain to catch up with every other part of me." Toby's eyes glistened again.

Ollie cupped his face. "I'm not mad, sweetheart. I'm so damn proud. You're sticking up for yourself and doing what's best for you, which is how it should be. I'd be mad if you said yes and hadn't been truthful to your heart."

"It's not my heart that's the problem," he muttered.

Toby stared down at the ring, and Ollie hoped he liked it. It was white gold with turquoise and tourmaline gems inset alternately. He hadn't been able to find a decent teal gemstone he was happy with, so he'd had to compromise.

"I know it's not teal, but I thought it would remind us of our initial conversation."

"I love it."

Having known it wasn't a foregone conclusion that Toby would accept, Ollie had decided not to make a big deal of it, regardless of the answer. When they arrived back at the little cottage, he set to work making dinner. Despite not getting the answer he wanted, his words to Toby were true. He was so proud of him for taking the time to think about things. Ollie didn't feel like he'd said no, even though he hadn't said yes, either. At least he didn't have to tell anyone about it because no one had known he was going to propose.

When dinner was ready, he slipped into the living room and found Toby fast asleep on the sofa. What stopped him from waking him to eat was that Toby's fingers and thumb were holding on to the promise ring, even lax in his sleep. He had hope for the future. No matter how long he had to wait, he would. And if Toby was never ready, then so be it. Ollie wouldn't find another boy he wanted as much as Toby, and he'd stay like they were for the rest of their lives if that was what Toby wanted.

He was about to put dinner aside to warm up later when Toby stirred. He crouched beside his boy, running a hand over his hair. "Hey, sleepyhead. Do you want to sleep some more, or do you want some dinner?"

Toby clicked his tongue a few times before answering. "Dinner, please. My tummy is rumbling."

Ollie grinned. "I've got a hungry pup, have I?" He stood and held out his hand. "Come on, then." He tugged Toby to his feet, holding him against him while he got his bearings.

Toby rested his cheek against Ollie's chest. "You're so warm."

"Is that a good thing in summer?" Ollie joked.

"Yes. I like you warm."

Ollie manoeuvred him to the table and settled him in a chair. He dished up the sausage casserole and slid the plate in front of Toby, then sat beside him.

"Tomorrow, I was thinking we could visit the main town and see what's around. We can get some trinkets or something for our friends," he said.

Toby's eyes lit up, and he nodded while finishing his food. "Yes! We'll have to get some postcards, too."

Ollie frowned. "I think we'll get home before the postcards get delivered."

Toby giggled. "Not to send, silly. Just some of the areas we've visited. As memories. Maybe we can start a scrapbook or something."

"What about a memory box? You could decorate the box, and we could put in all the things we get on our travels that you don't want to put on display."

"Yes! We might need several boxes if we're planning lots of holidays."

Ollie chuckled. "Lots of holidays, huh?"

Toby bit his lip, unable to hide his smile. "We could bring the dogs next time."

"We can." Ollie tilted his head. "You like it here then?"

"I do. I mean, I don't think I could live in such isolation all the time because I'd miss my friends too much. But as a getaway, I really like it." He frowned. "It's like a reset button. Forgetting real life and being able to do what we usually can't is nice."

"I'll forget our plans for later if you don't want to do what we usually do," Ollie said, forking some food into his mouth.

"I don't mean we can't do what we usually do." He frowned. "What did you have planned?"

Ollie pretended to consider the options, tapping a finger on his chin. "Well, I had thought we could watch a movie and cuddle, then maybe head to the bedroom for some fun. And I brought one of your birthday gifts to maybe try out." He waggled his eyebrows, then straightened his face. "But it's okay. We can do something else instead."

Toby clambered from his chair and into Ollie's lap, knocking the table as he wrapped his arms around his neck. He grinned. "I always want that with you. No matter where we are."

Ollie laughed. "I know, sweetheart. I was teasing."

"What gift did you bring with you?" Toby's expression went from a scrunched-up face to wide eyes and a gaping mouth. "You didn't?"

Ollie grinned. "I did. I'd love to see what you look like with a tail."

Toby stood. "I've finished eating!"

"I haven't, and you need your energy." He continued eating, knowing it would make his boy impatient.

"Please, Daddy!"

Ollie's chair screeched across the floor as he stood and lifted Toby into his arms. His boy wrapped his legs and arms around him, fusing their mouths as he stumbled towards the bedroom.

He bumped his shin on a small table in the hallway but ignored the pain. They fell to the bed in a tangle of limbs, barely removing their mouths to undress or breathe. When they were skin-to-skin, Ollie slowed things down, skimming his fingertips across Toby's skin and allowing his lips to follow. Once he'd kissed the length of his body and back up again, ignoring the place Toby wanted him to focus, he reached across to the bedside table and pulled out the gift he'd stashed there. He rose to his knees and dangled it in front of his boy.

"Would you like to be a pup tonight, sweetheart?"

Toby's eyes heated further, if that was possible. "I'd like to try a tail for a bit."

"Let's get you prepared then."

It didn't take long for Toby to be taking three of his fingers, and Ollie flipped him over to his hands and knees. He lubed the dildo and held it at Toby's hole.

"Ready, sweetheart?"

"Oh, god, yes."

Ollie dropped a kiss on his hips as he pushed the dildo against the ring wanting to keep it out. Toby bore down, and it slipped inside, earning a gasp from his boy. Ollie thrust and withdrew, giving Toby slightly more each time. When it was finally all the way inside, Ollie's heart skipped a beat at the fluffy brown and white tail trembling between Toby's ass cheeks.

He tugged at the tail, and Toby moaned and arched his back. "How does that feel?"

"Oh, god. It's... It's weird. I can feel the fluffiness touching my skin, and every time I move, the dildo presses against me." He moved his hips from side to side. "Every sway of the tail moves it, too. It's..." He blew out a breath.

"You look sexy as hell, though."

Toby smirked over his shoulder at him. "You like me as a pup?"

"I like you as you are. What's making my cock fucking hard is the way you're moving to make that plug touch you inside. You probably don't even realise you're doing it."

"Doing what?"

Ollie smiled. "Moving your hips to sway the tail. Clenching your fingers into the covers. Arching your back. I could watch you all night."

"Please, Daddy."

"Please, what?" Ollie moved closer, knowing exactly what he wanted to do.

"Please!" Toby's movements increased, his eyes closing.

Ollie laid on the bed on his back and slid until his mouth was in place for Toby's cock. When Toby circled his hips forward, Ollie sucked his dick down.

"Oh, fuck!" Toby's limbs trembled, but his hips increased their thrusting. "Yes, Daddy! More!"

Ollie sucked harder, and Toby's arms gave way. He choked on the sudden mouthful of cock, and Toby apologised, trying to move. Ollie gripped his hips and held him steady, continuing to tongue Toby's shaft, focusing on the underside.

"Oh, god, Daddy. Oh, god! Oh, god!"

Toby's trembling increased further. Was he close? Ollie reached between Toby's legs and tugged on the tail gently.

"Oh, fuck!"

Within seconds, Toby's release coated Ollie's mouth, and he drank it down, waiting for a few seconds longer before tugging on the tail again. Toby swore again and pulsed, and Ollie reached higher, gripping the base of the dildo; he slid it partially free and thrust it in again.

"Fuck, fuck!"

Toby's cock jerked in his mouth and released a little more. Ollie continued withdrawing and thrusting the dildo until Toby sobbed for him to stop. Then he pulled it free and dropped it to bed, cleaning Toby's cock before pulling off. He slid out from under him, and Toby collapsed to the bed.

Ollie laid next to him and rubbed a hand over his back, soothing him down from the release. He was hard himself but didn't feel the need for an orgasm. Toby had been beautiful in the throws of arousal. Even though Ollie hadn't been able to see his face, the sounds he made and the taste of him would forever be etched into his memory.

He slipped from the bed and grabbed a flannel, wetting it and returning to the bed, where Toby was still in the same position—and fast asleep if Ollie had interpreted his breathing right. He gently cleaned his ass and took the flannel to the washing basket, then lifted Toby so that his head rested on the pillow and slid the covers over him. Ollie put away the dinners they'd left, made sure everything was turned off in the cottage and that the door was locked, and then climbed into bed with him.

The climb would've exhausted anyone, but all the excitement of the day would've been too much for Toby. It was why Ollie had mentioned the dildo. It was enough of an enticement to get him into bed and enough of an energy-expelling activity that he was out for the count.

No doubt, the following day, Toby would be upset that Ollie hadn't come, but he had plans for that, too.

Ollie rolled to his side and snuggled against Toby's back. They'd needed this break. Taking them away from real life, as Toby called it, was good for them. Now everything with his ex was sorted—as much as it could be, anyway—they needed to find their way back to normal. Ollie might have ruined it with his proposal, but only time would tell. He had everything he could ever need, and if Toby never said yes, then that would be okay. And if he did say yes, Ollie would make him the happiest man alive. He'd make sure he spent the rest of his years giving Toby everything he could ever need or want.

Yes, he'd spoil him.
More than he already did.
His boy was worth it.

27

TOBY

It had been two months since Ollie had proposed, and Toby still hadn't felt like he could get past how scared he was. Two days ago, he'd had an epiphany, if he could call it that. He didn't know what had caused it, but one minute he'd been fighting a zombie, and the next he froze, staring at the screen as the zombie killed him because he'd started crying. The idea that Ollie wouldn't always be there with him was prominent in his mind, and he'd sobbed his heart out.

Luckily, it had been a couple of hours before Ollie was due back up from the garage, so he'd had time to calm himself. When he'd calmed, he'd known what he wanted—to marry Ollie. And he knew just how to let him know it.

That day had arrived in the form of Ollie's birthday. It hadn't seemed like a day since they'd celebrated Toby's, but Ollie had refused anything big. He wanted to spend the day with Toby and no one else—although they'd had to compromise with visiting Ollie's mum and sister for dinner, which was a small price to pay. That weekend, they were going to celebrate with their friends at a bar. But from the moment Ollie woke, they would spend several hours together.

Toby had got up early to get breakfast ready, although he didn't start it. He'd do that once Ollie woke. He had presents ready on the table, and both dogs had bows on their collars. While he waited for his Daddy to get up, he sat on the sofa with a cup of tea and fiddled with his promise ring. He removed it from his right hand, twirled it around several times, then nestled it back on his finger—his left finger. Ollie had told him to swap it over when he was ready, and he was. But he was going to see how long it took for his Daddy to notice the difference. Would he figure it out straight away? Toby thought he might because Ollie was always playing with the ring when they held hands. It wouldn't take much for him to realise.

How wrong could he have been?

Three hours later and his Daddy still hadn't noticed, even though Toby was blatantly using and showing that hand. He was going to explode if he wasn't careful. He didn't know what else he could do to get him to notice.

He made one last attempt before he'd spill.

"Daddy! Come dance with me!"

Ollie groaned but got up and slid his arms around Toby.

Toby giggled. "No, properly. Hold my hand."

Ollie sighed and changed posture, sliding one hand into Toby's and resting his other on his waist.

"You like formal dancing?"

Toby shook his head. "Not bothered, really, but we need to practise for Friday."

Ollie snorted. "I doubt there'll be formal dancing at the reunion."

Toby wiggled his hand, threading their fingers together. He rested his cheek on Ollie's shoulder. Waiting. Hoping. For him to...

"Toby?"

"Yes, Daddy?"

"Please tell me I'm not hallucinating?"

"About what?" he asked innocently.

Ollie pulled away and gazed into his eyes for a long moment before dropping them to their hands. Toby bit his lip as Ollie took his left hand in both of his. He was quiet, but when he looked up again, he had tears in his eyes.

"Toby?" he croaked.

"Yes, Daddy. For as long as you'll have me." He answered the unspoken question.

Tears spilt over, and Ollie dragged him close, burying his face in Toby's neck. Hot, wet breath sawed out of him and onto Toby's skin, and Toby gripped him.

Ollie lifted his head, his face blotchy, and smiled. "Thank you. I love you so much. I didn't expect this but thank you, thank you, thank you." He punctuated each word with a kiss on his face.

Toby laughed. "I love you, too, Daddy. Happy birthday."

"Best birthday ever!" Ollie dragged him to the bedroom, and they spent several hours locked away from the world.

When they finally surfaced, it was time to visit Ollie's mum, so they went over on the bike. Ollie was vibrating with energy, too excited by the news they had to tell them. If Toby hadn't been feeling so happy and energised, he would've teased him about acting like a boy instead of a Daddy.

They hugged Bea, and Ollie stopped her before she headed down the hallway. "Mum, we have something to tell you."

"Sounds serious." She frowned, glancing at each of them.

"It is." Ollie pulled Toby's hand forward. "We're engaged," he said solemnly.

Bea's expression froze for a second before the words seemed to register, and she covered her mouth with her hands as tears filled her eyes. "You are?"

Ollie grinned and nodded. She glanced at Toby's hand, then at him, then at his hand again before taking his hand with her own and gushing over the ring.

"You have good taste, Ollie. I never would've believed it until you brought Toby to us."

"Hey! I had taste before Toby got here." Ollie huffed. "There's no getting away from us now, sweetheart." He slipped his arm around Toby's waist.

"Not going anywhere," Toby said.

Bea started walking towards the kitchen, murmuring to herself, but Toby caught part of it.

"How can I make the cheesecake a celebration cake?"

He would've told her not to bother if it would've changed her mind, but it wouldn't. He'd expected a little pushback about how long they'd been together, but she was as accepting as Toby's mother had been when they'd called her before leaving for Bea's house. Maybe they understood more than he thought they would.

He smiled up at his Daddy, the returning smile making his heart beat faster. He lifted his chin. "I love you."

Ollie captured his lips, wrapping his arms around him and holding him close. His reply was in the way he held him, and Toby didn't need words.

"Are we really doing this?" Ollie said, fussing with his jacket.

"Of course we are! We have to show them what we've made of ourselves," Denny said. "Plus, I want to see what Frankie Roberts has done with his life."

"You had nothing to do with him at college," Ollie said.

"He was your boyfriend. I covered for you several times."

Ollie scoffed. "Yeah, because he was a closeted asshole who kept promising to come out for me before he dumped me."

"Yeah, you're well rid of him. But I still want to know if he's still closeted or not." Denny winked at Toby.

Toby loved their banter. Even when they were pissed at each

other, they couldn't help the back and forth; they would've won a gold medal if it was an Olympic sport. He was going to love seeing them at the reunion, which was being held at the sports hall of the college they'd attended. He couldn't wait to see where they'd gone to college.

"You don't have a date, though, do you?" Ollie grinned.

Denny cleared his throat. "Actually, I do." He checked his watch. "He should be here any minute."

Ollie gaped. "Who did you ask?"

Denny grinned. "You'll have to wait and see."

Toby distracted Ollie from replying by removing his tie and unbuttoning the top button of his shirt. "You don't need that," he said, throwing the tie over his shoulder. "You look gorgeous either way, but I want you comfortable.

"I will be comfortable with you around. Just don't go off with any college friends."

Toby chuckled. "I won't. Promise. I can't get what I need from them. Only from you."

Ollie smiled and slid his arms around Toby's waist, nuzzling his neck. "Same."

"Come on, then. Let's go," Denny said, heading for the stairs.

"I thought we were waiting for your date?" Ollie said.

"He's downstairs." Denny descended the stairs at a jog and opened the door.

Toby heard murmuring, and he pulled Ollie in their direction. Who was it? When he got to the bottom of the stairs, he blinked at the man standing with Denny. "Preston?"

Preston glanced over his shoulder and smiled. "Hi, Toby. How are you?" They hugged, and Toby held onto his biceps for a second longer.

"This is a surprise."

Preston rolled his eyes. "He wouldn't let up. Kept asking and asking." He shrugged a shoulder. "I didn't have any plans for tonight, so I thought, why not? A night out on him." He tilted his head towards Denny, who watched them with narrowed eyes.

Toby laughed. "Why not, indeed." There was something between them, but he had no idea what. He only had his own experiences with them and Ben's information about Preston to go on, but he could see where the attraction was between them. Even if they might not want to admit it. They'd look good together, but could they give what each other needed? That wasn't for him to decide, but he couldn't help but hope they found what they were looking for.

"Shall we go?" Denny asked, stepping close enough that his shoulders touched Preston's.

"Sure," Toby said when Preston didn't. He moved over to his Daddy and pursed his lips. "Something is going on there," he whispered as he passed him to get into the car.

"I agree, but what, I have no idea."

"That's for them to sort out, I suppose."

He climbed into the car and clicked his seat belt into place. Ollie got in the driver's side and started the engine. Toby watched in the side mirror as Denny and Preston spoke for a few seconds, then Denny waved his hand towards the car, and Preston nodded. Denny opened the door for Preston, closing it once he was in, and jogged around the back of the car to climb in his side. Toby tried to hide his smile, but if the squeeze he received on his thigh from his Daddy was any indication, he didn't succeed.

"Let's party!" Denny said.

Plenty of cars sat in the car park as they arrived - fashionably late, of course - and when they entered the hall, it took Toby back to his teenage years. Why did people think that decorating like they were back in the 90s was a good thing? He understood it was a reunion that was supposed to take them back to those years, but why decorate it that way? Modern decorations were just as good. He shook his head and refocused on Ollie.

"Oliver Young! Well, I never."

Toby stared at the tall, slender woman who wore baggy trousers and a crop top as if she was part of the Spice Girls. It looked good on her, but it made Toby worry if they were supposed to have dressed up.

"Melinda. How have you been?" Ollie said, tightening his hold on Toby as if worried he was going to leave him alone to fend her off.

"I'm good, thanks. I wasn't expecting to see you tonight, even though you RSVP'd. Didn't think this was your thing. How are you?"

Ollie smiled, though Toby could tell it was forced, and he nodded in Denny's direction. "Had my arm twisted. I'm great, thanks."

"Denny, Denny, Denny," Melinda said, shaking her head. "How much have you changed? Any?"

Denny grinned. "I don't think so. I wouldn't be myself if I had."

"Ain't that the truth?" Melinda chuckled. She reached for some paper from the table she stood behind. "Well, here are your name tags. I haven't done tags for your plus ones, but there are spare ones here if they want to have one."

Toby waved his hand. "I'm good."

Melinda smiled at him. "Bet you've got your hands full with this one. I remember what he was like." She tilted her head towards Ollie.

Toby narrowed his eyes. He didn't like her implications. He lifted his left hand and scratched his chin, making sure his ring was in full view. Melinda's eyes widened. "Nah, he's got his hands full with me." His tone made it clear what he was implying.

She cleared her throat, her cheeks flushing. "I'm sure. Have a good evening."

Ollie steered him towards the doors, and when they were inside, he burst out laughing, Denny and Preston joining in.

Toby sighed. "I didn't like what she said. I'm staking my claim here and now."

Ollie panted to get his breathing under control and dragged Toby into his chest. "No, I am." He lowered his head and took Toby's lips in a fierce and deep kiss. Everyone else disappeared as he lost himself to the feeling of being in his Daddy's arms. It never grew old.

"There. That should do it." Ollie sounded smug, but Toby didn't care. He could claim him every minute if he wanted to.

"I need a drink," Denny said, heading over to the bar.

"We all do. This is going to be hell on earth," Ollie said.

Once they had drinks in their hands, they found a space to call their own and chatted—at least until people started coming up to them and talking about college experiences he was sure Ollie and Denny hadn't wanted to be reminded about. During a brief lull, Ollie tensed, and Toby glanced at him.

"Are you okay?"

Ollie's gaze was on something across the room, and Toby followed his gaze. A man dressed in jeans and a polo shirt stared back at them. Toby frowned, wondering who he was, but braced himself for more veiled insults as he made his way over to them.

"Ollie," the man said.

"Frankie."

Toby knew who it was then, and he stepped closer to his Daddy, wanting to comfort him as he faced the man who had made him feel worthless.

Frankie glanced at him, and Toby saw pain in his eyes. When he refocused on Ollie, he said, "How have you been?"

"Great, thanks. You?"

"Better now." Frankie sighed. "I'm sorry for back then. It's no excuse, but my parents were...phobic. I wouldn't have been able to deal with what I did at that age. I had to grow up more first, but I'm sorry you were on the receiving end of that."

Ollie shifted. "Are you out now?"

Frankie smiled, small though it was. "Yes." He glanced over his shoulder and waved at someone. "I'm married." He slid his arm around a small guy who joined them. "This is Linc. He helped me through losing my parents when I came out."

Ollie's shoulders lowered, and he held out his hand for Frankie to shake. "I'm sorry for your loss, but look what you've gained. Nice to meet you, Linc." They shook hands, each smiling at the other until Ollie let go and pulled Toby close. "This is Toby, my fiancé."

Toby grinned at the introduction and shook hands with them both. Not wanting to keep them out of the conversation, he pointed to Denny. "You remember Denny?"

Frankie blanched. "Yes. Hi."

Denny held his hand out. "You deserved it."

Frankie hesitated but shook hands with him and nodded. "I did."

"Deserved what?" Ollie asked.

Denny worked his jaw but didn't answer, but Frankie did. "He punched me when I dumped you."

Ollie backhanded Denny's shoulder. "I told you to leave it alone!"

"You're my best friend, Ollie. I was so *not* going to leave that alone."

"Asshole."

"Reprobate."

Frankie laughed. "They've not changed that much," he said to Toby.

Toby grinned. "I hope they never do."

28

OLLIE

Fifteen months later

Ollie was nervous, though he shouldn't be. Toby wanted to get married. Ollie wanted to get married. There wouldn't be anyone who stood up to say why they couldn't get married, so why the hell was he so nervous?

He'd wanted to give Toby the wedding of his dreams; therefore, he'd made them wait over a year. Asking Toby to wait until December so they could celebrate the date they'd met was pure torture for them both, and several times, he'd wished he'd rescinded the words. But he wanted their wedding to celebrate two years of knowing each other as well as their official joining.

In the past year, they'd met so many boys and Daddies through Gareth and Ben's Daddy's Boy app and the events they hosted, which Toby still helped with. Their list of friends had grown substantially, and therefore, so had their guest list. Everyone who mattered knew of their lifestyle, including their families, because they hadn't wanted to pretend to be something other than themselves. It had taken a lot of courage from Toby before they had spilt the beans, so to speak. Funny thing was Toby's brothers' eyes lit up when they found out. Ollie was certain they would join the app—if they hadn't already—but he wasn't bringing that to Toby's attention.

His front door opened, and footsteps thundered up the stairs.

"Where are you?" Denny yelled.

"Where do you think I'd be?" Ollie called back.

Denny poked his head in the doorway. "I'm not answering that." He whistled. "Look at you, all spiffed up."

"Why did I agree to have you as my best man?"

"Because I'm *the* best man, you know."

"That's...bloody true. Well, one of them anyway."

A second set of footsteps sounded, much more sedate this time, and he waited until Enno entered the room, pushing Denny aside, before he said, "And here's the other."

He'd refused to choose between his two best friends, so he'd chosen them both as best men. He wouldn't be here without either of them, and they both deserved the title.

"I won't ask what you're talking about," Enno replied, handing him a takeaway drink cup. "Don't spill it," he warned. He handed another cup to Denny, then set the tray on the bedside table and held his own. "Okay, time for a toast."

"Isn't that supposed to happen at the reception?" Denny asked, stepping closer.

Enno sighed and glared at him. "This is different." He raised his eyebrows at Ollie. "Are you sure you want him to speak during the reception? You can still back out."

Ollie grinned. "I can't wait to hear what he says."

"Your funeral." Enno held his cup up. "A toast. To the two best men I know. Yes, even you, Denny." Denny grinned and tugged Enno to him with an arm around his shoulders. "Where would life have taken us if we hadn't become friends? It's a question I'd asked myself for years, but now I realise I don't want to know the answer. Life would be too quiet without you both, and I, for one, wouldn't change it for the world."

Ollie tapped their cups together. "That sounds like something you would've said on *your* wedding day."

Enno chuckled. "I probably would've if Denny hadn't pissed me off that morning."

"I never—" Denny started.

"—always—" Enno interrupted.

"—piss you off," Denny finished.

Ollie laughed, then sobered. "I hear you, Enno, and I raise you a 'you're both fucking amazing.'"

He hugged them both, being careful to keep his cup upright. They finished their drinks and headed down to the waiting car.

Only it wasn't a car.

"Where's the car?" he asked.

Denny and Enno smiled at him.

"Toby asked for a change of vehicle to get you to the wedding as a surprise," Enno said.

Ollie stared at the two Harley-Davidsons decorated with white ribbons. Tears filled his eyes, but he refused to free them.

"How the hell did I get lucky enough to find him?" he whispered.

Denny clapped him on the shoulder. "I'd like to know that, too."

Ollie backhanded him. "Fuck off." He exhaled. "Let's go."

Denny climbed on one and gestured at the back. "I'm just glad the weather held out. I would've hated to ride in the rain. You're on mine, bucko."

Ollie snorted. "Bucko?" He climbed on.

"What? You'd prefer something else? Boomer? Buckaroo? Buddy?"

"Enno, can I go on your bike?" he asked in jest.

Denny revved the engine, and Ollie chuckled. They put on their helmets, and Enno set off in front, Denny following. They didn't race through the streets, happy to keep a sedate speed as they aimed for the park the wedding was being held at—after all, how could they have Flossie and Ghost attend if they were in a building?

They parked the bikes in a space that was cordoned off for the ceremony. It had taken some wrangling, but the council had allowed them the ceremony in the park. They had wanted things to be official rather than behind anyone's back, and they'd been lucky.

Ollie handed his helmet to the assistant, who would look after the bikes. He headed down the path to where the "aisle" started. Chairs on either side of a white, heavy-duty carpet runner held their guests, and he greeted many of them as he walked down to where he'd stand to wait for his husband-to-be.

"Gareth, glad you could make it."

Gareth chuckled. "It was more than my life was worth if I said we couldn't. Ben's already deserted me for Toby. I'm glad I have company." He gestured to his side, where Preston, Victor, Andy and Scott sat.

"Hi, guys. Thanks for coming," Ollie said to them.

A hand touched his shoulder. "You need to get into place," Enno said.

"In a moment," he said when he spotted someone. He walked over to Rio and his daughter. "Hey, man. Thanks for coming."

"Wouldn't have missed it." He tapped his wheelchair. "Congratulations."

"Thanks."

Rio had made huge progress in learning to walk, but he couldn't be without his wheelchair for too long. One day, Ollie was sure he would, but he wheeled himself into the garage every day, and they'd set up a small room on the ground floor as an office for him. He loved being part of the garage, and Ollie would never stop him from doing so. Maybe he'd eventually want to be a mechanic again, but so far, he'd refused.

Enno tapped his shoulder again. "Okay, okay." Ollie exhaled and raised his eyebrows. "Time to go."

Rio smiled. "Enjoy it. And breathe."

Ollie chuckled. "I will try."

He settled at the front, after petting the dogs so they would be less likely to interrupt, and smiled at his mother, then at the picture they'd framed of his father that sat on the seat next to her. It was probably stupid, but he liked the idea that his father might be watching down on them.

Music started, and he focused on the aisle. The rumble of a motorcycle filled the air, and he frowned as the noise got louder and louder. He saw a Harley Davidson jump the curb and roar down the path, stopping at the end of the aisle. Someone jumped off the back and pulled the helmet off, revealing a beaming Toby. His hair was mussed, but he was gorgeous. He stopped at the end of the runner while his father joined him—the man who would walk him down the small stretch of carpet separating them.

Ollie couldn't keep his eyes off his boy. He wore a black suit and white shirt with his leather jacket over the top, and it wouldn't have surprised him if he kept the jacket on, but Ben joined him and held out his hand. He could see words being spoken and Toby frowning, then huffing before he slipped the jacket off and gave it to Ben. Ollie rolled his lips inwards at the display, having an idea of what Toby would've said. Then Toby slipped his arm through his father's, and they started down the aisle to the music they had chosen.

His heart raced the closer Toby came, but the smile on his boy's face was one of pure happiness. Ollie's worries about anything going wrong disappeared.

Toby's father left him at Ollie's side with a smile and joined his wife and sons. Toby beamed at him, and Ollie returned it, holding his hand and turning them to face the officiant, who smiled and nodded.

"Welcome, guests. We are here to celebrate the joining of Oliver and Tobias." He cleared his throat, and his cheeks reddened. "I apologise. We are here to celebrate the joining of Ollie and Toby." Ollie chuckled. "The vows they will recite today will be unique to them. They requested that they be relevant to their lives. Therefore, Ollie, will you please repeat after me..."

Ollie repeated, "I, Oliver Young, will love, support, protect and care for Tobias Neesham from this day forth to the best of my ability. But I will also ask for help when I need it and allow Toby to help hold me up when my legs can't take the weight. I promise to pander to his wishes as much as I am able but to say no when Toby needs to hear it." Laughter flowed through the guests.

"And now, Toby..."

Toby smiled at him. "I, Tobias Neesham, will love, support, protect and care for Oliver Young from this day forth to the best of my ability. But I will also ask if I'm not getting what I need and remember that love is stronger than anything else. I promise to not push for more dogs than our house can accommodate, but I do not promise to not request a larger house at any time." Laughter sounded again.

"Could we have the rings, please," the officiant asked, and Sarah stepped forward, placing them on the open book. "Thank you. Repeat after me as you place the rings on your partner's finger."

"With this ring, I thee wed and promise to love you through whatever trials are thrown our way. Through thick and thin, through light and dark, through oil and water. I will hold your love within my soul, keeping it burning throughout our years."

"It is with great joy I can pronounce Ollie and Toby as husbands. Congratulations. You may kiss to seal your vows."

Ollie grabbed Toby and fused their lips, tasting salt but not knowing which of them it was coming from. He buried his face in Toby's neck and tightened his hold, whispering, "I love you."

"I love you," Toby replied.

They stepped aside for a few minutes to sign the documentation to go along with the ceremony, and then they faced the guests who were on their feet, clapping and cheering for them. They walked down the aisle, hand in hand, to the waiting bike. The assistant handed them a helmet each and Toby's jacket, and Toby climbed on before he could. Ollie chuckled.

"You're driving, are you?"

"Hell, yes."

Ollie climbed on behind him, sliding his arms around Toby's waist. "Let's go, husband."

Toby trembled but set off carefully. He had received his licence but was still a little unsure. Ollie wasn't, though. He knew Toby was more than capable of holding his own on a bike.

"To the hotel!" he heard someone shout from behind them, followed by a loud cheer.

They arrived at the hotel they had hired for the reception lunch. Toby handed the bike keys over to another assistant. Toby told him they would ensure the bike was returned to where it needed to be. Before they entered the hall, Ollie pulled Toby into his arms again.

"I never thought this day would arrive. I love you."

Toby beamed. "I love the sound of being Toby Young. I've been practising my signature for months."

Ollie chuckled and pecked him on the lips. "Roll on two hours when we can disappear."

"Sooner, if we can manage it."

He kissed him once more and guided him into the hall, where they waited at the door for their guests to enter. They greeted every guest they'd invited before they sat at the large table at the front of the room that faced everyone else.

Ollie stood, pulling Toby to his feet also, and clinked his glass to garner everyone's attention. "Thank you for being here to celebrate with us. We appreciate it more than you know. There will be some speeches later, but for now, the buffet is open. So please help—" He paused when a chair scraped across the floor, and Denny raced from his chair. Ollie snorted. "So, please, grab some food before *he* eats it all."

Everyone laughed, and their guests made their way to the tables full of food.

Ollie and Toby settled back into their seats, not needing to go anywhere because their food would be delivered to them as part of the wedding package.

"Are you happy?" he asked. Though he knew the answer, he needed the confirmation all the same.

"Ecstatic." Toby kissed him, brushing his thumb against Ollie's cheek. "The only way I'll be happier is when we get on the ship."

"Yes, two weeks on a cruise sounds like bliss." He frowned. "As long as I don't get sea sickness."

Toby chuckled. "We have all possible antidotes for that, so you'll be fine. If not, I'll look after you."

"You didn't tell Denny about the free food, did you?"

Toby shook his head with a smile. "I thought we could tell him afterwards. We don't want an unexpected guest to tag along."

"Definitely."

"So," Toby started, staring down at their joined hands. "Is it too early to talk about kids?"

Ollie's heart lifted, and he cupped Toby's face. "I want as many as you do."

"Two might be nice. Do you want a surrogate or to adopt?"

"Either. I'd love to have some mini-Toby's running around, but I also love the idea of giving someone a home who doesn't have anyone."

Toby nodded. "Same. Maybe we can start looking into it when we get home."

"Sounds like a plan."

Their food arrived, and they both ate their fill before Denny and Enno stood to make their speeches—or rather speech because it was one long rambling effort of embarrassing stories from Ollie's childhood. Then Toby's father stood, being interrupted several times by Toby's brothers before their mother clipped their hands to shut them up. Sarah stood up for Toby, too, and then Ollie's mum surprised him.

"I know what Ollie's father would've said if he could've been here. He would've offered eternal congratulations and would've probably cried. But I know he would've loved Toby as much, if not more than I do. You are part of our family now, and I wish you every happiness."

Ollie's tears won, and he sniffled even as he smiled at his mum and mouthed, "Thank you."

It was a shame his father wasn't there to see him, but Ollie knew he'd want him to live his life to the best of his ability, and he'd already promised that to Toby. He had no qualms in promising to the sky where his father, hopefully, watched over them. And if he was able to bring a child into their family as well, they would grow up knowing their grandfather and the legacy of the garage, though they didn't have to work the garage themselves if they chose another path.

Anyway, he was getting ahead of himself. He couldn't wait to have Toby completely to himself for two weeks, away from everything.

Two weeks of sightseeing.

Two weeks of free food.

Two weeks of optional clothing.

He would be in heaven.

29

TOBY

Five months later

"I wonder how long it will take to have a child placed with us?" Toby said while they were watching a film.

"I'm not sure. But we can help several children by fostering instead of adopting, and we can both be here with them as much as needed," Ollie said.

"I suppose now it's just a waiting game. We've been through enough training that I think we'll cope well enough, and the dogs are great with kids."

Ollie chuckled. "Those dogs will roll over for anyone. Even burglars."

Toby tapped his chest. "Not true."

"They don't even growl when the post arrives."

"Doesn't mean they'll let anything happen to us."

"True."

Their decision to foster instead of adopt came after a meeting with an adoption official. They had mentioned their ages and suggested fostering instead. And once they'd mentioned how many children needed foster care, Toby glanced at Ollie and raised his eyebrows. After that meeting, they'd spent several hours discussing the good and bad points, and they believed their abilities would be better put towards fostering. They weren't getting any younger, that was for sure.

They'd been through five months of training and had received their final clearance earlier that day. Now, they just had to wait for the call to ask them if they could take a child.

As soon as he'd had that thought, Ollie's phone rang. He frowned and put it on speaker.

"Hello?"

"Mr Young, it's Izzy from the foster department. I know you have only just completed your training, but we have an emergency family that needs a haven. Would you be willing to take two children tonight? It should only be for a day or two until we figure out where they can go for long-term care."

Ollie raised his eyebrows at Toby, and Toby nodded. "Of course. We'd be happy to help."

"Wonderful. We'll be with you within the hour. Thank you."

Ollie ended the call and stared at Toby. "We got our wish quicker than expected."

Toby stood. "We need to get the room ready."

He headed for the spare room they'd set up for when the children came. They'd built a bunk bed on the off chance they had more than one child on the advice of their fostering support advisor. He was glad they had now.

He grabbed two sets of covers and sheets and made the beds while Ollie grabbed two cuddly toys from the stack they had in the room. His Daddy placed them on the finished beds, and Toby knew those cuddly toys would go wherever those children went after they left their home.

"I wonder if they'll be hungry?" Ollie asked, heading to the kitchen. "I'll make a snack plate for each of them in case they are. If they don't eat it, it can go in the fridge for tomorrow."

Toby smiled as Ollie disappeared. He would be a wonderful dad to children. He was an amazing Daddy to him, so this was just an extension of their lifestyle. Following in his wake, Toby made sure there were spare towels and toothbrushes in the bathroom and sat on the counter in the kitchen while Ollie pottered around. Toby was nervous, but they were both capable of taking care of children. But as much training as they had been given, would he be able to cope when they left? That was something he'd have to figure out.

When the knock came, Ollie exhaled and stared at him before following Toby to the stairs.

"You go. I'll wait up here," Ollie said. "I don't want to overwhelm them in such a small space."

Toby nodded and descended the stairs, opening the door.

A young woman with blonde hair tied in a ponytail smiled at him. "Mr Young?"

Toby nodded. "One of them, yes."

She held out her hand. "Izzy Barnard. Nice to meet you." She looked down at the two children by her side, and Toby followed her gaze. "This is Olivia, and this is Sammy."

Toby smiled. "Nice to meet you all. Would you like to come in? We have hot chocolate ready to go if you'd like some."

Sammy's eyes lit up, but he stared at his older sister without answering. Toby glanced at Olivia, who narrowed her eyes at him. "With marshmallows?" she asked.

"Is there any other way to drink hot chocolate?"

"Unfortunately," Olivia replied, sounding much older than her appearance advertised, and stepped past him, dragging her brother with her.

Toby hid his smile and gestured up the stairs. "Up the stairs. You'll meet Ollie at the top. He's the cook of the two of us."

They climbed slowly, and Toby closed the stair gate once they were all up.

"Izzy, Olivia, Sammy. This is Ollie, my husband."

Izzy shook hands with him.

"Hi. You must be Olivia," Ollie said, pointing to Sammy.

Sammy snorted into the blanket he held. "No! I'm Sammy."

Ollie clapped his forehead. "Oh! Sorry. Nice to meet you, Sammy." He held out his hand, and Sammy hesitated before shaking it. "Nice to meet you, too, Olivia."

The girl shook his hand briefly, then asked, "He said you have hot chocolate with marshmallows?"

Ollie grinned. "Always. Would you like to help make it?"

Olivia hesitated but nodded. "I would." She glanced at Sammy. "Would you like to help?"

Sammy scrunched his nose. "Do I have to?"

Olivia peered at Ollie, who shook his head. "Not if you don't want to. You can sit in here and watch, or Toby can show you the living room where you can watch TV for a few minutes before bed."

The children stared at each other as if they were having a silent conversation, and then Olivia smiled and nodded at him.

"Can I watch TV, please?" Sammy asked.

"Sure you can," Toby said, holding out his hand. "This way."

With a last look at Olivia, Sammy let go of his sister's hand and slipped his smaller one into Toby's. Toby's heart skipped a beat, and he settled the little boy on the sofa with an animated film. He settled on the opposite side of the sofa when Izzy settled in the armchair.

"I have some information for you, but I won't talk too much while they're still up. They have been in this situation a couple of times before, but this is the end." She stared at him. Did she mean they weren't going back or something else? "They are supposed to have school tomorrow, but I think they would benefit from staying home. However, that's something you can decide in the morning and after a discussion with the children. They might want to go, and if they do, accept their wishes."

Toby nodded. "I will."

Soon, Ollie and Olivia—wasn't that a cute thought—carried cups of hot chocolate to them, and they settled around the coffee table, drinking. Olivia asked a few questions, whereas Sammy was quiet, his eyes blinking blearily at the screen. Toby didn't think he'd last much longer, so after a few more minutes, he decided to take the reins.

"Right. I think it's time for bed. Would you like to see where you're going to sleep?"

Neither child said anything, but both stood when Toby did and followed him down the hallway. "Here we go." He turned the light on and stepped inside but stayed by the door.

The children wandered around, looking but not touching. Izzy stopped beside him with a small suitcase he hadn't noticed before.

"Here are some of your things. There should be pyjamas and clothes as well as some other things from home," she said. "If you want anything else from there, let Toby or Ollie know, and they'll contact me, okay?"

Olivia nodded absently. "Which one do I sleep on?"

"Whichever you want to," Toby answered.

Sammy stepped towards the ladder. "I want the top!"

Olivia chuckled. "Okay, pipsqueak. I'll have the bottom."

Toby bit his lip to stop his tears. Was it because this was the first children they'd had, or would he be like this with every child who came through their door?

"Great. I'll leave you to get changed. Just shout when you're ready, and I'll show you where the bathroom is, and we can brush our teeth."

They left the children in the room, and he pulled the door not quite closed before joining the adults in the living room.

"I'll be quick," Izzy said. "Their parents died, though, at the moment, the children believe they were asleep when they left. Drug abuse. They severely neglected the kids. They've been taken away from their parents before. Personally, and if you ever repeat this, I'll deny it, they should've never been given back the first time." She held up her hand. "But that's not my call. We try to give parents the benefit of the doubt as much as possible."

"What about abuse to the children?" Ollie asked.

"No signs of physical abuse, but definitely emotional. As for mentally, well, we'll have to wait and see. We will arrange counselling for them, no matter what. Especially as the news of their parents' deaths will have to be broken to them."

"Anything else we need to know?"

Izzy shook her head. "I don't think so. If I do, I'll message you instead of calling unless it's urgent."

"Thanks," Toby said.

"I'll stay until they're in bed if that's okay."

"Sure."

Izzy clasped his forearm. "You're doing fine."

"We're ready!" Olivia called.

Toby inhaled and headed for the hallway, seeing the kids waiting at their bedroom door. "Okay, that is mine and Ollie's room if you ever need us, and here is the bathroom. You have a towel should you need it, and here is a toothbrush each if you don't have one."

"It's green!" Sammy shouted. "It looks like a monster!"

Toby chuckled. "It does a bit." He spread toothpaste on their brushes and watched as they brushed, helping Sammy when he needed it. "Good job. Time for bed." They went into the bedroom. "Do you like stories?" he asked when they were settled.

"Yes!" Sammy said.

"Toby?" Olivia said.

"Yes?"

"What are these cuddly toys for?"

Toby smiled. "They are for you and Sammy if you would like them."

She didn't look at him, but her hand reached for the bear. "For us to keep?"

"If you want them." Olivia peered up at him and nodded once. She didn't say anything further, so he chose a book. "Ollie is going to come in for bedtime, too, okay?"

Both children nodded, not seeming to worry about the adults in the house. It eased something in him, having an idea that they were not afraid of adults. During the training, that was something they were told to watch out for. It usually meant some harm had come to them, but it seemed Izzy's words were true to form, and it was emotional and possibly mental abuse they'd suffered. Time would tell.

Ollie entered the room and settled on the floor beside Toby's chair. Toby started reading the story, and soon enough, Sammy was asleep, softly snoring. When he finished the story, he met Olivia's gaze.

"Are you okay?" he asked, leaning forward.

Olivia blinked at him. "Thank you for looking after us," she whispered.

His heart broke, and only Ollie's hand on his back stopped the tears from flowing. "You're very welcome." He tucked the cover over her shoulder. "Goodnight, Olivia."

"Livvy," she said.

Toby raised his eyebrows. "You prefer Livvy?" She nodded. "Okay, Livvy it is."

"Goodnight, Toby. Goodnight, Ollie."

Ollie tucked the covers over Sammy, and they switched the light off, closing the door. Toby kept his wits about him until he reached the living room, and then Ollie guided him to the sofa.

"Are you okay, Toby?" Izzy asked.

He nodded. "It's just so sad. Olivia—Livvy is so grown up. How old is she?"

"Eight, and Sammy is six. She is well beyond her years, I agree.

She's been looking after her brother for far too long. We now need to find a home for them so she can learn to be a child again."

Toby glanced at Ollie, who chuckled. "What happened to fostering, sweetheart?"

"But they need a home." Toby's cheeks heated.

Izzy tilted her head. "I thought you were just interested in fostering, not adopting. Adoption is not on your file."

Ollie exhaled. "Originally, we wanted to adopt, but our advisor told us it would be more difficult because of our ages. It's why we chose to foster instead."

Izzy's expression darkened. "Bullshit! Who the heck told you that? We don't discriminate like that."

Toby's heart pounded. "It's an option?"

Izzy nodded. "If they settle well here, then yes, definitely. You can foster them long-term, to begin with, then we can discuss it further."

Toby bit his lip and stared at his husband. "What do you think?"

"I'm happy either way."

"I'll put you down as potential long-term with potential adoption. I want you to think about it over the next couple of days, and then when I come back on Thursday, we can discuss it further. How does that sound?"

Toby smiled. "Good."

"Right, I'm going to leave you now. Here's my number should any problems occur. You can get me day or night on that." Izzy stood, and Ollie saw her to the door.

Toby stared at the blank TV, startling when Ollie settled beside him again. "Are you sure?"

"It's what we wanted to begin. Why would I change my mind now it's a possibility we weren't sure we had?"

Toby rested his cheek against Ollie's chest and closed his eyes. "I don't want to hope."

"I know, sweetheart. I know. But you can make a wish."

So he did.

And ten months later, they formally adopted Livvy and Sammy into their family.

And also another two dogs, courtesy of their children.

Life was certainly not quiet, and Toby couldn't be happier. He had his Daddy still taking care of him, two children whom he loved, and four dogs who didn't know when to quit.

Life was perfect.

ACKNOWLEDGMENTS

Thank you, as always, to Renee for being there for me every step of my journey. You're the best. Don't ever stop being you.
Emma, you're amazing. I'm so sorry to keep you so busy!
Thank you to Christine L for naming one of Toby and Ollie's dogs, the grey Great Dane called Ghost – I love this name!
And thank you to you, my reader, for being here and trusting me with several hours of your life every time you pick up one of my books.

BOOKS BY ELOUISE EAST

Boys, Daddies, Snuggles & More
Need Him
Trust Him

Daddy
Love Me, Daddy
Soothe Me, Daddy
Spoil Me, Daddy
The Complete Daddy Series Box Set

Illuminate Matchmaking
Ignite
Blaze
Kindle
Scorch

Club Royal
Royal Firsts
Rogue Royal

Star-Crossed
Protecting the Thief
Sizzling Chauffeur

Elouise R East (taboo)

Dark & Divergent
Forbidden Temptation
Too Many Secrets

Collide
When Fantasies Collide
When Dreams Collide
When Pleasures Collide
When Cravings Collide

ABOUT ELOUISE EAST

Elouise East writes sweet and steamy connections in gay romance. She also touches on taboo stories under the name Elouise R East.

Books that tell the stories where friendship and family are the focal point - be it blood family or chosen - are very important to her. That's why she includes a variety of personalities, talents, ages, situations and abilities as she believes a story or character needs. She wants her characters to be real, to be relatable, to be free to have whatever views they tell her they have. And trust her, most of the time, she does not have *any* say in the matter!

Her characters come to life on the page for her as well as her readers. Their stories unfold in front of her as she writes, and she has very little input into how they want to be shown. Just like real life, the lives of her characters change with every choice, every interaction and every conversation. And she wouldn't have it any other way.

She writes books that are emotionally realistic, even if liberties are taken with other aspects of the stories. She doesn't know any other way to write. It comes from deep inside.

Who is she? A single parent to two children living in the UK. An avid reader who still tries to devour every book she can get her hands on. A student of learning about any subject that takes her fancy. An author of books she would read herself. And a romantic at heart who loves anything cheesy.

Who's joining her on her journey?

Follow her here...
Website : https://elouiseeast.com
Newsletter : https://elouiseeast.com/newsletter
All links : https://elouiseeast.com/links